Praise for
CAROL LEA BENJAMIN's
RACHEL ALEXANDER Mysteries

"Rachel Alexander is someone who holds your interest and makes you keep turning the pages."
New York Times bestselling author Nevada Barr

"Benjamin combines expert storytelling, wry humor, and a flair for bringing unusual characters to life."
Ft. Lauderdale Sun-Sentinel

"[A] first-rate murder-mystery series."
Orlando Sentinel

"Her high quality of prose and convincing way with dialogue may surprise and delight first-time readers."
Chicago Sun-Times

"Benjamin keeps the tail-wagging to a minimum, relying instead on solid private eye basics. Dash . . . is nevertheless a dependably entertaining companion among murder and mayhem."
Denver Rocky Mountain News

"The adventures of private detective Rachel Alexander and her pit bull partner, Dashiell, hooked me."
Seattle Times

Books by Carol Lea Benjamin

WITHOUT A WORD
FALL GUY
THE LONG GOOD BOY
THE WRONG DOG
LADY VANISHES
A HELL OF A DOG
THE DOG WHO KNEW TOO MUCH
THIS DOG FOR HIRE

And coming soon in hardcover from
William Morrow

THE HARD WAY

CAROL LEA BENJAMIN

WITHOUT A WORD

A RACHEL ALEXANDER MYSTERY

AVON BOOKS
An Imprint of HarperCollins*Publishers*

This is a work of fiction. The characters, incidents, and dialogue are drawn from the author's imagination and are not to be construed as real. Any resemblance to actual events or persons, living or dead, is entirely coincidental.

AVON BOOKS
An Imprint of HarperCollins*Publishers*
10 East 53rd Street
New York, New York 10022-5299

Copyright © 2005 by Carol Lea Benjamin
Excerpt from *The Hard Way* copyright © 2006 by Carol Lea Benjamin
ISBN-13: 978-0-06-053902-3
ISBN-10: 0-06-053902-X
www.avonmystery.com

First Avon Books paperback printing: July 2006
First William Morrow hardcover printing: September 2005

Avon Trademark Reg. U.S. Pat. Off. and in Other Countries, Marca Registrada, Hecho en U.S.A.
HarperCollins® is a registered trademark of HarperCollins Publishers Inc.

Printed in the U.S.A.

10 9 8 7 6 5 4 3 2 1

For Stephen, my sweetheart

WITHOUT
A WORD

CHAPTER 1

Leon Spector had dead written all over him, not the kind where they put you in a box, say a few words and toss the earth back over you, not the ashes-to-ashes kind of dead, but the kind that lets the world know that whatever the battle was, you lost, the kind that says that sometime, a long time ago, you were beaten into the ground by circumstances beyond your control. I didn't know what those circumstances were in Leon's case, but on a particularly sunny afternoon at the Washington Square Park dog run the month I turned forty and my pit bull, Dashiell, turned five, Leon apparently planned to tell me.

He met me as I was closing the inner gate, a wide, multicolored camera strap slung around his neck, his Leica hanging low on his chest. I'd seen him at the run before, not with a dog but with his camera, and I'd seen him taking pictures on other occasions as well, the opening of the new park along the river, the annual outdoor art show, the gay pride parade. Someone said he was a freelance photographer. Someone else said he was working on a book. Until that afternoon, that was all I knew about Leon, but not why he carried not only a camera everywhere he went but also the weight of the world. You could see it pulling him toward the ground, as if the gravity under Leon was working overtime.

"I've been looking all over for you," he said as I bent to unhook Dashiell's leash. "I couldn't call you because . . ."

I looked up. Leon stopped and fiddled with the strap of his camera.

"Because I'm not listed?" I asked.

Leon shook his head. "I never got that far," he said. "The person who told me about you, who said what I needed was a private investigator and that's what you . . ." He stopped and shrugged. "It is, isn't it?"

I nodded.

Leon nodded back. "She just said she'd seen you here and that your dog wore a red collar with his name on it and that you had," he made a spiral with his left pointer, "long, curly hair. She didn't know your last name."

I didn't know his last name either, at least not yet, but I didn't say so. Leon didn't look in the mood for small talk.

"What's the problem?" I asked.

Instead of answering me, Leon put the camera up to his face and looked through the viewfinder. I wondered if he had a deadline of some sort or if he was just one of those people who talked better if he was doing something else at the same time.

I heard the shutter click and looked in the direction Leon's camera was pointing. There was a little girl of about nine or ten sitting alone on a bench, watching the dogs. She was wearing dark glasses and a shirt that looked three sizes too big. Next to her, on the bench, there was a small see-through plastic purse the shape of a lunch pail, with something color-ful inside, but I was too far away to make out what it was.

I waited. Sometimes, doing something else or not, I let the other guy do the talking, see what comes out before adding my own two cents.

"I need you to find my wife," he said.

I guess that explained the sagging shoulders, the hangdog look. He'd been a good-looking man once, you could see that. But now he looked faded, used up, worn out. You could feel the effort it took for him to form sentences, as if he could barely muster the energy to speak.

"It's not for me," he said. "It's for my daughter. She's in trouble and she needs her mother."

Dashiell was busy digging a hole in the far corner of the run, a hole I'd have to fill in before I left. I turned to look at Leon now to see if his face might tell me what his words hadn't. But Leon's face wasn't talking either.

"Where is her mother?"

"That's the whole point. I don't know, not since she walked out on me and Madison."

I took out a small notepad and a pencil. I wrote down, "Madison."

"Divorced you?" I asked.

He shook his head. "Nothing so . . ." He scratched at the dirt with the sole of his shoe. "Nothing as clear as that."

"Missing, you mean?"

Leon nodded. "I do," he said. "Every day."

I nodded. I knew what it was like to miss someone who was gone. I figured, one way or another, just about everyone did. But Leon had a bad case of it, not only being abandoned, but being abandoned with a kid.

"Come on," I said, "let's sit down."

We walked over to the closest bench.

"No clue as to why she left," I asked, "or where she went?"

"You ever notice the way things look one way but they're not, they're another?"

"How did you think things were?"

"Permanent," he said.

I felt that little stab that sometimes comes along with an unexpected truth, simply stated.

Leon lifted the camera to his face again. But this time I didn't hear the shutter click. I wrote down, "How long is wife missing? How old is Madison?"

"After the initial shock of it, the police investigation, all of that," he moved the camera away from his face and turned to look at me, "everything just a dead end, I managed okay." He tilted his head left, then right, as if he were arguing with himself. "At least that's what I thought. Not perfect. Far from perfect. But okay. Considering." He shrugged. "But now." He shook his head. "I don't know how to handle this."

If his daughter was pregnant, I wondered if there might be some female relative who could help. Or a neighbor they were close to. Was this just an excuse to try to find his missing wife again? I was about to ask when Leon started talking again. Perhaps he was finally on a roll.

"She went out one night and never came back," he said, covering his face with the camera. He was pointing it at the southern end of the run where a Weimaraner had dropped his ball into the water bucket and was trying to fish it out with his front paws, but I had the feeling Leon wasn't actually looking through the lens this time.

"Your wife?"

Leon moved the camera away and nodded. He hadn't taken a picture this time either. "Just like that," he said. "Went for a walk. Didn't take a thing with her."

"No money, no passport, not even a change of clothes?"

"Just a change of heart, I guess. And Roy."

"That was the man she ran off with?" I asked quietly, sympathetically, finally getting it.

Leon shook his head. "That I could understand, if that's what she had done."

"But it wasn't, is that what you're saying?" Wanting to

shake him by now. "Spit it out, Leon. I'm going to be a member of AARP before you get to the point."

"Roy was the dog," he said.

"The dog?"

Leon nodded, though it was sort of a rhetorical question. "See, what I don't get is that Sally never wanted him in the first place. She said, 'No matter what you say now, Leon, I'm going to be the one taking care of it. I already have more than I can handle with the kid, going to school at night and you, Leon. What the hell do I need a dog for?'" Leon shrugged again. "Guess I was the one who needed a dog. Guess that's what she was saying. So I said I'd take care of him. I figured that would take care of the problem, you know what I mean?"

"But it didn't?"

"One night she says, 'I think Roy needs a walk. I think he needs to go.' So I get up to take him out, but she flaps her hand at me, picks up the leash and walks out the door. That was the last time I saw either one of them." He scratched the side of his nose with his thumb. "I guess she was the one who had to go, not Roy."

"The police . . ."

He shook his head.

"What about Roy? Did he . . ." I stopped to consider how to word what I wanted to say. But was there anything I could say that Leon hadn't thought of a thousand times over? "Did he ever turn up?" I asked.

Leon shook his head again. For a while, we just sat there. Leon didn't say anything and neither did I.

"That's why I was looking for you," he finally said, "to ask if you could find her for us."

"How long has she been gone?"

"Five years, two months, eleven days." He looked at his watch but didn't report back to me.

"That long?"

Leon nodded.

"Without a word?"

He nodded again.

"How do you know she's still alive?"

"I don't," he said.

"There was no credit card activity that night? Or afterwards?"

"She didn't have it with her." He shrugged. "She'd just gone out to walk Roy."

"Did she have a driver's license?"

"We didn't have a car." As if that answered the question.

"What about social security payments made under her name? Did the police follow up on that?" I asked, thinking she could have a new name, a new social security card, a new life.

Or not.

"They didn't come up with anything," he said. "No sign of . . ."

I nodded.

He was probably in his forties, but he could have easily passed for sixty, the hair sticking out from under his baseball cap a steely gray, his skin the color of honeysuckle, that yellowish white that looks great on a plant and really lousy on a person. But it was mostly his eyes that made him look so old, his sad, dead eyes.

"Look, someone gone that long," I shook my head from side to side, "Leon, if your daughter's pregnant and that's, that's a problem, there are only a few choices that can be made. Why go through all this . . ."

"Pregnant? Wouldn't that be . . ." For a moment I thought he was going to laugh, but then he looked as if he was about to cry. "Madison's not pregnant," he said. "She's suspected of murder."

"Murder?" Why was he talking to me? His daughter didn't need her mother, she needed a good lawyer.

"They say she killed her doctor in a fit of rage. She gets them sometimes."

"Fits of rage?"

Leon nodded.

"And did she?"

Leon looked shocked. Then his old, sad eyes looked even older and sadder. "I don't think so."

"But you don't know?"

Leon shook his head.

"Did you ask her?"

"I did."

"Well, what did she say?"

"She didn't say anything. Madison doesn't speak. She stopped talking three days after her mother disappeared." He glanced around the run, as if to assess whether anyone might be listening, but there wasn't a soul near enough, and besides, a Jack Russell had spotted a squirrel on a branch and was barking his fool head off. "I was hoping if you could find Sally for us," he whispered, "maybe Madison would start to talk again. Maybe she'd say what happened that day instead of letting people who weren't there say what was in her heart and what she did."

"Does she respond at all? Does she write things down? Does she nod for yes, shake her head for no?"

"Sometimes she draws pictures, but even then, you can't always know for sure what she's thinking. There was a picture on the doctor's desk, a heart with a scraggly line going into it."

"Stabbing it?"

"It could look that way."

"And was she angry with her doctor?"

Leon nodded. "She has these tics and he was treating her with Botox, to paralyze the muscles so that she'd . . ."

"Look more normal?"

" 'Pass for normal' is what he said. Can you imagine saying that to a patient? To a kid?"

Pass for normal, I thought. Isn't that what we all tried to do?

"But the last shot he gave her, he screwed up." Leon looked straight at me. "He said it would go away, that it would wear off, but meanwhile it made one eyelid droop and she was really freaked out by it."

"So was the picture an expression of her anger, maybe a threat, is that what the thinking is?"

He nodded. "She was his last patient of the afternoon. The receptionist was there when Madison showed up but not when she left. When she went back to the office, she found him, Dr. Bechman, dead."

"Stabbed in the heart?"

"With the Botox injection that Madison had refused."

That did it for me. No way could I turn down the case now.

"Alexander," I said. "It's Rachel Alexander." I gave him a card with my landline and my cell phone numbers.

It took him a while to find his card. It was in the third pocket he checked. I explained my fees and the advance I required. I said there might be some expenses in a case like this and that he'd have to cover those, too. And finally I told him I couldn't guarantee I'd find Sally after all these years, that there was only the slimmest chance of that, but if he still wanted me to try, I would. He said he did.

As for Madison, I hoped there'd be some other way to prove her innocence, if she was innocent, because even if I found her mother and even if the kid started talking again, told the cops what happened on that terrible day, said the blame wasn't hers, who says anyone would believe her?

Leon and I shook hands. Looking at his sad face, I wasn't

sure who needed Sally more, the husband or the daughter. And I had no idea at the time what I was committing myself to and how it would change my life.

"So the receptionist found the doctor when she got to work in the morning?" I asked, wondering why no one had called earlier to say he hadn't arrived home. "That must have been a shock."

"It wasn't in the morning. She went back that night."

"Why would she do that?"

Leon shrugged.

"You think maybe his wife called the receptionist—if he had a wife?"

"He did. He kept her picture on the desk. They all do that for some reason."

"So maybe she called the receptionist at home to ask where he was, if there was some meeting or conference or business dinner he'd neglected to mention?" Why call 911, I thought, when it might just be miscommunication, or a lack of communication?

"I wasn't told why she went back, just that she did."

"And the doctor was there, dead?"

"That's correct."

"What about Madison? Was she there?"

"No. Madison was at home. She came home right after her appointment."

"And did she seem upset?"

Leon didn't answer my question.

"Were you there when she arrived home, Leon?"

"What I say to you, what you say to me, it's confidential, right?"

"It is as far as I'm concerned."

He nodded. "Well, then," he said, "I wasn't at home when she got there, at least not right at that exact moment. I got home about an hour later."

"How do you know she was home an hour if she doesn't speak, if she doesn't communicate with you?"

"She always came straight home from . . ." Leon stopped and looked at me.

"So when you got home that day, did she seem upset? Was anything different, anything off?"

Leon shrugged.

"Not that you noticed?"

"No."

"And when did the police show up?"

"Late. After Madison had gone to bed."

"Were you asleep as well?"

"No."

"And when they came, they told you what had happened?"

"Yes."

"And they showed you the drawing?"

"No. They described it to me."

"And what else did they say?"

"That no one else was there, just Madison and Dr. Bechman. And then they said that the receptionist had gone back and that she'd found him."

"But they didn't tell you why? They didn't say she'd been called, nothing like that?"

"I never thought about it, about why she went back. They were saying that Madison was the only one there and that Dr. Bechman was dead. That's what was on my mind."

"What else did they say?" Wondering if they'd gone beyond implying to accusing.

"One detective said they'd been told that Madison had a history of violence and that she'd been very angry at Dr. Bechman for the perceived harm he'd done to her. Can you imagine? 'The perceived harm.' Then the second detective, he said they were told the doctor had ruined her eye. You see how it was going?"

I nodded, wondering what the cops thought about Leon that night, first his wife had gone missing and now this, the man getting agitated just telling me about it.

"What happened next?" I asked him.

Leon rubbed the back of his neck, looking away, looking anywhere but at me.

"Leon? I'm on your side. Speak up."

"I kind of . . . I got angry. She's my daughter and . . ."

"So you said what?"

"That they should be ashamed of themselves implying that a child with a disability had committed murder."

"Good. That's good you said that. And what was their . . . ?"

"I was yelling—well, yelling softly, if you know what I mean. I didn't want to wake Madison. But they remained calm. Cool. It was almost spooky. They asked if I was there. You know how they do that? They knew I wasn't. Trying to trip me up, to make me out to be a liar, the way they did when Sally disappeared." Leon's lips tight for a moment, his hands balled into fists. "I told them I hadn't been there. So then they asked what time Madison got home." He stopped again, looking at me, then looking away.

"Confidential, Leon, straight down the line."

"I said she'd come straight home, that she was home by five forty-five. Then they asked if she'd been upset when she'd gotten home, if anything was out of the ordinary, and I said no," talking faster now, "that she was fine, that she did her homework before dinner, watched TV afterwards, went to bed on time, everything as usual."

"But you weren't home."

"No, I wasn't." Looking me in the eye now, letting me know he'd do anything to protect his kid.

"And where were you?"

"In the darkroom. It's in the basement of the building where we live. So technically . . ."

"Yeah, I get it. Technically you *were* at home, just not in the apartment."

He nodded. "So I wasn't seen out," he said. "So no one could say they saw me elsewhere."

"Meaning no one could tell the police you weren't at home?"

"Right."

"Not even Madison."

Leon blinked. "That's right."

"But?"

"They're not finished with this. With her. That's why I need your help."

I nodded. I was sure he was right but I didn't say so. Why tell him something he already knew, that the police probably knew he was lying and that there were other issues working against him, the question of a missing wife, a daughter's rage.

"Had Madison ever been violent?" I asked.

Leon struggled with what to say, his brow furrowed, his eyes pinched. He licked his lips, too, letting me know his mouth was dry. There was water at the run for the dogs but none for the people. I waited. I had the feeling his face was telling me more than his words would.

"She's been destructive," he finally said. "She's been out of control on occasion."

"What do you mean by 'out of control'?"

"Breaking things. Ripping up mail. Kicking furniture. She scratched me a few times. Once she broke the dishes."

"All of them?"

"It was cheap stuff. It didn't matter."

"I see. Leon, is it unusual for Madison to go to the doctor herself, for you not to go with her?"

"She . . ." He stopped to think. He seemed to be a cautious man, always concerned he might be choosing a less than perfect word. "She's very independent," he said, nodding.

"Independent?"

"She likes to do things on her own. By herself. She doesn't respond well to . . ."

"Suggestions?"

Leon smiled but his eyes stayed sad. "Yeah. You could say that."

"You're saying she's difficult?"

"She's had a difficult time."

"What about medication? Is she on anything, besides the Botox injections, any kind of tranquilizer or antianxiety medication?" Thinking just about everyone was on something nowadays, thinking that some medications had really serious side effects, some made patients psychotic, thinking if she did do it, maybe it wasn't her fault. But how would we know what she did or didn't do if she wasn't talking?

"She's not on anything. There wasn't anything that could help her, not without terrible side effects. That's why the Botox seemed like the way to go. Dr. Bechman talked about it as if it would be a miracle, as if it would . . ."

Okay, I thought, not medication. Maybe Leon was right. Maybe there was only one thing to do.

"Got any pictures?" I asked.

"Of Madison?"

"No. Of Sally."

"Just the one."

"What one is that?" I asked.

"The one Madison didn't rip up after Sally disappeared."

"Why not that one?"

"She didn't know about it. It's the one in her high school yearbook, those pictures they take of everyone in the graduating class."

My own looked more like a mug shot than the marking of

a milestone and I doubted I still had it. Did the existence of her high school yearbook mean Sally was a saver? And if so, might there be other things she held on to that could help me find her? In which case I'd need a more recent picture because I wasn't all that sure I'd be able to recognize a woman in her forties from a thumbnail shot of her at seventeen.

"What about negatives?" I asked.

Leon turned away. I let it go for the moment. Something about him made my heart grow heavy. It wasn't only what he was saying, it was something about Leon himself.

"I'd like to meet Madison, too. Would that be possible?"

Leon didn't answer me again. He got up and headed for the gate. When he got there, he motioned for me to come, a man of few words, a man of gestures and images. I held up one hand and went over to the hole Dashiell had made in the far corner of the run, shoving the dirt back in with the side of my shoe, then tamping it down. When I headed for the gate, a woman came in carrying two pugs, and the little girl who had been sitting on the bench diagonally across from where we were standing left. I could see what was in her purse now. There was a plastic palm tree, a leaf of lettuce and a live turtle.

I caught up with Leon, and we headed toward the closest exit, Leon stopping once to take a picture of a drug deal in progress, the buyer and seller sitting on the wall behind the chess players.

"Where are we going?" I said.

"You'll need that picture, won't you?" He began to walk again, then remembered his manners and turned around. "Madison," he said to the little girl with the purse who was walking in the dirt next to one side of the path, "this is Rachel. She's going to help us try to find Sally."

Madison looked my way. The oversize shirt was the kind a repairman might wear. Or a soda jerk. The name Tito was embroidered over the chest pocket in navy to match the collar and the trim on the short sleeves, sleeves that came down past her elbows. I walked over to the side of the path and held out my hand. "Hi, Madison," I said, "I'm pleased to meet you."

She lifted her free hand but not to take mine. She was reaching for her sunglasses, taking hold of them, sliding them off. The eyelid over her right eye drooped badly. The other moved quickly from left to right a few times and then stopped. Standing in front of her, Madison just staring at me, I had the same experience I sometimes got before I became a private investigator, when I used to train dogs for a living. I was suddenly privy to information that seemed to come from another creature without benefit of words. Back then, and now, it always made me want to run for cover. Have a good look, Madison seemed to be telling me, at why my mother left in the first place.

Dashiell took a step forward and put his face up to the plastic purse, his tail slapping against my leg. Madison ignored him. She put her glasses back on, turned and walked after Leon, who was already leaving the park. For a moment, I just stood there watching them, the father looking in one direction, the kid in another, the empty space between them, space where Sally could have walked were Sally here. They stopped at the corner to wait for the light to change, then crossed the street and headed down the block, neither one turning back to see if I was with them. I tapped my leg to let Dashiell know we were going and hurried to catch up.

CHAPTER 2

We walked pretty much in silence, or rather we walked from Washington Square Park to Greenwich and Bank streets with the accompaniment of sirens, helicopters, pneumatic drills, horns honking, dogs barking, cell phones and bicycle bells ringing, babies crying, people shouting, the usual cacophony of a big city, but without a conversation of our own.

Leon and Madison lived in a brick apartment building on the west side of the street; there was a restaurant on the east side and a supermarket on the northwest corner of the intersection. Leon unlocked the inner lobby door, and we walked up a flight of stairs to the second floor, Leon taking the lead, Dashiell next, then me, Madison and her turtle bringing up the rear. Like most kids over ten or eleven, Madison had walked home as if she were by herself, sometimes ahead, sometimes behind, sometimes off to the side, but never right alongside her parent and never, as far as I could see, holding hands.

When Leon unlocked the door, we entered a short hall with a hugely overcrowded clothing rack full of coats and jackets, then a small foyer with a desk, a laptop, a printer and a wall of books. The bookshelves continued around the next wall and down one side of the living room, all the way to the far wall of windows facing east and overlooking Greenwich Street. The small kitchen, at the far end of the foyer, had a window, a real prize in New York City. Between the office area and the doorway to the kitchen, Leon had an oversize dining room table covered with books, tossed-off clothing, newspapers, magazines, cereal boxes, empty soda cans and unopened mail.

As soon as we were inside, Madison disappeared down a hallway just beyond the archway to the living room. A moment later, I heard a door slam, but before Leon had the chance to offer me a glass of water or a place to sit, she was back, this time without her shoes and without the turtle. Or so I thought. But then she walked up to Dashiell, opened her hand, and there it was, smack in the middle of her small palm. When Dashiell leaned closer to get a good sniff, Madison took a step backwards, retreating in slow motion and taking Dashiell along with her.

"Leave the door open," Leon said, turning to me and raising his eyebrows as a way of asking if it was okay for Dashiell to go off with Madison. But before I had the chance to answer, we heard the door to Madison's room slam again, this time louder. And a moment after that, Dashiell was back, the door apparently having been closed in his face.

Leon shook his head. "Twelve," he said. "Just. But eleven wasn't any better. Neither was ten."

There was a daybed under the living room windows, a small, faded love seat against the wall to the left. I sat on the love seat. Leon walked over to the wall of books opposite where I was sitting, taking a few books off a high shelf, pulling out one that had been lying flat against the back of the bookcase.

"She was the most beautiful thing I'd ever seen," he said, his voice barely above a whisper.

"Sally?"

Leon nodded. "Sally," he repeated, grateful, I thought, for any chance to say her name.

He sat down on the edge of the daybed.

"I couldn't take my eyes off her."

"Where did you meet?" I asked.

"I was her teacher," he said.

"College?"

"No," glancing down at the book in his lap, "high school."

"Oh," I said.

"She got pregnant so I married her."

"How old was she?"

"Sixteen. Fifteen really. She was in the twelfth grade. She was, is, very bright and she'd been skipped a couple of times."

"Wasn't there some kind of trouble about this, Leon, you getting a fifteen-year-old kid pregnant?"

Leon looked at me for what seemed like a very long time before responding. "I left the school. I left teaching actually. That's when I began . . ." He touched his camera, still hanging around his neck, lifting the strap over his head and putting the Leica down on the round wooden coffee table that sat between us.

"And what about Sally? Did she get into any kind of trouble over this?"

Leon shrugged. "We moved here," he said. "I got her into another school for the rest of her senior year. She graduated with honors."

"How'd you manage to marry a fifteen-year-old?"

"We drove down to Delaware. Pregnant teens can marry there without parental permission."

"So her parents . . ."

"It was just her mother."

"And?"

"It was bad."

"Did it ever get better?"

Leon shook his head.

"What? They never spoke again?"

"No."

"So you're saying Sally was fifteen when you got her pregnant and her mother disowned her?"

"Something like that."

"So Sally's mother never got to see her granddaughter?"

"No."

"Not even after Sally left?"

"She was gone by then. Cancer."

I shook my head. "You'd think she'd taken an Uzi and shot up the school. High school kids get pregnant. It's not great, but it's a fact of life."

Leon nodded.

"Let me get this straight, okay? Sally was a senior in high school at the time?"

"That's right. She was in my honors history class."

I stopped for a minute to make some notes.

"And you got married in Delaware when she was only fifteen."

"And a half."

I nodded.

"She got to graduate," he said. "That was good."

"Then no one knew?"

"Only her mother."

"Did her mother get you into any kind of trouble, with the law?" I whispered, thinking for just the briefest of moments whom it was you'd look at first when a wife disappears, then pushing the thought from my mind, at least for now. If the police hadn't suspected Leon, why should I?

"No, not really. It, it got worked out."

"Because you married her?"

Leon didn't answer me.

"It's still considered statutory rape, isn't it, when a girl is only fifteen?"

He nodded.

"But even with an irate mother, you weren't charged?"

"No, there were no charges." Leon turned away, but not before I could see the pain in his face.

"I see," I said, putting the pen down. "Had you or she ever considered terminating the pregnancy?"

"No, we never did. It never came up."

"And no one else knew?"

He shook his head. "She made it all the way through graduation without showing. Madison was born in September."

"What about her girlfriends? Did she confide in any of them?"

Leon shook his head again. "After we came back from Delaware and moved here, she kept pretty much to herself."

"She lost touch with her old friends?"

He nodded. "She didn't want any of them to know."

"What about new friends at the new school?"

Leon turned the yearbook over, as if the answer to my question might be on the front cover. "No. She read a lot."

"So she'd be what now, twenty-eight?"

Leon nodded. "June fifth," he said. "She graduated at sixteen. She's an extraordinary . . ."

He looked toward the end of the living room where the little hall to Madison's room began, before opening the yearbook to where there was a picture of Sally among the graduates. He put his finger next to it, but she was the only Sally on the page, Sally Bruce, it said, talented newcomer, and above that, the picture, a pretty girl who didn't look much older than her daughter was now.

"How did this come about, Leon, you dating a student?"

Leon held up one hand, as if warding off a blow. I let it go. I had agreed to try to find her because Leon thought it might help Madison. What had happened all those years ago wasn't really the point. Or was it?

Had Sally loved him back then, I wondered, when he was her teacher? Or was it the excitement of the forbidden, an older man, the aura of romance, the fact that it had to be kept secret? Those were powerful aphrodisiacs, but aphrodisiacs don't last. Had she been happy to marry him? And then what? Somewhere along the way, as happens to so many of us, had she stopped loving him? If she ever had.

And what about Madison? Had Sally loved her? Had anyone loved Madison back then? Did anyone love her now?

"Do you have anything of Sally's I could borrow, or look at? A diary, school papers, letters, computer files, anything at all?"

"There are a few things I have put away."

"Would you rather we do that when Madison is in school?"

"She's not in school now. I'm keeping her with me for the time being." Leon looked very uncomfortable.

"Can you just do that?" I asked, wondering what he'd told them, if he'd said she had the flu or sprained an ankle, something that would explain the time out of school. Or had he told them the truth, that there was the possibility she'd killed someone and he didn't want her running around loose?

But all he said was, "They're faxing me her lessons," and I let it go. There were more important issues at hand.

"Can she hear us?" I whispered.

"I don't know."

"You said she was a suspect. Then she hasn't been charged?"

"Not yet," he whispered. "Doesn't mean they're not trying." He looked toward the foyer again.

"So they're attempting to make a case, but they haven't yet. Have they talked to Madison?"

"They tried. They came again the next day. Madison was here and I didn't know what to do."

"So you let them talk to her?"

He nodded.

"And?"

"What you'd expect. She listened. She stared at them. Then she went to her room and closed the door."

"Slammed it?"

"No. Closed it quietly. She didn't seem in the least bit angry."

"What did she seem?"

"I figured she didn't want to . . ."

I waited while Leon surfed for just the right words.

"She wasn't going to deal with it," he said. "That's how she is, since Sally left."

"She was only seven then."

"Correct. But that's when it started. It was all part of the package, not speaking and this, this shutting down. She'll almost always listen to what you have to say, but if Madison decides she's not dealing, there's no changing her mind."

"Did they ask to have a psychiatrist examine her?"

"They did. But I said I'd have to think about that. When they left, I called a lawyer. He told me that unless there was a court order, I should refuse. So that's what I did."

"And you're keeping her with you . . . ?"

"To protect her," Leon whispered. "She's in a bad place right now. She's in grave danger. And she's my daughter."

I nodded. Leon had the yearbook on his lap, both hands pressing it down as if, but for that, it might fly away and disappear.

"So how do you want to do this?"

"I'll get together whatever I have," he patted the year-book, "and call you when it's ready."

I picked up the pen and pad. "How do you spell her doctor's name?" I asked him.

Leon looked surprised for a moment and then reached for the pad and pen, writing down the doctor's name. "I'll work on the things you need after Madison goes to sleep," he said.

I nodded. "I'd like to say good-bye to her, to Madison."

Leon got up, and Dashiell and I trailed after him past the bathroom to Madison's door. Leon knocked and waited but there was no answer, nor was there any sound coming from inside that would make you think Madison might not have heard the knock. When he lifted his hand again, I shook my head.

"Another time," I said.

There was a horseshoe hung over the apartment door, open side up to catch good luck. If any family needed it, it was this one.

Walking home along Hudson Street, I thought about the chess players we'd passed in the park, hunched over the in-laid boards at the small square tables in the southwestern corner of the park, the kibitzers standing all around watching every move. It was getting kind of cool for outdoor chess but the players would be there until the snow came, maybe even afterwards. That's how it was when you had an obsession. Something that would make another person stop and think, or turn away, foul weather, say, or the fear of running afoul of the law, might not even slow you down. Was that the way it had been for Leon? And what, I wondered, had it been for Sally?

CHAPTER 3

I unlocked the wrought iron gate that leads to the tunnel formed by the town houses on either side, picked up my mail and watched Dashiell run ahead into the cool October light that filled my garden. The small brick back cottage I rented was in the far left corner of the garden, an herb patch I'd planted on the side facing the town house my landlords owned, a cobalt blue water bowl on the far side of the stairs where Dashiell was taking a long, noisy drink. I sat down on the steps leading to my front door and opened the mail, three offers of credit cards, all preapproved, a free pass to one of the local gyms, an envelope full of discount coupons, three catalogs.

I unlocked the door and left it open for Dashiell, who was inspecting the land, first checking the perimeter, then quartering the yard looking for something that would require his attention. Today was also the day we'd check out the town house to make sure no one had broken in and that everything was working properly, the job that earned me a rent so low I could afford to live in Greenwich Village, the increasingly unaffordable neighborhood where no matter what changed, I still felt most at home.

Leon had a different kind of deal. I knew the building

anyway, but the signs were all there as well, no doorman during the day, a small, no-frills lobby, halls that could have used a paint job. Leon's deal was called rent stabilization, one of the factors that gave the city its remarkable diversity, allowing the old, the young, the newly arrived, the fresh out of school as well as artists, writers, actors and photographers to live here. The young managed by taking on roommates. Others, the newly arrived, lived in the outer boroughs, the Russians in Brooklyn, the Chinese in Queens. And the luckiest ones, many of the city's elderly and everyone in Leon's building, survived because their landlords were bound by laws which limited the percentage they could raise a tenant's rent.

I picked up the key to the town house, whistled to Dashiell, and we went back out the front gate, locking it behind us. We went up the steps to the front door of the town house, unlocking both locks and stepping into the small hall that led first to the library and next to the living room. The Siegals had been home only for three weeks in the last six months and the house looked more like a museum to me than a home. The Siegals' house, since they owned more than one, was not crammed full of a lifetime of personal artifacts. But even with the ones that were here, photos of their parents and their children, the collection of hand-carved wooden animals from all over the globe, the paintings of flowers in the living room, the house didn't seem to have the personal feeling of a lived-in space.

Leon's apartment was different, and though the living room had a sparse coolness to it, little furniture and black-and-white photos on the white walls, the rest of the apartment, at least the parts I had seen so far, were cluttered with the detritus of the occupants—peeled-off clothing that had been tossed on the backs of the dining room chairs, piles of negatives and contact sheets on Leon's messy desk, a red wagon, like the one I used as a coffee table, filled with toilet paper parked between the kitchen and the bathroom. There were canisters on the kitchen counters, tea and coffee, perhaps cookies in one, signs of life that were missing in the Siegal house. In fact, on those occasions when my landlords blew into town, they ate out every night, went to the opera, the theater, a museum or two, and then they'd be off again, to England or Italy or Greece.

Would the way Leon's space looked make more sense when I got to know him better, the blackboard scribbled with notes over his busy desk, the dining room table covered with at least a week's worth of mail, most of it not yet opened, and then the stark living room? There were no plants, no rugs, no knickknacks, no doodads, nothing collected in a trip to Denmark or Kenya, no photos of Sally or any other family member, just the three of Madison and those weren't in the living room. They were over the dining room table. I'd stopped there for a moment on the way out. Madison at two holding a small wooden giraffe. Madison at what looked like four reading a book, precocious like her mother. Madison at six holding up a drawing the way kids do, proffering favorite artifacts to the eye of the camera. Nothing more recent. Nothing, it seemed, since her mother had disappeared, as if she, Madison, had disappeared along with her.

Dashiell and I took the stairs down to the Siegals' huge kitchen. I checked the windows, he checked the odors. With nothing out of the ordinary there, I sent him on ahead to check all the rooms, following slowly behind him. Anything I found might need a glazier or perhaps a plumber. What he might find would be of more concern, and while I checked for signs of break-ins, too, Dashiell was the one who would actually find the intruder were there one. There was nothing to worry about this time. When I got to the top-floor bedrooms, I opened the back windows to give the place some air. I'd stop back and close them in a day or two.

We always left by the back door, emerging into the light of the garden. Dashiell followed me into the cottage and up to my office on the second floor. I sat at the desk, thinking about Madison, about the tics that the late Dr. Eric Bechman was treating with Botox. I turned on the laptop and Googled Botox to see what I could find and discovered that Botox is not only used for wrinkles, but that it's used medically as well, to mitigate the pain of migraine headaches and to stop the muscle spasms of Tourette's syndrome. Leon hadn't mentioned Tourette's. He hadn't mentioned any disease, just the fact that Madison suffered from tics. I wondered if it was Tourette's, and if so, what the timing was in Madison's diagnosis and her mother's departure.

Botox, or botulin toxin A, paralyzes muscles. That had been the point, of course, in injecting it into the muscles that controlled Madison's eyelid. And even though it had caused ptosis, or drooping, rather than merely stopping the tics, Dr. Bechman, it seemed, had planned on injecting the other eyelid. Wasn't that why there'd been a hypodermic needle there, already filled?

It didn't take a genius to figure out what that injection might do to any other muscle, including the heart. Even a kid, say a twelve-year-old, could figure that out.

I thought about the little girl I'd met that day. She wasn't the same little girl I'd seen in the three portraits her father had taken. The little girl in the pictures was serious, not smiling at the camera for Daddy. But the little girl I'd met in Washington Square Park was seething with anger, and from what I had already learned, with good reason.

And what about her mother? Had Sally been angry, too, trapped by a pregnancy at fifteen? I thought about the girls who got pregnant when I was in high school, Amy Mandel and Claire something or other. Amy had married her boyfriend. They were both seventeen. They had a boy. I heard later that they got divorced and that Amy and the kid had moved back home, to her parents' house. Claire disappeared for the rest of the term, and when she came back to school she was neither married nor did she have a child. Someone said she gave it up for adoption. Someone else said that since she was a devout Catholic, abortion had been out of the question. But apparently sex hadn't been.

I didn't know of any other girls at school who were pregnant before graduation, but I'm sure there were a few others. And I didn't know of any girls who were having sex with their teachers, something frowned upon by society in general and by the state of New York in particular. But we all knew things happened. Every girl in the school knew never to be caught alone with Mr. Margolies. We called him the Groper. And there were rumors about two of the gym teachers as well, Ms. Edison and Mr. Morris. Mr. Morris was married, but still the rumors flew that he liked boys. Ms. Edison looked like a truck driver and everyone said she lived with another woman. If you got her for gym, she'd pat you on the ass when it was your turn to play, or if you got a basket, ran faster than you had the day before or simply stood close enough for her to reach you.

Leon said no one knew that Sally was pregnant. I wondered if that were so. I wondered if it might be possible to find someone who had gone to school with Sally Bruce, someone with a good memory and a loose tongue. I took out the little pad and made some more notes, then I transferred my questions to three-by-five cards and tacked them up to the bulletin board over the desk.

Sally's classmates, one note said. I was sure Leon would put the yearbook in with the papers he was going to collect for me. But the one with her picture in it wouldn't help. What I needed was the yearbook from Sally's old school. That's where her friends had been and that's where, if there had been any rumors, they would have been. I bet the school library kept all the yearbooks. I added, "Name of high school where Leon taught and Sally went?" to the card.

After she'd married Leon, Sally didn't make new friends. Or so Leon said. I'd have to check that out, too. And find out what she liked, what she did, who she was, all of which seemed to have changed when she got pregnant. And wasn't that the case when I was in high school, too? Plans to go to college, hanging out with friends, senior trips, after-school clubs, all became a thing of the past. Suddenly everything was about the baby, the baby you didn't plan for, the baby you didn't want in the first place.

Leon hadn't said what kind of dog Roy was and there were no pictures of him hanging over Leon's desk, over the dining room table, on those stark white living room walls. Had Madison torn up the pictures of Roy, too?

I'd been hired to find Sally. In order to do that, I'd need to know more about whom she chose to take with her and whom she'd left behind. If there was a chance in the world she could be found in the first place.

I went downstairs to fix Dashiell's dinner and think about my own, whether to order in a salad with some grilled chicken from Pepe Verde or a pizza. The *Times* was sitting unopened on the small table outside the kitchen where I'd dropped it after Dashiell had brought it in from where the delivery lady slid it through the curlicues in the fence. I got a card from her every Christmas. "Season's Greetings from Estella Gonzalez, your *New York Times* delivery person," it said, my reminder that a tip would be appreciated. I took the paper over to the couch and began to page through the depressing news, one page of it after another, stopping to read an article with the headline "Body Found at LaGuardia."

"A headless body," it said, "and a head, floated to the surface of the East River near a runway at LaGuardia Airport
yesterday morning, the authorities said, but it was unclear
whether they were from the same person."

Who was I kidding, I thought, or more accurately, who
was Leon kidding, hiring me to find his missing wife?
Sooner or later, most missing people turn up dead like the
poor chap who was found in the East River just yesterday.
The body, the article said, was male, apparently a young
man in his twenties. "No details about the head," it said,
"were available yesterday."

What if it turned out that Sally Bruce Spector wasn't
alive and well in, say, San Francisco? What if it turned out
that she was dead? Then what? Sure, I would have done my
job, but what about Madison?

I dropped the paper and went back upstairs to my office,
first looking in the phone book for a Dr. Eric Bechman and
writing down his address. Then I did an Internet search to
see what was out there, what if anything I could learn about
the man Madison had supposedly killed.

CHAPTER 4

Everything was on the Internet now, instructions for making bombs, herbs guaranteed to enlarge your penis, sites listing the side effects of drugs, people's family albums. No more little black corners needed to affix your precious photos in a real-life album. Now you could use a virtual one. Instead of baby books, infants had their own Web sites starting with their sonograms, scanned and put online as baby's first picture.

Eric Bechman had no Web site, which wasn't surprising, but something useful did come up when I searched, a two-paragraph article that had been in the *Times* two days after the murder. The article said that Eric Bechman, fifty-one, a pediatrician, had died suddenly and that the police suspected foul play. They were "following some leads," an unnamed spokesperson for the department was quoted as saying, and the case was "under investigation." There was, I was relieved to see, no mention at all of an underage suspect. I imagined that because of Madison's age, any information about her had been withheld.

In the second paragraph it said that the doctor was survived by a wife, Marsha, and two sons, Alan and Rubin, all of Larchmont.

I checked the card tacked up over my desk. The doctor's office was on Washington Square North, which meant it was in one of the capacious town houses along the north side of Washington Square Park. Not a bad commute, probably not much more than an hour, door-to-door. But perhaps the doctor stayed over in the city one or two nights a week anyway, the better to be at the hospital early in the morning or late in the evening. The better, sometimes, to have an evening or two away from the family and in better, or at least different, company.

I took another file card from the top left drawer and wrote down Bechman's name and address again and under that a few questions that had come to mind. Did the doctor have a pied-à-terre in the city? Did the doctor stay over in the city during the week? Did the doctor have a girlfriend, preferably, I thought, an irate one? Where had Marsha Bechman been at the time of her husband's murder?

I wondered if Bechman had one of those shared offices, two or three doctors together to keep the expenses down, almost a necessity nowadays what with people suing over every little mistake doctors made and malpractice insurance being so high. In fact, I suspected that for someone injecting Botox into the faces of children, the insurance would be even stiffer than usual.

I stopped writing and checked the time. It was too late for a doctor's office to be open and too early for Dashiell's last walk, but I had the sudden yen to walk over to Washington Square Park and see how many names were on the doctor's bell. As soon as I stood up, Dash did, too. He was always willing to drop whatever it was he was doing, in this case taking a nap, in order to accompany me on a walk of any length, one of the many things I liked about dogs in general and Dashiell in particular.

I grabbed my cell phone, my keys, a twenty-dollar bill

and Dashiell's leash, checking the pockets of my jeans for pickup bags and finding three. We headed out the door and turned right, walking a couple of blocks to West Fourth Street and then taking that toward the park, skirting it when we got there, then looking for Dr. Bechman's address. The town house his office occupied was about a third of the way up the block, a stately building with views that at one time were more elegant than they are today, unless there were drug dealers and the homeless in the park then, too. Even so, the doctor was in a classy spot, not far from the newly renovated Washington Square Arch and just around the corner from Fifth Avenue.

I didn't need to open the low gate that led to the two steps down to the doctor's office. I could read the three brass plaques from where I stood on the sidewalk. Dr. Bechman was, according to the plaque with his name on it, a plaque that was still there a week and a half after his death, a pediatric neurologist, something I didn't know existed before that moment. Dr. Hyram Willet, who had the top plaque, was an oncologist and Dr. Laura Edelstein, a pediatrician. My guess was that Dr. Willet worked only with children, too, because there was no way an adult with a diagnosis of cancer would sit in a waiting room full of screaming kids.

The fact that Bechman had been part of a shared practice was good news. It meant the office was still open for business, that the receptionist still had a job and I had a chance of wheedling some information out of her. What I wanted, of course, was a complete patient list as well as any personal gossip about the late Dr. Bechman I could get. At the very least, I wanted someone else's take on Madison Spector. Since she herself wasn't talking, and since I believed her father was holding things back in order to protect his daughter, something I couldn't really fault him for, I had to find people who were willing to speak openly about Madison. I needed to know more about her.

I looked at the card I'd taken off the bulletin board and pocketed, and dialed Dr. Bechman's number. Standing in front of the doctor's office, I listened to the recording tell me what hours the office was open and when Dr. Bechman was, or in this case used to be, available: Mondays, Tuesdays and Thursdays from noon to five and Fridays from one to four.

I took the stairs, a wide, long stoop up to the front door, which led to the parlor floor of the town house, just as they did in the smaller version I took care of on West Tenth Street. I had a penlight in my pocket but found I didn't need it. The light hanging over the doorway, brass and etched glass, lit the name on the bell. There was just one. Apparently Dr. Willet lived in the rest of the town house and Drs. Bechman and Edelstein commuted. I made a note to check under Bechman again in the phone book to see if there was a residential listing as well.

Standing at the top of the stairs I reminded myself that whatever Dr. Bechman had done, with or without Botox, it was unlikely he deserved his early demise. I had to be sure that in my zeal to get Madison off the hook, inspired not by my belief in her innocence but by the fact that the likelihood of finding her mother was so slim, I did not fall into the trap of blaming the victim. I didn't plan to do anything with whatever I discovered unless I was sure it impacted on the case. I was just, for the moment, doing what my job had taught me to do, following every thread, no matter where it went, because you never knew what it could reveal.

I dialed Leon's number next. He answered on the first ring.

"Are you planning to be with Madison every second of the time until this case is resolved one way or another?"

"Rachel?"

"Sorry. I should remember to say hello first."

I expected Leon to laugh at that but he didn't. I doubted he'd had much to laugh about for a very long time.

"What are you talking about?" he asked. Then he whispered, "Do you think it's odd that I don't want her on her own now, Rachel? After all . . ." His voice trailed off, but I didn't need Leon to finish his last sentence.

"No, it's not odd."

"I don't understand. What is it you want?"

"I was thinking I'd like to spend some time with Madison, just the two of us. Would that be possible?"

There was silence on the phone while Leon processed my request.

"Why? She's not going to tell you anything," he whispered. "She's not going to talk to you, if that's what you're thinking."

I looked at my watch wondering if Madison was still up and if that was why he was whispering.

"Even if you had a court order saying that you had to keep her with you, you'd probably still be able to occasionally hire a responsible person to take care of her when you weren't able to."

"There is no court order. She hasn't been arrested."

I ignored his comment. "Hire me," I said. "I'm responsible and my rates can't be beat."

Silence.

"Don't tell me you couldn't use a break, Leon? I'm offering you a break."

"What's this all about?"

"You're going to have to trust me on this, Leon," I told him. Then the silence was coming from my end. "I'm not sure what it's all about but I think that in order to do the job you hired me to do . . ." Stopping in mid-sentence, sounding more like Leon than myself. "Here's what I'm doing, Leon. I'm exploring every possible connection to Sally in the hope that someone or something will eventually lead me to her. That's all I can do after all these years and that's what spending time with Madison is all about."

"But Madison . . ." He stopped. I figured I knew what he was going to tell me but I didn't say so. "She won't talk to you, Rachel. And even if she did, she was only seven when Sally left. I don't know how much she remembers or if any of it would be useful to you. And she's difficult. You won't find it easy being with her. You can see that already, can't you?"

"I don't have a lot of options, Leon."

I heard him blowing his nose. Then coughing. "Okay," he said. "You do what you feel is best. I'll explain it to Madison."

"No, don't do that," I said much too quickly.

"Don't explain it?"

"What would you say?"

"I'd say that . . ." He stopped, unable to answer my question. "What would I say?"

"Does Madison understand the arrangement and the reason for it?"

"I believe so."

"So she knows you're not willing to leave her alone right now?"

"Yes."

"Fine, then tell her that you have to do something on Saturday morning and you can't take her with you. Tell her that I'm going to stay with her." There was another silence on the other end of the phone. I couldn't even hear Leon breathing. "Leon?"

"Oh," he said.

"Oh, yes or oh, no?"

"Oh, yes. I was nodding. I forgot you couldn't see me."

"I'll be there at ten," I told him. "Day after tomorrow."

"I'm working on the papers for you."

"Good. When will I be able to get them?"

"Tomorrow night, after eight. Madison goes to sleep at eight."

"I'll be there," I told him.

"Just ring the bell. I'll bring them down."

This time I was the one who nodded, but not until after Leon was off the line. It wasn't that I'd forgotten that Leon couldn't see me. I was nodding to myself, agreeing with my plan to try to get to know Madison. As I walked home, that's all I could think about, wondering how I might connect somehow with this unreachable person, wondering when I did, if I did, what her response would be, wondering if she had, indeed, killed Dr. Bechman in a fit of rage, as the authorities presumed.

When I got home, Dashiell and I stayed outside for a while. I thought I'd sit on the steps, look up through the branches of the oak tree in the center of the garden and watch the stars. But it was cloudy and there wasn't much to see, the sky an inky black with just the occasional wisp of silver-gray cloud visible beyond the tree. Dashiell sat next to me, on the top step, waiting to see if I might toss a ball or order a pizza, or perhaps just waiting with no other purpose in mind. I thought we'd stay out for a while and then go in and go to bed, but I couldn't stop thinking about Madison.

What if Sally were still alive? What if I were able to find her? What if I could convince her to come back and try to help the daughter she'd abandoned five years earlier? And suppose she did that, suppose she agreed and suppose, as Leon wished, seeing her mother, Madison began to talk again? And suppose when she did, she said she had killed

Dr. Bechman, that she was guilty as charged? Or rather as not yet charged.

I worried at first that even if Madison did speak up, no one would believe her. But that would only be the case if she claimed she hadn't killed Dr. Bechman. I was pretty sure that if she confessed to the crime, everyone would think she was telling the truth, the whole truth and nothing but the truth, even her own father.

Was that why I was so concerned about this angry, un-communicative little girl, because in the end she might have no one else on her side? I hadn't even been hired to solve the crime she'd been thought to have committed. I'd only been hired to try to find Sally.

Sally.

Had she planned to disappear, wouldn't she have left when Leon was out working and Madison was in school? She could have taken some things then, some clothes, some money. She could have left a note.

But that's not what had happened. She'd gone out to walk Roy. And then what? Had someone snatched her off the street? Had her body floated to the surface somewhere like the one that had turned up near LaGuardia Airport? Was Sally dead and gone, buried in potter's field or in some woods in New Jersey, her bones, perhaps, dug up and carried away by animals, one or two at a time?

Or was it something else entirely, a lover, say, closer to her own age, someone she'd met quite by accident at the su-permarket or in the drugstore, someone she'd been seeing and couldn't find a way to tell Leon about?

Or had she just wanted some air? And once outside, once she'd started putting distance between herself and the life she'd been living, she found she couldn't go back. Who hasn't imagined that scenario, I thought, walking out of the house one night, letting the door close behind you, never going back. You wouldn't necessarily know where you were headed. That wasn't the point. You'd only know where you had been, and that it was a place you didn't want to be, a place you couldn't be, not ever again.

CHAPTER 5

After a swim at the Y, I stopped at home to drop off my wet swimsuit, make a couple of phone calls and pick up Dashiell, heading back where we'd been the night before, to Dr. Bechman's office. It seemed that Dr. Bechman wasn't the only one who didn't have hours on Friday morning. According to the two recordings I'd just listened to, the entire office would be closed Friday morning. Dr. Willet's recording said that in case of an emergency, he could be reached at St. Vincent's Hospital. His pager number was repeated twice. Dr. Edelstein had hours from one to four on Fridays, the same as the late Dr. Bechman. It was still early and no one answered the bell. I crossed the street and leaned against the park fence to wait.

An hour earlier, floating in the pool after doing laps, letting my mind wander along with my body, I thought not about Madison Spector or her missing mother. I thought about my sister Lillian, on the day her son was born. My brother-in-law, Ted, had called to give me the news and I'd gone straight to the hospital to see the newborn Zachery, his tiny dimpled hands in fists he held to his face, like a boxer protecting a glass chin. The moment I picked him up, I felt a lurching in my chest, something opening to embrace him,

to make room for this small being in my heart. It was difficult to take my eyes off him, but when I did, I saw my sister
watching him, too, the expression on her face one I'd never
seen before.

"It's as if the whole world was in black and white," she
whispered, "and now, all at once, it's in color."

I was sitting on the edge of her bed, the baby's head
against one arm, his almost weightless body on my lap,
watching his lips work, practicing for his first big meal.

"I saw him being born," she said. "And the strangest thing
happened." My sister pale, her hair still damp against her
brow, her hand on my arm, the backs of her long fingers
against the baby's head. "It was as if I was finally ready to
start my life. No one ever told me," she said, taking her hand
away, reaching for the cup of water on her nightstand. "No
one ever said I would feel like this."

Waiting for someone to show up and open the office, I
wondered how Sally had felt when Madison was born, if
she, too, felt that her life was about to begin. Or did she feel
it had just ended? Instead of the brightness my sister had
experienced, my sister who always felt she'd been born to
be a mother, did Sally feel the world closing in? From that
moment on, everything she wanted to do would have to be
preceded by an answer to the question "What about the
baby?" Had the tiny person she held in her arms repre-
sented not the freedom to be herself, the way it had for my
sister, but a kind of prison, a taking away of everything
she'd ever wanted?

Turning the corner from MacDougal Street, a woman
caught my eye. Was it the brisk, no-nonsense walk, the fact
that she was heading for the place I was watching, or was it
something else, some hard-to-pin-down quality that said *receptionist*? Did she somehow appear to be the person whose
voice was on all three recordings? Or was it the white uni-

form, white stockings and white shoes? I wondered if she really was a nurse or if she just played one on the bus coming to work and, perhaps, in the office, doling out sage advice and urgent warnings along with the little white card with the next appointment on it.

I crossed the street and met her at the gate that led to the garden floor of the town house. When her eyebrows rose, I realized I hadn't planned what I was going to say. I wasn't related to Madison. I hadn't even been hired to do the work I was attempting to do. I had no right to ask anything. Could I tell her I had some questions to ask her because I was just curious? When I didn't speak, she reached for the latch to open the gate, but her manners and her training took over and she didn't continue on inside.

"Yes?"

"I'm not sure," I said, trying to gather my thoughts. Since lying when I was on the job was one of my specialties, in fact, lying for a living was as good a definition of undercover work as I'd ever heard, I was surprised to find myself tongue-tied. I knew what I wanted, but for once in my life, not how to try to get it. "It's about Madison Spector," I finally said. "I've been hired to find her mother."

She didn't say anything but she was shaking her head, holding her hand out the way you might hold a cross out to ward off a vampire. She looked startled, almost afraid, then angry, her face a slide show of emotions.

"I was the one who found him," she said. She shook her head again. "Whatever it is you want, I'm *not* the person to ask."

"I'm only trying to understand a child who doesn't talk," I said. "Her father thinks that if I can find her mother, Madison might be willing to speak again, might be able to tell us what happened."

"Oh, we *know* what happened."

"Do you?"

"I guess you're new on the scene," she nearly spat out at me. "I guess you haven't spent much time with her." She cocked her head and waited for my reply.

"That's correct," I told her.

"Do you think this is the first time she's acted up?" Shaking her head, frowning. "Well, it's not. Only this time—"

"Was there yelling?" I asked.

"Yelling? She doesn't make a sound." She dropped her voice to a whisper. "It's just one of her many ways of manipulating the people who are forced to deal with her."

"So there was no yelling?"

"Well, Dr. Bechman would never have yelled at a child. At anyone. So the answer to your question is no, there was no yelling."

The little tag pinned to her chest uniform said "L. Peach."

"So you didn't hear anything, Ms. Peach, anything at all?"

She inhaled sharply through her nose but said nothing, a woman in her sixties, neat in her white uniform, hair pulled tightly back off her full face. Her cheeks were doughy and she was wearing too much makeup. Behind her bifocals I could see she was fuming. A second later, I thought she was about to cry.

"She was the last person here. She, she . . ."

I just waited, Dashiell sitting close to my leg.

"I heard him before I left for the day. I heard him saying what he'd said before, what he'd told Mr. Spector when he came in with her right after it happened," pointing to her eyelid, "that the effects of the Botox were temporary, that that's why she was supposed to come in every three months for shots, because it wasn't permanent. Anyway, this shot was supposed to be for her other eye. He did one at a time. He was very conservative in his treatment of . . ."

"Yeah, yeah. And then what?"

Ms. Peach looked puzzled.

"You heard him explain to Madison that the effects of the Botox were temporary. And then what happened?"

"I left. I had no idea, of course . . ."

"Nothing else before you left?"

"Yes. One other thing."

This time my eyebrows went up, but whatever it was Ms. Peach was going to say, it wasn't coming easily.

"A kick."

"A kick? You heard a kick?"

"It sounded as if she kicked the desk." In control again. "Have you ever seen one of her fits, Miss . . ."

"Alexander. Rachel Alexander. No, I haven't. I only met her once. The thing is . . ."

Ms. Peach was shaking her head again. "Then you have no idea, simply no idea."

"That's why I came to you," I told her.

She nodded, then looked around to see who might be watching us. "Nasty," she whispered. "A real terror."

"Did you know her before?"

"Before *what*?"

"Before she stopped talking."

Ms. Peach sighed. She shook her head.

"How long have you been working here, if I might ask?"

"Nearly five years, as if that's any of your—"

"And the person who was here before you?"

"You mean the temp?" She rolled her eyes.

"No. The person who held the job before you."

"Oh, you mean Celia?"

"Yes, Celia. How long had she been here?"

Ms. Peach's brow furrowed. No free Botox for employees, I thought.

"Was she here before Madison stopped talking?"

"Well, yes, she was, but . . ."

"But what?"

"Two weeks after Madison was diagnosed, that's when her mother disappeared and Madison became silent. So Celia would have only seen her five or six times."

I nodded. "It's Tourette's syndrome, is that right?"

She began to shake her head. "I can't discuss that with you, Ms. Alexander. You're not a blood relative of the child's, are you?"

"I understand," I said. "But I'm confused now. Mr. Spector mentioned her, Celia, as one of Madison's favorite people."

"Celia?"

I nodded.

Ms. Peach snorted. "So *that's* what she did with her time."

"What do you mean?"

"Well, she certainly didn't pay attention to the files. I can attest to that."

"They were disorganized, inaccurate?"

"You wouldn't believe what I had to deal with."

"How long had she been here?"

Ms. Peach compressed her lips and waited for me to come to my senses and stop asking her questions she knew she shouldn't be answering. Or perhaps it was something else. Perhaps Ms. Peach was upset because she had already told me things she shouldn't have. She reached into her purse and took out her keys and turned her back to me.

"Some people just don't have the knack for it."

"For?"

"For keeping things in order. For staying on top of things."

"What a nightmare for you," I said, "coming in on something like that, everything a total mess. I bet you put in a lot of overtime fixing the mess she left."

"For months," she whispered. "I never got home before eight at night." She shook her head. "I was brought up to have pride in my work."

"It's amazing to me how few people there are like you nowadays. How does someone like that even keep a job?"

Ms. Peach inhaled through her nose but didn't respond.

"I'm trying to remember what else he said about her."

"Who?" she asked.

"Mr. Spector. Something about Celia being especially kind to Madison at such a difficult time," I said, continuing to make it up as I went along, keeping an eye on Ms. Peach as I spoke. "Was it Storch, Celia Storch? I'm sure it started with an S, is that right?"

But Ms. Peach was on to me. She was frowning now, looking down at her keys, perhaps thinking it was time to get to work, time to get rid of the snoopy stranger.

I went on as if nothing had happened. "I wonder, Ms. Peach, is there any way you could help me out here?"

"In what way?"

"I wonder if I might talk to any of the other parents of the doctor's other patients?"

"You know that's impossible. And what on earth do you want to do that for?"

"I just wonder if any of the other children had a run-in with Madison," I said.

"Oh, I couldn't possibly give you the names of any of the doctor's other patients. That would be against the law."

"I understand. But you could tell me that, couldn't you?"

"Certainly not. Anything that goes on here is private, confidential."

"Even in the waiting room?"

"Yes, even there."

"I guess you're right," I said. "Well, how about just letting me peek inside at the doctor's office, for just one minute?"

Ms. Peach stood taller, somewhat appalled by what I was asking. "Isn't that a bit ghoulish?"

"No, no, no," I said, "it's not what you think. It's just so that if the child tries to communicate something to me, I'll know what it is. I'm told her communications, her pictures, are kind of cryptic."

"Not the one I found on the doctor's desk."

"Do you still have that?"

"Certainly not! The police took that."

"Not even a copy?"

"Of course not. I wouldn't have touched anything. It was a crime scene."

"Not even the doctor? To make sure he was dead?"

"That's different. Naturally I felt for a pulse."

"And did you see the needle at the time, when you knelt next to Dr. Bechman to feel for a pulse?"

Ms. Peach put both her hands against her chest. "It was lying next to him. It must have fallen out when he fell."

"Did you pick it up? Or did you go straight for the phone?"

"I went straight for the phone," she said, a little too quickly.

"His or yours?"

"What on earth do you mean?"

"I mean did you just reach over, as anyone would, and pick up the closest phone, and did you see the drawing Madison had made at that time? Or did you carefully back out of the office and use your own phone, so as not to disturb any possible evidentiary material?"

Ms. Peach's mouth opened but nothing came out.

"The detectives who were here had no issues with any of my behavior," she said a moment later.

"Not that they mentioned," I said.

"You're making it sound as if I had some part in this when it's clear it was Madison who—"

"No, no, no," I said. "Nothing like that."

Ms. Peach nodded.

"You mentioned that Madison was a terror. But you didn't say whether or not she'd ever hurt anyone before, you or another child or, of course, Dr. Bechman."

Ms. Peach leaned closer. "I shouldn't be telling you any of this. I shouldn't even be talking to you, but since you are being so persistent, yes, she did hurt other children here. That's why Dr. Bechman started having her come last, when the other children were gone. Are you satisfied now? You're barking up the wrong tree, Ms. Alexander, if you think by snooping around here you'll find out that Madison didn't do this. I don't know when I've ever seen a child as full of rage, as mean-spirited."

"Tell me about the children she hurt."

Ms. Peach pulled her breath in, her chin along with it.

"Please, it's important I understand. If I am, as you say, barking up the wrong tree, then shouldn't I know it? Shouldn't I stop wasting my time and poor Mr. Spector's money?"

"Well, I'll give her this. She never started any of the fights. But if another child asked her a personal question," she pointed to her eye, "or teased her, well, they could be twice her size, it wouldn't matter to Madison. She'd never back down. She'd go after them like a wild animal."

"I don't understand. Why would a child get teased here?"

"Not all the children who come here have facial tics, Ms. Alexander. First of all, there are Dr. Edelstein's patients, who are normal children coming in for checkups and shots. But not all of Dr. Bechman's children had visible disabilities. Far from it."

"I see. So Madison would get teased and she'd react, is that what you're saying?"

Ms. Peach snorted. "React? Overreact would be closer to

the truth. If you'd seen her . . ." She flapped a hand at me. "You don't want to know."

But of course I did.

I'd seen dogs like that, dogs who I'd been told wouldn't start a fight, but would never shy away from one if challenged. Show me a dog who won't back down and I'll show you a dog who starts fights. Was that the way it was for Madison, too, that in one way or another, she'd provoke fights because she needed an excuse for venting her terrible rage?

"And what was the teasing like?" I asked, thinking of the kids who said that's why they'd shot up their schools, killed teachers and classmates, because they'd been shunned or teased.

"Oh, the usual thing. Another child would ask her what was wrong with her eyes," she said. "Or imitate her."

"Anything else you think I should know, Ms. Peach?"

"If she had to wait for the doctor, she'd pace around the office, or sit and bang her feet against a leg of the chair. Sometimes she'd come over to the desk and pick up my things, examine them, put them down in a different place."

Clever girl, I thought. She knew exactly how to play Ms. Peach into a frenzy. And I'd best be clever, too, because there was no doubt in my mind that Madison Spector would be turning that very cleverness on me the following morning.

"She filched things, too, at least two times."

"Like what?"

"Money, for one thing. She was here first thing that day and asked me for a glass of water. I hadn't put my purse away yet and—"

"How did she do that?"

"Well, when I went to get her the water, she must have—"

"No, how did she ask for the glass of water?"

"Oh, I see what you mean. Let me think. Well, it was very hot out and . . ."

"She looked all sweaty, is that right? So you offered her a drink of cold water?"

"Yes, I guess that's . . ."

I shook my head. "You read her mind."

Ms. Peach flushed.

"So it wasn't only Celia who was kind to Madison, was it?"

"Well, she . . ." Ms. Peach took a deep breath and let it out slowly. "I did try to . . ."

"And what was the other thing she stole?"

"One of the books from the reading nook. It was there that morning and missing when I cleaned up. It could have been one of the other children, of course, but it was a story about a turtle."

"She brought the turtle here?"

"Emil/Emily? Oh, yes. Mr. Spector even *introduced* me to the turtle. When I suggested that Madison leave it out here when she went in for her examination, she swept everything off my desk onto the floor."

"And what did her father do then?"

Ms. Peach snorted again. "Her *father*. Do you see the way he lets that child dress? Whose clothes are those she's wearing? They're certainly not hers."

I thought I had an idea whose clothes they might be, but I didn't say.

"Half the time he'd wait for her in the park, with his . . ." So angry she couldn't say the word; she mimed taking a picture instead. "He cared more about that than—"

"Oh, I hardly think—"

"It's getting late and I have work to do," checking her watch. "If you want to see the office, you best come in now."

She looked at Dashiell, then back at me, her head going from side to side. "But not with . . ."

Pointing at him.

Hadn't anyone ever told her it was rude to point?

"You'll have to tie him up out here," she said.

"I can't do that."

"Why on earth not?"

"Someone might steal him," I told her.

"Him?" Staring now. Even worse than pointing.

"I did," I said.

Ms. Peach looked up, reluctantly, as if it were difficult to take her eyes from Dashiell's eyes.

"That's how I got him," I said, neglecting to add that he'd been a puppy at the time and that by removing him from where he was, I'd saved him from a life, or a death, in the pit, the dirt-floored ring where illegal dogfights took place.

"He's house-trained," I said, "and anyway, we'll be in and out in a minute."

She opened the gate and then turned to face me. "I don't guess there'd be any harm in it. But I'll be right there with you every minute."

"I wouldn't expect anything less," I said, following her into the small courtyard. She unlocked the wrought iron gate and then two locks on the inner door.

The waiting room, not unexpectedly, was full of toys and books, with cheerful pictures of animals on the walls, every-thing in pale peach, including the carpet. Ms. Peach punched a code into the alarm system to disarm it.

"I bet you're the one who's responsible for this," I said. "It's perfect."

Ms. Peach beamed, opened a drawer on the other side of her desk, dropped in her purse and locked the drawer. "Dr. Willet wanted to redecorate shortly after I was hired. He asked me to find someone. I said, 'Why spend all that extra money? I did the office at my last job,' I told him. 'I can do this one, too.' "

"And he agreed?"

"He was delighted."

She led me to the second office down the long hallway. She opened the door, stepped back and let me pass.

Dr. Bechman's office was done in beige, and like the waiting room, walls and carpet were in shades of the same color. His rather imposing desk was in the center of the room, bookshelves were to my right, three chairs faced the desk, a place where the child and his or her parents might sit and talk to the doctor.

Dashiell dipped his head and began soaking up the scents on the rug, right at the place where Dr. Bechman must have fallen.

"What is he doing?" Ms. Peach asked, as if it was now registering for the first time that I'd brought a dog into the doctor's perfect office.

"Just checking out the scents on the carpet," I told her.

"There are no—"

I held up my hand. "That's just the way dogs view the world," I told her.

She watched him a moment longer, as if he might do something untoward in this sacred space, while I looked around the room. Behind the desk, on the windowsill, facing the patients' chairs, were the obligatory photos of the doctor's family, an expensively turned-out wife who, my guess was, looked years younger than her age and two well-groomed teenage boys.

"That would be Mrs. Bechman," I asked, pointing, "and the children?"

"A lovely person."

"You've met her?"

"Just on the phone, of course."

"Never here?"

She shook her head.

"So she doesn't work in the city?"

"Mrs. *Bechman*?" Ms. Peach smiled, the kind of smile that lets you know how perfectly silly your question was.

"No shopping trips and then lunch with the doctor?"

"Oh, Dr. Bechman never went out for lunch. He just worked straight through, same as Dr. Willet and Dr. Edelstein, busy, busy, busy."

I took a step toward her. For a moment, I thought Ms. Peach would take a step back, but she just stiffened.

"I've been so rude," I said in a stage whisper. "I should have asked you right away. Was it Dr. Bechman who hired you? Is your job in jeopardy now?"

"Oh, no. I mean, yes, it was Dr. Bechman, but I work for the whole office. I'm sure . . ." And then the doubt I'd planted was written all over her face.

"I imagine they'll find someone else to share the office, or buy his practice. After a decent interval, of course."

"Of course."

Ms. Peach was fussing with her hair.

I picked up one of Dr. Bechman's cards. "Another pediatric neurologist, perhaps."

"I'm sure Mrs. Bechman will sell the practice. It's customary."

I nodded. Dashiell lay down.

"We've had several inquiries already," she whispered.

I nodded again, picking up a heavy paperweight from the doctor's desk, turning it over in my hands and then putting it down an inch or so from where it had been. Ms. Peach reached by me and moved the paperweight back to its proper place.

I took a step toward the bookshelves. "The cops have been by a lot, I bet." My back to Ms. Peach.

"They've been wanting to take Madison's records, but they need a court order. Anything between doctor and patient—"

"Right," I said, turning back to face her. "And there's been no court order yet?"

She shook her head. "Dr. Willet is adamant that the police can't look through the files without a court order."

"The files? Not just Madison's?"

Now she was whispering, though we were the only ones there. "That's the hitch. They've asked for everything. Dr. Willet is adamant about protecting the rights of patients, particularly minor patients."

"Why everything?"

Ms. Peach tightened her lips again.

"Maybe they want to see if any of the other children suffered harm from one of the doctor's treatments." I waited, but Ms. Peach had no comment. "Just being thorough, I guess, perhaps because no one actually saw Madison slam that needle into the doctor's heart. Do most of the kids come with their parents?"

Ms. Peach nodded. "Except for Madison. She usually came alone. She was, is, a very strange child. Don't you think so?"

"I couldn't say, Ms. Peach. As I already told you, I've only met her once."

"Yes," she said, "I recall now, you mentioned that." She squared her shoulders and backed up a step to the doorway, waiting for me to pass by into the hall.

"I can't thank you enough, Ms. Peach. And I wish you all the best."

Again, Ms. Peach looked nervous. Perhaps, when I left, her eyelids might twitch the way Madison's did, as she wondered why I needed to wish her all the best.

I looked at the locks on the door again on the way out, the

heavy iron gate, the gated windows, all backed up by an alarm system. If I were to get Dr. Bechman's patient list, it couldn't be by coming back here at night and jimmying the locks with a credit card. It could only be through Ms. Peach.

"I'm sure everything will be all right," I said as she saw me out.

"What do you mean?" Her voice an octave higher than it had been.

"With your job," I whispered. "With leaving while the doctor was still with a dangerous patient."

I took another step, then stopped and turned back. Ms. Peach did not look well.

"Was the door locked?" I asked her.

"Locked? What door?"

"The front door, Ms. Peach. This one. Had you locked it behind you when you left?"

I could see the panic creeping into her eyes, then the anger.

"Of course not. The child had to be able to leave."

"Couldn't the doctor have let her out? Wouldn't that have been a safer solution?"

"Why, no, we've never—"

"So then the alarm hadn't been armed, is that correct? And since you were gone and the door wasn't secured, isn't it possible that after Madison left, someone else entered the office, while the doctor was returning phone calls, say? You didn't mention which phone you used to call the police?"

"The closest phone," she said, her face flushed now. "As anyone would in an emergency."

"Was it on the hook or off when you reached for it?"

"On the hook. I see what it is you're trying to do, Ms. Alexander, and I understand why. But you're wrong. No one else came in after Madison. She was the one who killed Dr. Bechman. Doesn't the note tell you that?"

"The note?" I said.

Ms. Peach wheeled around and walked around her desk, opening the top left drawer, reaching under some papers and pulling out a single sheet. She came back to where I was standing and shoved it at me. "The note," she said, too upset to remember that moments earlier she'd told me she hadn't copied it. "The way Madison says what's on her mind."

It was a rather crude drawing, a heart with a shaky line going into the middle of it, just as it had been described to me.

I stood staring at it. Then I looked into Ms. Peach's smug brown eyes.

"Why?" I asked her.

"Because of the droop," she said, pointing to her own eyelid. "She had an absolute fit about it."

"No, why did you copy the drawing?"

Ms. Peach just stood there, her face a perfect blank, as if she had been given Botox after all.

"Well, since you did," I whispered, "how about if you make one more?"

She began to shake her head, but I interrupted.

"Surely making a copy of your copy wouldn't be against the law, Ms. Peach."

She went back to her desk and put the drawing in the copy machine. I heard it click and whir, saw the lights flashing.

"Were her fingerprints on the note?" I asked. "Madison's?"

Ms. Peach turned to face me. "I don't know, Ms. Alexander, but I was told they were on the needle."

I flapped a hand at her, as if the bad news she'd just given me were nothing at all. "You just told me she handled everything, didn't you?"

Ms. Peach didn't answer my question. Instead she carefully put the copy of Madison's drawing in a large manila envelope, as if it were a medical report or an X ray, and handed it to me.

"Anyone could have made that picture," I said, as if I were talking to myself. "I certainly could have." I stopped short of suggesting that Ms. Peach herself could have made the drawing. But I was sure she'd gotten the point anyway.

Ms. Peach headed for the door, opening it for me.

"You said you were the one who found the doctor?"

"Yes, and I can tell you it was quite a shock."

"So you were the first one in that morning?" I asked her as casually as I could.

"It wasn't morning. I found him that evening."

"I don't understand. You said that you left when the doctor was in his office with Madison. I didn't know there were office hours in the evening."

"There aren't. I came back."

"Back to the office? Whatever for? Was it when you realized you hadn't set the alarm?"

"No," she said, her face red, her hands trembling. "I forgot my book."

"Your *book*?"

"Will you *please* stop repeating everything I say," she shouted.

"It's just that—"

"After dinner, I realized I'd left my book at the office and I wanted to finish it that night. It's not that far and so I—"

"How long after you'd left was that?"

"About two hours."

"Two hours?"

"See. You're doing it again. If you don't stop that compulsive mimicry, I'm going to have to ask you to leave."

"Must have been a good book," I said, ignoring her outburst.

Ms. Peach opened the door. "I have work to do."

"So the doctor's wife hadn't called to inquire where he was. That's not why you came back?"

"No. He had a meeting. It would have been a late night. She wasn't expecting him for dinner."

I nodded. "And she wouldn't have called you anyway, isn't that so? I mean, the doctor must have had a pager."

"Of course."

"And no one called the office to see why he'd missed the meeting?"

"Of course not. It's not as if he was the *speaker*."

"Just one more question, Ms. Peach."

Her eyebrows went up.

Then I shook my head. "Another time," I said. "You've got work to do."

This time I left without looking back, crossing the street toward the park. The phone call I had to make could be made there as well as anywhere else, and while I had just been cruel to Ms. Peach, very cruel, I'd done so for a reason. But there was no reason I could think of to be cruel to Dashiell by having him this close to the run and not giving him some time for R & R. As I entered the park at the corner and turned onto the path, his ears went up. I could hear the barking, too, a pleasure after the suffocating beigeness of Dr. Bechman's office.

CHAPTER 6

I called Leon from the dog run.

"I was just at Dr. Bechman's office," I said.

"Oh."

"I was told Madison's fingerprints were on the needle."

"It doesn't mean anything," he said. "That's why I didn't mention it."

"Leon . . ."

"If it meant something conclusive, she'd be charged, wouldn't she? And what does this have to do with finding Sally?"

"Maybe nothing," I told him. "Maybe something. I have to toss a wide net, then eliminate what I don't need, what doesn't help. It's not as if she left a trail of bread crumbs. I don't know where I'm going to find what I need to get me started in the right direction. Okay?"

"Okay."

I sighed. So did Leon.

"I need the name of the high school where you were teaching when you met Sally."

"Abraham Lincoln. On Ocean Parkway in Brooklyn."

"And do you remember the names of any of her friends?"

"She was never a big talker."

"No best girlfriend?"

"She never said."

"And you never met any of her friends?"

"No, I never did."

"No one in history class she came in with, sat next to, left with?"

"Not that I noticed."

"What about her other teachers?"

I waited while Leon thought. "I can't recall."

"One more question for now, Leon. Do you recall the name of the receptionist who worked for Dr. Bechman before Ms. Peach, Celia something?"

There was a silence on the line. I figured Leon was trying to dredge up the name. But then I heard a chair scrape, something fall, a muttered curse. I waited some more. Dashiell had found a willing playmate and they were racing from one end of the run to the other. An elderly man was sitting across from me, a small brown mixed-breed dog on his lap. The dog's face came to a point, his ears seemed too large, erect and rounded at the top, like mouse ears, and he seemed alert but placid. For some reason, that's what I pictured when I thought of Roy. I thought I'd ask Leon about Roy when he got back on the line, another piece of trivia I thought I needed to know, wondering if any of it would help me find Sally.

"Abele," he said. "Celia Abele."

I never mentioned the little dog across from me. Or Roy. What did he have to do with anything at this late date? Why even assume that Sally would have kept a dog she'd never wanted in the first place? She might have just given him away. I remembered a dog I'd been given once when I was a child. I'd said he was cute and asked to pet him. The lady holding the leash asked if I wanted him. I'd nodded, hardly able to believe my good luck, but when my mother saw him, she was furious. She asked where the lady lived and I said I didn't know. She asked me where I was when the lady had given me the dog, but we'd just been on the sidewalk, two blocks from where I lived, and after she handed me the leash, she'd gone around the corner and disappeared. I begged and pleaded and my mother said, "We'll see," but in the morning, the dog was gone. She never said what she did with him, no matter how many times I asked, no matter how hard I cried. "See," my sister had said the next night when my parents were out of earshot, "I told you so."

I thought it was strange that Leon hadn't asked me why on earth I'd gone to Bechman's office. He hadn't asked me why I wanted Celia's last name either. What if he did ask questions? What if he asked me how far I'd gotten or what I thought? What could I say to him, that at this point I had no reason to think that Madison *hadn't* killed her doctor, nor any reason to feel hopeful about finding Sally, alive or dead? Or would I mention I'd put some terrible doubt in the mind of Ms. Peach in the hope that next time I showed up, she'd break a few laws on behalf of a kid she clearly couldn't stand?

"Well, then," I'd said after thanking him, "I'll see you around eight."

"Instead of ringing the bell," he said, "call my cell when you're on the way and I'll wait for you out front," he'd said.

I told him I would.

The dog Dashiell had just been playing with was gone, and now he was chasing an Irish setter in great circles around the perimeter of the run. Suddenly they stopped, dropped and began to wrestle in the dirt. Some people think adult dogs don't need to play, that play is only for puppies. If they visited the dog run, they'd change their minds fast. Not only was playing good for dogs, honing muscles, reaction time and social skills, but like exercise and gaming for humans, it was a stress buster, the best there was. It seemed to have the same effect on the onlookers, too. There was always someone leaning on the fence and looking in, watching the dogs living in the moment.

I'd taken the long way around, walking Dash past the chess players at the southwest corner of the park. Two of the kibitzers were kibitzing here now, at the run, their arms hanging over the fence, watching a different kind of game. The woman was tall and horsey, long face, long nose, big chin and hair pulled back so tight it made her ears seem to stick out. Her coat looked worn, even from across the run, and while it wasn't cold out, and that may have been why she had it unbuttoned, it might not have fit across her considerable girth. The man was small, shorter than I am, lost in a hunter's orange jacket at least two sizes too big for him, a watch cap on his head, the hood over the cap, aviator glasses, unlaced workman's boots with unmatched socks peeking over the top. They might have both been homeless, having picked their outfits out of the trash, neither willing to look a gift horse in the mouth. Even if your coat won't close, or the color of it gives the impression that someone is about to start shooting deer in Washington Square Park, you can't be fussy about size and color when winter's coming and you're lucky enough to find something you can get into that will keep you warm.

When I got home, I checked my Brooklyn directory and located Lincoln High, way the hell at the far end of the borough. Then I checked under Abele, to see if Celia lived in Brooklyn. There was a Claire Abele on Bedford Avenue, a Richard Abele in Brooklyn Heights, and that was it. I tried the Manhattan directory next. There were six Abeles in Manhattan, Audrey, Harrison, J., Louise, Philip and a C. Abele on Bethune Street, a block from Leon's apartment and just a short walk to her former job as receptionist for Drs. Willet, Bechman and Edelstein.

Of course the Celia Abele who had worked for Dr. Bechman at one time could live in Queens, the Bronx, on Staten Island or in New Jersey. She might have relocated to Denver, Colorado, or Wake Forest, North Carolina. Nothing said she'd remained close by or that she even had the same last name now that she did then. For all I knew, she'd left her job to get married to an Eskimo who lived fifty miles north of Fairbanks.

Still, I wrote down the address and the phone number, but I didn't plan to call. I thought I'd walk by, see how big the building was, see if there might be some way, by hook or by crook, to talk to Celia Abele face-to-face. It was too easy to hang up the phone, and too tempting, too, especially with the glut of telemarketers invading what used to be the privacy of your home.

I turned on the computer and typed in Classmates.com. They'd been after me weekly to sign up and get in touch with my old classmates, something I had no desire to do. What would they think of the life I'd chosen? I couldn't imagine. Or maybe I could and that was why I'd had no desire to get in touch. But I did finally accept Classmates.com's invitation, signing up not as Rachel Kaminsky, the name I'd had in high school, but as Sally Bruce because it was her long-lost friends I was hoping to hear from, not my own. I backtracked to the year she would have graduated, then back four from that to give the range of time she'd attended Lincoln. Now all I had to do was wait and hope.

If Lincoln was like any other New York City public school, its senior class would have had around a thousand kids in it. I didn't know the chances of anyone recognizing Sally's name and responding. I figured they were slim, like everything else in this case. All the more reason to try anything I could think of.

At a quarter to eight, I called Leon. Dashiell and I headed a block and a half west to Greenwich Street, then a few blocks north to Bank Street. I could see Leon sitting on the steps out front, a black gym bag on his lap.

He handed me the bag. "I hope this helps."

"Me, too," I said. I weighed the bag by hoisting it up and down. "Not much in it."

"I wasn't sure what you wanted."

"A diary would be nice," I said, thinking I'd get a smile.

"There was one," Leon said. "But when the police came, I couldn't find it."

"You don't think she took it with her?"

"She didn't even take a purse. Just a light jacket, her keys, some pickup bags."

"And Roy."

Leon nodded.

"Did it ever turn up?"

"Excuse me?" I had the feeling that even with something this important, Leon only half listened.

"The diary?" I sat on the top step, putting the bag on my lap and unzipping it, hoping to see the diary lying on top.

"Never did."

I looked inside the bag. There were some notebooks, the kind you use in school, the yearbook Leon had showed me with Sally's graduation picture in it, a manila envelope with two rubber bands around it. "What happened to her books," I asked, "her clothes, her stuff, you know, hairbrush, bracelets, ice skates, bowling ball, family pictures, cartoons she cut out of the *New Yorker* and hung on the refrigerator, anything that might tell me something about her, something that might give me a hint where she might have gone?"

"Madison has her clothes and some of her things."

"She didn't tear those up?"

Leon shook his head. "The books are upstairs. Do you want to see them?"

"Yeah, I do."

Leon got up. I reached for his arm. "You can show me which ones were hers when I come in the morning."

"All of them," he said. "Well, most of them. Not the photography books. Not the history."

"I'll see you in the morning," I told him, not wanting to tell him I was heading out on what no doubt would be a fool's errand, not wanting to tell him any more than I had to lest I get his hopes up only to dash them a moment later. I was going to wait until he went inside, but Leon stayed put, waiting for me to go. So I headed back the way I'd come, and when I got to Bank Street, I turned back to see if he was still standing there. The stoop was empty. I walked back that way, passing the entrance to Leon's building and heading for the corner of Bethune Street. When I glanced up, I saw the light go off in Leon's living room. I wondered what that meant. Surely, he wasn't going to go to sleep at eight-twenty. Did he watch TV in the dark, I wondered, or listen to music with his eyes closed?

Canned pears and Mop & Glo were on special at the D'Agostino's on the opposite corner. I turned west and started watching the addresses, looking for the building where the C. Abele I'd found in the phone book lived, someone who might or might not be the person I hoped to find.

The address in the phone book turned out to be a medium-sized brick apartment building. Like many buildings in the city, you could enter the vestibule without a key but not the lobby. I did so and checked the names on the bells. Again, it said C. Abele. There was one more place to check. The mailboxes were on the opposite wall. I looked for the one for 3F, then looked to see the name in the little slot. It said Charles Abele.

Dash and I walked along the river before going home. The water was choppy, those small peaks everywhere, and it seemed to flow in stripes, every other one heading for the ocean, the ones in between going back from where they came. There was a good breeze, even better when we walked out onto one of the piers. I sat on a bench at the far end, putting the gym bag next to me, the Statue of Liberty overseeing the harbor to my left, New Jersey across the way. Looking downtown, I could only be aware of what was missing, a hole in the skyline where the Twin Towers used to stand.

Dashiell lay down on the pier near my feet. We stayed for a while, listening to the water sloshing against the pilings, letting our thoughts drift. Then we headed home to open the gym bag once again and see if there was anything in what Leon had collected that would help me find his missing wife.

CHAPTER 7

When I got home, I sat on the living room couch and dumped the gym bag out next to me. Then one by one I picked up the things Leon had packed and put them on the glass-topped red wagon that served as my coffee table. There was a Post-it in the high school yearbook indicating where Sally's picture was. I opened that first and was going to prop it open with a stationery box that had been the last thing to tumble out of the bag. That, like the manila envelope, had rubber bands around it. I slid them off and took the lid off the box to see what was inside. Photographs. These looked like family shots, mostly old, mostly small, some cracked or missing corners. I thought they might have been slipped out of an album, maybe her mother's, shortly before Sally moved out. I couldn't be sure who was who, and there were no names written on the backs, but I thought I was looking at Sally's parents, some aunts and uncles or family friends, a grandmother, from the shape of her face probably her maternal grandmother, and a couple of pictures of Sally as a little girl.

Sally's mother, or the woman I supposed was Sally's mother—and would it have broken Leon's hand to add a few Post-its with the names of these people?—was a tough-looking old bird. She looked to be one of those women who grit their teeth through life, expecting nothing good to happen, and thus not getting disappointed. She had a round, peasanty face. I couldn't be sure about her hair color because the picture was black and white and not all that good, perhaps the work of a small point-and-shoot camera, if they had those then. She was stocky, grim-faced, and dressed without style. In the most recent of the pictures of her, she would have been no more than forty or forty-five, but she looked older than her years, the way Leon did, from grief, perhaps, or disappointment, or a sour, unloving upbringing.

Sally's father was blond, unless he had white hair by age thirty. It was from her father, clearly, that Sally had gotten her good looks. I picked up the yearbook, opened it to where Leon had put the Post-it and held one of the two pictures of the man I thought was Sally's father next to the picture of Sally. They had the same-shaped face, the same fair coloring, the same clear eyes and sensual mouth. A large corner was broken off one of the pictures of her father. The other was worn in places, as if it had been handled a lot. Yet the small box and its contents had been left behind. Either Sally hadn't done much advance planning or she had only gone out to walk the dog, just as she said, and someone else's planning had been the reason for her disappearance.

There were four pictures of Sally as a youngster. She was alone in all four. Like her mother, she didn't smile at the camera. She looked down or off to the side, enduring or obeying, but not shining. I never thought of anyone that beautiful as being shy, but Sally, at least in her photos, appeared to be just that.

I looked at the other unnamed people, a man and woman standing about six inches apart and staring at the camera, the old woman, probably Sally's grandmother, with the same forbidding expression that would later mark her daughter's face.

I looked back at the yearbook, picking it up, leaning against the arm of the couch and holding it under the light. Not grim like her mother and grandmother. Not smiling like her father. Not much of anything. I scanned the other pictures on the page and on the facing one, all the girls and about half of the boys were smiling, happy to be graduating or because the photographer told them to. But not Sally, Sally who had been pregnant with Madison when that picture was taken. She was looking at the camera but there was no hint of what was going on underneath. How ironic. She could have been a model for a Botox ad, a pretty face without emotional expression, without history, blank as a fresh sheet of paper.

I put the book back and picked up the manila envelope, taking the rubber bands off and pulling the flap out from where Leon had tucked it in—more photographs. Had he found some of Sally as an adult, photos he didn't know he still had?

But when I slid them out, it wasn't Sally I was looking at. It was Roy. He wasn't a little brown mutt with a pointy face and large batlike ears. Roy was a Border collie. Now how on earth did Sally get anywhere with no money and a dog that big? True, Roy wasn't full grown yet. He probably weighed no more than thirty pounds, so Sally could have lifted him. But to what avail? He was too big to fit into a carrier, not that she had one or even the money to buy one. Nor would there have been an open pet store had she had the money for a carrier. Without a carrier, she couldn't have taken a bus, a train or a subway. Unless she'd ditched the dog first. Had Leon checked with the shelter? And would she have done that, just left him alone on the streets of New York? People did. People dumped dogs out of cars, left them in parks, tied them to fences or trees and just walked or drove away, maybe figuring some kindhearted dog lover would take up the responsibility they had let go of. Maybe not giving it a second thought. Is that what Sally had done? She hadn't wanted a dog in the first place. Leon had made that clear.

The next three pictures were of Madison, the same pictures that were hanging over the dining room table. And after that, one more, a picture of Madison at seven holding the puppy Roy on her lap. She was sitting on the floor in what might have been her bedroom, looking at the pup but not touching him, her arms bent, her hands held high as if she were showing someone the height of something. I set that one aside and put the others back in the envelope.

I picked up both notebooks and sat back with them on my lap. Sally had been going to New York University at night according to the schedule taped inside the first book, studying American literature and third-year Spanish, attempting, it seemed, to get a degree. I turned through the pages of the book, notes from class, drawings in the margin of the professor and of other students. Her handwriting was small and neat. The notes proficient and detailed. I wasn't sure why Leon had put these in the bag, nor why he'd saved them, but I supposed it was one more thing about Sally I ought to know, that she'd abandoned not only her husband and child, but her plans for a degree as well. No way the cops would have neglected to check and see if Sally had requested a transcript so that she could continue her studies at another institution in another city. No way Sally wouldn't have known that to do so, to attempt to preserve the work she'd done so far, for, possibly, all the years she was married, would be to give herself away, something she'd done once and perhaps didn't want to do again.

Or was this another reason to think that Sally Spector was no longer alive? Would someone work that hard, at night, after caring for a young child all day, and then simply drop it?

I picked up the picture of Madison and Roy again, holding it under the light. Something about Madison made me think she was frightened. Was it Roy she'd been afraid of? She didn't seem scared of Dashiell. If not Roy, then what? Or who?

CHAPTER 8

Leon opened the door and looked more than ready to bolt. He had a heavy-looking camera bag over one shoulder, the shoulder hiked up to keep the bag from slipping off. "When do you want me back?" he asked, already moving sideways to slip by me.

"In a couple of hours. That okay?"

"Madison," he called over his shoulder, "Rachel's here. I'm going."

He waited. I did, too. Nothing happened.

Leon shrugged.

"See you at twelve, twelve-thirty," I said.

Leon hesitated.

"Just go," I said, flapping my hand at him.

After closing the door, I unhooked Dashiell's leash. He headed straight for the short hallway that led to Madison's room. I heard a door open. I heard Dashiell's nails clicking on the bare wooden floor, then the door closed. I waited, but Dash didn't return.

Standing quietly in the vestibule next to Leon's desk, I listened for more, some sound coming from Madison's room. But there was none. Was it wise to let Dashiell be alone with her? I wasn't naïve enough to think that, because of her age, Madison couldn't have killed Dr. Bechman. But if she had, she'd done it for a reason. She'd have no reason to harm Dashiell, I thought. At least none that I knew of.

I walked down the hallway to Madison's room and stood there listening, to what end I didn't know. Did I expect to hear Madison chatting away to Dashiell? I waited a moment, then knocked, expecting what had happened last time, no response. But the door opened and there stood Madison, Dashiell at her side, Emil/Emily in her free hand. She backed up, leaving the door open. I took that as an invitation and walked in, immediately feeling like Alice falling down the rabbit hole. Madison's walls were blue, not a pale blue wallpaper with little rosebuds on it, not a Wedgwood blue with white molding, not a sky blue with blue-and-white-striped curtains. Madison's room was the blue of the ocean, the walls covered with enormous fish, a coral reef, underwater reeds curving gracefully as if from the flow of the water and, of course, turtles. It was the kind of painting a proud parent might tape up on the refrigerator, but it was huge, floor-to-ceiling and wrapped entirely around the room, as if the room itself, and Madison, were underwater.

"This is fantastic. Did you do this?" Forgetting I wasn't going to get an answer.

Madison walked over to her desk, which was under the window that faced the D'Agostino's on Bethune Street, through which I saw a homeless man with a plastic bag full of empty plastic bottles sitting on the ground, leaning against the brick wall, his eyes, like Madison's, hidden behind dark glasses. There were two more windows over the bed, facing Greenwich Street, the sun pouring in from those. Which might explain why Madison was wearing her sunglasses indoors, if I didn't know better. I could see one eye twitching when she leaned over to put Emil/Emily into the tank that sat on one side of her desk. There were a few inches of water in it, enough so that the turtle could swim, and a big rock that he/she could climb up on to get out of the water. Madison picked up a book, sat on her bed and began to read, as if I weren't there.

Dashiell hopped up on the bed and lay down next to her, leaving me standing alone between the doorway and the desk and, if I had anything else to say, talking to myself.

Dashiell had no trouble understanding Madison. He didn't need words to get along or know what someone was feeling. Well, maybe I didn't either. After all, I'd been a dog trainer and had no trouble understanding the dogs I was hired to train. And I'd done pet-assisted therapy with autistics. No words there, either.

Madison seemed absorbed in her book, not the kind of fiction with a lesson to be learned in the end that most kids end up reading, but a book on photography. So I sat on the end of the bed and looked around the room. I saw the camera on her desk, one that fits in your pocket, digital, I figured. It was sitting next to her computer. There were two closets, the door to the one closer to me ajar. Half the clothes seemed the size to fit a smallish twelve-year-old. The rest of the clothes must have been Sally's, an odd collection of retro things that looked as if they'd been bought secondhand. There were sweaters folded on the shelf, shoes tossed in on the floor. A backpack had been thrown in the corner, and from the looks of it, it was full of books.

Madison was wearing clothes that fit her this time, and I had the feeling that the beads wrapped around one wrist had been her mother's necklace. There was a ring on her thumb, a plain silver band, and she was wearing a necklace, but I could only see part of the chain. Whatever it held was under Madison's T-shirt. She wore a watch, too, like the one I wear when I swim. Like most of her things, this, too, was too big, the face almost comical against her thin arm, the band so loose the watch slid up or down her arm when she moved it, too big for her because it was most likely the watch Sally had left behind.

"Do you want to go out for a walk?" I asked, forgetting that I'd decided to try to communicate without words. No matter, I thought. I always spoke to Dashiell, didn't I? And surely, even though Madison didn't speak, she understood what was being said to her.

To my surprise, Madison responded. She jumped up and walked out of the room, Dashiell behind her, me bringing up the rear. That's when I realized that I didn't have a key to Leon's apartment. If Madison didn't either, we couldn't leave because we wouldn't be able to get back in. No way could I handle this one without words. But it turned out I didn't have to. No sooner was I out in the dining area than Madison turned around and headed back to her room, closing the door before either Dashiell or I could follow her. A moment later I heard a hissing sound. And shortly afterwards, the odor of citrus seeped out into the hall, telling me that Madison was spraying her room with air freshener, her message loud and clear without a word spoken.

Dashiell went into the kitchen, caught my eye and glanced up at the sink, so I found a bowl, filled it with cold water and set it down under the window for him. I hadn't seen Madison communicate that way. I wondered how she indicated that she was hungry or what she wanted to eat for dinner, for example. I opened the refrigerator, not just because I was a snoop but to see the sort of care Madison was getting, though I was starting to have a pretty good idea. There was an open can of tuna in the refrigerator, a container of milk and one of orange juice, a carton of eggs, a bowl with wrinkled grapes in it, a package of American cheese, the kind where each slice is individually wrapped, peanut butter, jelly, butter and several packages that looked like they were from the deli section of the supermarket, perhaps sliced ham and turkey. There was a partial head of lettuce in the vegetable bin, probably for Emil/Emily, two kinds of soda, Coke and ginger ale, but no beer. The freezer was small and had only hamburger patties and some vanilla ice cream in it.

I poked my head out into the hallway. Madison's door was still closed. I picked up the kettle and filled it, putting it on the stove. Then I began to search for tea bags, finding some in a small canister on the counter. There were cookies in another one, sugar in a third. Waiting for the water to boil, I walked over to the bookshelves next to Leon's desk.

If the majority of the books had belonged to Sally, as Leon had said, she'd been not only a prolific reader but one with good taste. I didn't know how much of this reflected assignments from her classes and how much reflected Sally's own choices. I walked around the corner into the living room, scanning the shelves there as well, picking up books and seeing that Sally had underlined phrases, sentences and sometimes whole paragraphs. There were notes in the margins as well, sometimes questions. I wondered how Sally had had time to do anything else with all this reading.

Leon had a stack of contact sheets on his desk. I picked up the top one and found myself looking at some familiar territory, Washington Square Park, the chess players, the homeless, a misguided citizen with a bag full of torn-up bread. She may have thought she was feeding birds and squirrels, but much of the food would end up nourishing the park's rather healthy rat population. New York City could boast not only some of the fattest squirrels on the face of the earth, but also rats as big as Hummers. On the bottom row, there was Madison emerging from Dr. Bechman's office.

Even when Leon went with her, he apparently only went as far as the door.

I made a cup of tea, thought about offering something to Madison, then changed my mind. Leon had said there were things of Sally's here. Why would he have told me that if he hadn't meant for me to look at them?

I checked out the two hall closets, looking for anything that might have belonged to her, not sure if Madison had taken all of Sally's clothes into her room. The coat closet was crammed full of clothes and boots and hats, scarves, gloves and rain gear that seemed to belong to a grown man and a little girl. I wondered how big Sally had been, thinking of the shirt Madison had worn the first time I saw her. When I looked underneath the coats, at Leon's winter boots and Madison's, the closet seemed to go farther back than I originally thought. I put my hands in the middle of the clothes and pushed both sides apart as far as I could. There in the back, along with a few parkas for the coldest weather, was a jean jacket and a long black coat. I took them out. Too big for Madison. Not the right gender for Leon. I put the jacket on the back of Leon's chair and held up the coat with one hand, slipping my hand into the pockets with my other. Tissues, black leather gloves, thirty-six cents in change. The label was missing so there was no size. I slipped the coat on, to see how big Sally had been, one more tiny piece of information that would probably get me nowhere. The coat was snug in the shoulders and it was too short. So Sally was smaller than me, and Madison was built more like her mother than her father.

I never heard the door open, but when I turned around, Madison was standing at the end of the dining area, staring at me wearing her mother's coat. Before I had the chance to say anything, she'd wheeled around and returned to her room. And in case I hadn't heard the door the first time, she slammed it, opened it and slammed it shut a second time. Who said this kid didn't communicate?

Good job, I told myself. If there'd been a chance in hell I could get through to this kid, I'd just blown it. I took off the coat and hung it back where it had been. Then I reached for the jean jacket. It was a washed-out blue with silver studs around the collar and along the tops of the patch pockets. There was nothing in the left-hand pocket, a ten-dollar bill in the right. I left that where I'd found it. Then I walked down the hall to Madison's room and knocked. When she didn't answer, I opened the door.

Madison was sitting on the bed. If I expected her to look outraged that I'd invaded her privacy, that wasn't the case. Her face, at least whatever showed around her dark glasses, was, like her mother's face in her yearbook portrait, beautifully blank. Whatever harm I might have caused had already been safely stowed away.

"Look, Madison," I said, standing at the foot of her bed, the jacket over my right arm, "your father told you why he hired me, right? Well, I'm having a little trouble here. I can't even begin to try to look for your mother without knowing anything about her. And your father's not much more forthcoming than you are."

I waited a moment and then went on.

"I found her old coat in the back of the hall closet. I bet your father forgot it was even there. My guess is that she used one of the closets in here, because there's no way two adults could fit all their clothes in the two small closets out there. So you probably never went looking out there, am I right?

"Anyway, the reason I tried on the coat is that I wanted to know Sally's size. How am I supposed to find her if I don't know how tall she is or if she's fat or skinny? I don't know if she likes hot climates or cold, if she bowls, ice-skates, skydives, rides a bike. I normally wouldn't talk to a kid like this, but under the circumstances . . ." I stopped again to take a good look at Madison, her blonde bangs half under and half over her dark glasses, the length of her hair uneven, her nails too long not because it was a chosen style but because they hadn't been cut, her shirt tucked in in the front and hanging out in the back. "You do understand the circumstances, don't you?" I asked, so angry that no matter how hard I tried not to, I ended up shouting.

Should I just turn around, go sit in the living room and wait for Leon, I wondered, tell him this wasn't going to work? I could follow the slimmest thread, but I couldn't follow nothing, and nothing was precisely what I was getting.

But I didn't do that. I was already on the road to hell. Now I started running.

"I wish one of you would help me out," I said. "I wish one of you would tell me what kind of music she likes, if she had any friends, boy oh boy, the names of a few friends would be nice. Or even what she likes to eat, her favorite color, *anything*, just anything at all. But no, no one's talking. Are you listening? Good." Too angry to stop, not sure why.

"Here's the thing," I said, watching her left cheek twitch up and down, her eye, I guessed, along with it, but the way she was holding her head and with those dark glasses on, I couldn't see her eyes. "I don't know who I'm looking for, except that she's twenty-eight, shorter than I am, she's right-handed and she may or may not have a Border collie with her."

With that, the tics revved up. Madison took off her glasses, bent her head and cupped her palms over her eyes, then quickly put the glasses back on. As soon as she dropped her arms, the bed seemed to be shaking. But it wasn't the bed, it was Madison, her arms trembling as if she'd suddenly gotten very cold.

What the hell was I doing here? What the hell was I doing to this kid?

"I'm sorry," I said, my voice barely above a whisper. "You don't have to do a thing. I'll work it out. I promise." Thinking that now I was *really* being cruel; I was giving her hope.

"By the way," I said, holding up the jacket with both hands so that Madison could see it, "I found this, too. I think this would be perfect for you. What do you think?"

At first, Madison didn't move. She sat where she was, legs folded in front of her, the book leaning on her feet. Then she pushed the book out of the way and got up. She slid off the bed and came around to where I was standing, took the jacket and slipped it on. I heard the front door open, heard Leon walk into the kitchen, open the refrigerator and pop open a can of soda. I checked my watch. He'd only been gone an hour and ten minutes.

"Looks good on you, kiddo, real good," I whispered, giving her shoulder a quick squeeze. "Check the right-hand pocket," I whispered, walking out into the hallway before she did.

"How'd it go?" he asked.

"Swell," I said. I didn't tell him that I was dying from a lack of information. I didn't ask him who I had to fuck to get out of this job. I didn't tell him anything.

Leon's eyebrows went up. My mouth stayed closed. If Leon wasn't talking, neither was I. That's when Madison came out of her room, still wearing Sally's jacket.

"I'd forgotten about that. Where was it?"

"In the back of the closet," I said. "You mentioned that there were things of Sally's here. I hope you don't mind my looking around."

He shrugged his shoulders. Leon, it seemed, had nothing to hide.

"Hey, Madison, thanks for the visit. Maybe next time you'll come to my house, okay?"

Leon walked me out into the hall. I asked him about Madison's diagnosis and what the prognosis was. I told him I'd be in touch.

Walking home with Dashiell, I realized the morning hadn't been a total loss. I'd found out what didn't work with Madison. Now all I had to do was find something that did. I'd also seen evidence that Madison had problems other than chronic motor tic disorder. For one thing, there was a roar in the apartment. I wondered if it came from the street or if it was the result of some sort of air intake for the kitchen vent. But that made no sense. The kitchen had a window, so it didn't need a vent and probably didn't have one, especially in a building this old. Maybe it was just the hum of the city, something newcomers always heard and natives rarely did. In that case, why was I hearing it? Being a New Yorker, I shouldn't have noticed it at all. Instead, I couldn't get the sound, like the sound of the ocean from two blocks away, out of my mind. The only explanation I could come up with was really crazy, that it was the sound of Sally's absence, roaring through the house, not letting anyone forget she was gone.

As if that weren't enough, when Leon left the house, he hadn't offered to kiss Madison good-bye, and when he came home, he'd ignored her completely. Apart from Emil/Emily, the kid was pretty much on her own.

CHAPTER 9

It was almost lunchtime but I wasn't hungry. I was still angry and I couldn't shake it. But who was I angry at? Surely not Madison. She was a frustrating kid but she was managing any way she could, like the rest of us. She'd reacted to an extreme circumstance with extreme behavior, electing not to speak. Did that make her a criminal? Actually, it made her a survivor. Even the little turtle was helping her to survive, giving her some sense of control and a companion who couldn't walk out on her.

Was I angry at Leon? Wasn't he doing the best he could, too? Wasn't he trying to survive despite difficult circumstances and a severely broken heart? What more could I expect of him, or of Madison?

Walking down Hudson Street past the big playground, I found myself shrugging my shoulders, talking out loud, like the rest of the crazies in New York. I needed to do something to get my sanity back. I thought about the blue walls of Madison's room. I needed to get to the pool.

I dropped Dashiell off at home, grabbed the bag with my suit, cap, goggles and lock and headed for the Y on Fourteenth Street, still talking to myself on the way there.

I thought about my sister's kids, kids who had every privilege, pricey private school, horseback riding lessons on the weekend, braces to fix their crooked teeth, a summer abroad studying music for my nephew, one of those expensive summer camps for kids who want to act for my niece. And what about Madison? A nearly empty refrigerator, hair that needed trimming, an isolating chronic disorder, abandonment, neglect and now suspicion of murder.

Was that why I was so mad? Was I mad because there wasn't a roast chicken in the Spectors' refrigerator, because Madison's nails were long and dirty? Even given Leon's neglect, there were lots of kids who had it worse than Madison, kids without homes, kids who were abused by their own relatives, kids who lived with parental addiction or without parents at all.

There was a water exercise class on one side of the pool, families with kids swimming on the other, the dads and moms encouraging their kids to swim, praising every effort. There were only three lap swimmers in the available center lanes. I slipped into an empty lane and began to swim, all the thoughts that had been plaguing me gone for the moment. I swam hard, wanting to keep my mind empty, just to feel my body working as I moved through the water, leaving room for nothing but what I was doing at the moment. I concentrated on my breathing, stretching my arms as far out in front of me as I could, trying to kick away my anger. There was something calming about the blue world under the water, something that allowed me to push away all the chatter that had been going on inside my head.

But once I was out of the water, all the calm disappeared. Now there was a wall of noise from the kids, only a dozen or so of them but each one shouting as loud as possible. And as I walked toward the showers, all my own noise came back. Standing in the hot shower, I finally knew why I'd been so angry at Madison's house. It wasn't a coincidence that I'd been thinking about my sister lately. Because what had happened to me had happened to her as well.

I was only five at the time. Lillian was fourteen. My mother sat us down in the kitchen and told us that she was going away. We were bad, she said, and that was why she was leaving. I remember how cold the air seemed, how hard the wooden chair I sat on felt. Lillian asked when she'd be back. My mother, who had been sitting with us, got up and walked over to the sink. With her hands on the edge of the sink, her back to us, she said she didn't know. Without turning around to face us again, she left the room.

It was my fault. I knew it. Lillian was always so good. I was the one my mother got mad at time after time. I was the one she said would aggravate her to death. I was frozen with fear and guilt. Lillian ran after her. "If you don't love us anymore, then fuck you," she shouted. I didn't hear my mother's answer, if there'd been one, and even though I waited for Lillian to come back and tell me what to do to keep my mother from going away, she never did. I heard the door to my mother's room close. I heard Lillian's door slam. I sat in the kitchen for a long time, holding the seat of the chair as tight as I could with both hands.

When I woke up the next morning, my mother was gone. There was a strange woman in our kitchen. She knew our names and told us to call her Aunt Minnie. She was strangely pale, I remember, not like the dark-haired people in my own family, and she smelled funny, sour, not at all like the sweet way my mother smelled. Even when we were outside, Aunt Minnie's hands were always warm and moist. I wanted her to touch me and not touch me, all at the same time.

Unlike Madison, I was a very lucky little girl. My father kept telling us that our mother would come home "in her own good time," and a week after she had left, she did. She never told us where she had been or why she came back, but years later, when I was an adult, my aunt Ceil did. She said my mother had been thinking of leaving my father, that she'd gone away to think it over. But something in me, something that my mother had broken, remained the way it was. It's hard, nearly impossible, to alter the truths you learn as a child, even when you find out that what you were told had nothing at all to do with what was so.

My mother's mysterious disappearance made my sister, Lillian, want to be the best mother in the world, one, she told me years later, unlike the mother *we* had. It had the opposite effect on me. If it was possible to give birth to a baby and then one day abandon her, even for a week, I wouldn't be anyone's mother. That way I'd be sure I'd never do to a child of mine what my mother had done to me, what Sally had done to her daughter.

If Madison Spector had nothing to say to anyone, she surely had her reasons. Even without being told so, she would assume that Sally had left *her,* as indeed she may have. Ms. Peach said that Sally had left shortly after Madison's diagnosis. What other conclusion could this kid have come to given the timing of her mother's departure?

I stopped by Miyagi on the way home and got some sushi to go. I was anxious to get to the computer and find out more about the disorder that might have been part of what made Sally run.

Chronic motor tic disorder, which Madison might or might not outgrow, was considered to have a genetic cause despite the fact that the gene or genes that caused it had not yet been identified. I wondered if Sally had had a tic disorder as a kid. The more common kind was transitory, lasting only weeks or months. The kind Madison had lasted considerably longer, usually for years and sometimes for a lifetime.

Or was it Leon who'd had the disorder?

I stopped reading what little I'd found online when I got to a part that was particularly painful for me. All the symptoms common to the disorder, muscle spasms, tics, grimacing, odd recurrent movements and blinking, exacerbated during times of stress. I had gone to spend time with Madison in the hope that someway, somehow, I could make some connection with her, that she would be able, one way or another, to feed me some information about her missing mother. Instead, I vented my frustration, most of which had nothing to do with her or with this case, ranting at the poor kid while her face twitched, her eyes blinked and both arms began to shake and tremble, reminding me of the autistic kids I used to work with and what happened when you first tried touching them.

I owed Madison, I thought. But perhaps it wasn't that simple. Perhaps there was another side to getting her upset. Perhaps that would be the way I would find out what it took to get her to act violent. The question was, how far did I dare go and what would it do to Madison and to me if I pushed her again, if I pushed her even harder than I already had?

I printed the rest of the pages on chronic motor tic disorder and put them on the side of the desk to finish reading later. Then I wrote some notes and questions on file cards, tacking them up over the desk. It was early evening by the time I called Leon. "I have a few more questions," I told him.

"Shoot."

"Are there any of your neighbors that Sally was friendly with, another young mother perhaps?"

"Three-H," he said. "And four-F. There was another one, but she moved. And Ted. He's downstairs, the apartment under us."

"Names?"

"Three-H is Nina Reich. Four-F, the Goodmans. They have a girl Madison's age."

"Do the kids still see each other?"

"Not anymore. Not since the accident."

"What accident?"

"It was a couple of years ago. Madison accidentally pushed Alicia when they were on the stairs."

"And?"

"Alicia broke her arm. They haven't played since then."

"Was anyone with them? Were you there, or one of Alicia's parents?"

"Yeah, Nancy, the mother, she was there. She said it wasn't an accident. She might not even want to talk to you."

"I see. What did she say happened?"

"That Madison shoved Alicia down the stairs."

"I mean before that. What was the reason for her anger?"

"Whatever the reason, there's no excuse for that kind of behavior."

"Agreed. I'm just trying to understand. The kid, Alicia, did she make some comment about the tics? Is that what happened?"

"That's my guess."

"You mean Nancy wouldn't say?"

"That's right."

"Leon, has Madison had any therapy to help her deal with her disorder?"

"Yeah, she went to two different shrinks. Neither one of them worked out."

"Why is that?"

"Because she just sat there. She wouldn't speak."

"I thought they do play therapy with kids. Or art therapy. I would think they'd have some way to work with her, even without spoken language."

"Me, too. That's what I thought, but it didn't work out that way."

"Okay, and the last name, Ted? He's your downstairs neighbor? Sally and he were friends?"

There was no answer. Perhaps Leon was nodding again.

"What about school? Were there students Sally mentioned, anyone in the same class with her that I might be able to find? Anyone she'd have coffee with after class?" I asked, but I had the feeling that if there was anyone Sally spent time with, someone she could talk to, she wouldn't have told Leon.

"No, she usually came home right after class unless she had to go to the library."

Right, I thought. "Leon, were you happy?" I asked him. But Leon didn't answer me. That's not a question, I learned a long time ago, that everyone can answer. "Was Sally happy, do you think?"

"She was going to school," he said. "That's what she wanted to do." There was silence on the line. "At least that's what she said she wanted to do. I don't know," he said. "I don't know if she was happy. I don't know if I was happy. I never thought about it."

"The night she left?"

"A Saturday."

"What time?"

"Nine. Nine-ten, actually. I looked at my watch because I thought it was too early for Roy's last walk. I figured I'd just walk him again, after the eleven o'clock news, the way I always did."

"What was she wearing?"

"Sally?"

"Yeah. Do you recall?"

"A white T-shirt, not one of those oversize ones, one that

fit her, faded blue jeans, work boots. A light jacket, white, with a hood but she had the hood down. It was warm out. Summer. She had her hair pulled back and stuck up at the back of her head in a big barrette, but it didn't catch all the hair. There were these wisps that always slipped out and hung down around her face." Leon stopped, perhaps to take a sip of water, or wipe his eyes. "She never wore any makeup," he said, his voice cracking. "She didn't need to."

"She was that pretty?"

Again, a silence. "I found her watch," he said after a moment. "It was in the bathroom, on the side of the sink. She'd gone out without it."

"Did she usually wear it?"

"Always," he said. "She always wore it."

Maybe Leon hadn't been so hot at giving information because I'd been asking the wrong questions. Ask him something that required visual memory and Leon was all there. Or was that only so when it pertained to Sally?

"Thanks, Leon," I said. "Just one more question for now. Did either you or Sally have any kind of tic disorder when you were younger, or anyone in either family?"

"No," he said. "No one I know of."

Leon had put me in a visual mode, too. I was thinking in pictures, seeing a watch on the side of the sink in Leon's bathroom. Now why would Sally have taken off her watch if she'd been going out to meet someone?

"Leon," I said, "was there, by any chance, a phone call shortly before Sally took Roy out for a walk?"

"No, no phone call."

"You're sure?"

"Yes."

"She didn't make one either?"

"No. I would have heard."

"Leon, the night that Sally left, was she wearing a bra?"

"The police never asked me that," he said.

"I'm sorry, Leon. You must have figured out before you hired me that this wouldn't be easy. I can't be polite when there's something I need to know and you're the only person who can tell it to me."

"You're thinking . . ."

"I'm not thinking anything," I told him, not wanting to tell him what I had in mind until I tried it.

"No bra," he said. "She almost never wore one."

"I'll be in touch," I told him, wondering if you could be arrested for a hit-and-run when you'd done it verbally. Something I needed to know, I'd told Leon, as if that made it okay.

I went back to the computer to check my mail before I turned it off. There were eleven spam messages, which I deleted, and two messages addressed to the new e-mail address I'd set up specifically for Classmates.com.

Dear Sally,

What a total hoot to see your name here. I don't know if you remember me after all these years. I sat next to you in Miss Freibush's English class. I went to Brooklyn College for two years, got married and had two kids. Me. I can't believe it. I wanted to be a teacher but not one like Miss F with her bra strap falling down her arm and her slip showing half the time. My husband, Bob, is a chemist. We have a house in Paramus, New Jersey. I can't believe I'm writing this. It seems like five minutes ago when we were in school. Please write and tell me all about yourself. Maybe we could even meet, have lunch or something one day.

Barbara Tannenbaum Greene

I wrote Barbara back and said I'd like to get together. Or maybe talk on the phone. "Send your number. There's too much news for e-mail," I wrote, hoping for a face-to-face.

Dear Sally,

    I wondered where you went you disappeared so fast. Did you move or what? And where are you now?

Jim

Jim didn't bother with a last name. I wrote him back and asked if we could get together for a cup of coffee—"too much news for e-mail," I wrote again, hoping it would get me what I wanted. Jim didn't say where he was, but if there was a chance of learning something about Sally, I was willing to travel.

It was almost time to travel now, on foot, back to Sally's block. I put on a pair of faded jeans and dug my old work boots out of the back of the closet. I was already wearing a white T-shirt so I unhooked my bra, pulled my arms out of the sleeves and dropped the bra on the bed. I twisted up my hair and fastened it to the back of my head with a big barrette.

I checked my watch, then took it off. Sally hadn't been wearing one the night she'd disappeared and neither would I. I didn't have a white jacket with a hood. I wasn't Sally and Dashiell was no Border collie, but all I could do is work with what I had.

CHAPTER 10

I got to Sally's block around nine and sat on the stoop for what seemed like ten minutes, fully aware as I sat there waiting that no matter what I did that mimicked Sally's behavior that night, I wasn't a twenty-three-year-old gorgeous blonde, that Dashiell carried very different baggage than a Border collie and that this was now and not then in dozens and dozens of ways I couldn't begin to name. I knew that even if I were Sally, what happened this night might not reflect at all on what had happened five years earlier; you can't step into the same river twice. Despite that, I was going to give it my best shot.

If Sally had no money, maybe just a ten or twenty stuffed into her pocket along with the pickup bags, no credit cards and a medium-sized dog, how did she disappear? Was it even reasonable to think she hadn't been abducted, raped, murdered and dumped? Was there a remote possibility that her story didn't end with Sally's body weighed down with a concrete block and dropped into the Hudson or buried somewhere in New Jersey, but with Sally in Flint, Michigan, say, alive and well and living a different life under another name?

There was only one scenario I could think of that might have gotten Sally out of town. I walked downtown first, stopping whenever I saw a car, standing off the curb and sticking my thumb out, smiling hopefully. I tried Greenwich Street, where Sally lived, then walked a block over to Washington, which went in the opposite direction. I even tried hitching alongside the West Side Highway, although picking up passengers there would be dangerous and probably against the law. It was possible that hitchhiking was against the laws of New York City anyway, but that wasn't the point. Someone still could have stopped to pick up Sally and Roy. People broke laws all the time, for any reason you might imagine.

Not one car stopped for me during the first hour I tried hitching. It could have been because I wasn't seventeen years younger than I was, blonde and really beautiful. It could have been that with all the bad press pit bulls got, no one wanted a strange pit bull in their car. On top of everything else, Dashiell is white, and while everyone thinks there's nothing scarier than a black dog, and that may be so during the day, there's nothing eerier than a white dog in moonlight. Dashiell, glowing in the dark, his eyes an iridescent yellow in oncoming headlights, looked like everyone's worst nightmare. But some of the drivers never saw Dashiell. Twice he was hidden from view by parked cars. Once there was a Dumpster in the way. Still, no one stopped. No one even slowed down. People might stop, or not stop, for any number of reasons. I'd never know why, and worst of all, none of this told me whether Sally had been able to get a ride.

Near the end of the second hour, or what seemed like the second hour, I wondered what the hell I thought I was doing. But in some ways, I'm like Dashiell. Once I get an idea in my head, I have trouble letting go of it. So I kept trying. Halfway through the third hour, I got a better idea. I headed back toward Leon's block, wanting to try a different route, starting where Sally would have started, from her home. I walked north, turned the corner, and headed a block west to Washington Street and then north again toward the meat-packing district, where, for one reason or another, all the cars slowed down. I didn't think I'd pass for one of this particular stroll's transvestite hookers, not in my faded jeans, work boots and clean scrubbed face, but at least the traffic wouldn't be speeding by.

I began to read what was on the huge semis parked nose-in on either side of the street, another reason that traffic was slower as they negotiated the slalom path of the meat market during working hours. It was an off hour for deliveries, but there were still a lot of markets open, a lot of trucks pulling in to unload poultry from Kansas, pork from Ohio and Nebraska, beef all the way from Montana, the refrigerated trucks so loud it would have been difficult to hear anything else. The first truck stopped for me before I got to Little West Twelfth Street.

"Where you going, little lady?" he asked, leaning toward me, his hand on the passenger door. If picking up hitchhikers was illegal in New York, it was twice as illegal for truck drivers. Company policy forbade it and it said so right on the side of the truck.

"As far as I can get," I told him. "I've had it with New York."

He patted the seat. "Hop in," he told me.

I held up Dashiell's leash.

"Sure, your pooch can come, too."

"Where are you headed?" I asked.

"Back to Illinois. A little company will help keep me awake."

I nodded. "Thanks," I said. "I was thinking I'd go north."

"Suit yourself," he said, pulling the door closed. The truck made a sound as if it was exhaling right before he drove off.

I watched out for the hookers, careful not to impose on their territory, a gaffe which could get my throat slit with a razor blade. The next truck was going to Georgia, the one after that to North Carolina. While none of the cars stopped, about half the trucks passing did. Only one guy asked me, "How much?" The others were all clear that I wasn't that kind of girl.

I didn't need to stay out any longer. If I wondered if it were possible for Sally to get out of the city with no money, no credit cards and a dog, I had my answer. It was possible. Whether or not that had happened was another story altogether.

I liked walking Dashiell in the meatpacking district during the day. The side streets were pretty empty, even with all the recent gentrifying, pricey restaurants and pricier shops. It was a place I could take him off leash and not bother anyone, a place where there were always dog treasures to be found, a dropped work glove, an old boot, an empty water bottle. It would be the perfect place for Roy to get the chance to run, too, but Sally wasn't the one who walked Roy. It was Leon who often took the dog with him when he went out shooting. Had Leon worked in the meat market, a favorite location for fashion shots? Perhaps Roy had turned to the left, had looked at Sally with his round brown eyes, had led her this way. And then what? Had she just decided to go on the spot? Or had one of the trucks stopped to offer her a ride without her asking for it, the way the truck from North Carolina had stopped for me.

"Can I give you a ride home?" he'd said, a little guy, sitting on a couple of pillows to get high enough in the cab to see over the steering wheel. When he smiled, I saw he had a front tooth missing. "You look like you might be lost," he said when I hadn't answered right away. "This ain't no place to be walking your dog at night." And when I still hadn't responded, "I won't hurt you. You have my word on that."

He reached out his hand for mine, I thought to help me up into the cab, but then he said his name, "Fred White," as if that was the assurance I'd been waiting for.

When I shook my head, he shook his right back at me. "You take care, hon. Maybe walk him that way," he said, pointing toward Ninth Avenue. "These ladies here, they don't play nice." Fred winked, shut the door and drove off.

Dashiell and I headed home. No wonder there were so many people who disappeared and were never heard from again, I thought. It was so easy.

You could hitch a ride out of town, no problem. But then what? You get out of the truck the next day in Fayetteville, say, and go job hunting with your Border collie? So what if you could get out of the city. Wouldn't that just be the beginning of your troubles, not the end?

Sally would have needed a job, preferably one that included room and board. I checked my watch, remembering only afterwards that I'd left it at home. Sally would need a watch, too, I thought. If she got a job, she'd have to get there on time in order to keep it. But she couldn't buy a watch until she had the job—one of those dilemmas.

I thought it was probably too late to call Leon, ask him what work skills Sally had. We walked back along Greenwich Street, just in case. If I saw a light in Leon's window, I would have called. But Leon's window was dark. It was Madison's room that had the lights on, Madison up past midnight. I wondered if she was reading in bed. Or if she'd had a bad dream. I wondered if Madison were willing to talk, if she needed to talk, would Leon be willing to listen? I wondered if anyone had ever listened to Madison, and if no one had, maybe that was why she'd stopped speaking.

Why call Leon anyway, I thought, heading over to Hudson Street, crossing over to the side where the playground was, the sandbox empty, the swings still, no sound of little

kids having fun. What skills could Sally have had, knocked
up at fifteen, taking care of a baby all day when she was sixteen, then starting school at night? There wouldn't have been
a chance for her to work summers either. She'd been too
young. Maybe she'd babysat. Kids started that at thirteen or
fourteen, those without huge allowances and credit cards,
and I didn't for a minute think Sally fit into that group. Could
she have gotten a job as a nanny? That would have given her
room and board plus a little bit of money. But how would you
do that without references? And how would you do that when
you had a Border collie with you? If you had a Border collie
with you. If things didn't look too good for Sally, they looked
even worse for Roy.

CHAPTER 11

Not a nanny, I thought the moment I woke up. Or had I been dreaming? She couldn't have walked out on her own child to end up taking care of someone else's. I didn't believe that was possible.

After breakfast, I checked the want ads, looking for jobs that included food and lodging, or if not food, at least lodging. A place to stay, that would have been the first problem that needed solving. Of course, the jobs in the *Times* were mostly local. I didn't know what Sally might have found in other cities, or in a town so small it only made it onto local maps.

I thought about the truckers, most of them lonely, some of them trying to deal with their loneliness by spending a few bucks and a few minutes with a transvestite hooker. A lot of them willing to bend the law and pick up a woman and a dog, have company part of the way back home. If Sally had been picked up by a trucker, might someone have seen that?

The hookers were out on weekend mornings. After working all night, they looked like they'd been washed up on-shore someplace, beached and barely able to move. The ones who hadn't had electrolysis had beards showing by morning, not a pretty sight. But I wasn't interested in purchasing their services. I was interested in talking. Perhaps one of them had seen Sally and her dog get into a truck. Perhaps, I thought, sitting outside with a cup of tea, the cool morning air waking me up, I should have my head examined. The hookers were all hard-core junkies. They wouldn't remember yesterday, let alone something they might have seen in passing five years earlier. Hookers as witnesses? The cops say, if hookers clean up well, they can be great witnesses in court. But I doubted that these particular hookers could be cleaned up. By the time they hit *this* stroll, they were beneath rock bottom. Most of them wouldn't talk to me unless I offered money for conversation, and in that case, they'd give me what they thought I wanted to hear. "Yeah, baby, a little blonde with her dog. Sure, I remember, she got into a poultry truck, a beef truck, one of them pork trucks, whatever kind of truck you got in mind, she got into it. Never saw her sorry white ass around here again."

Did the hookers even live five years, the lives they lived, the work they did, the chances they took?

And what about the butchers? Very few were still open at night, and of those that were, none would rat out a trucker. They wouldn't tell me if they saw a trucker negotiating with a hooker. And they wouldn't tell me if they'd seen Sally getting into a truck with one either.

A witness in the meatpacking district? Not on a bet.

After feeding Dashiell, we headed over to Leon's building. It was Sunday morning, late enough for most people to be awake, early enough that they might still be home. I thought I'd start with the Goodmans, see if they would talk to me.

"I wasn't surprised to hear what happened," Nancy Goodman said. She was standing in the doorway but hadn't invited me in. "She's a very disturbed little girl."

"Not for nothing," I said. I waited for that to sink in.

"I suppose not."

"And no one could blame Alicia for not wanting to see her again."

"It wasn't Alicia's decision. Sam and I thought it would be a bad idea, too dangerous."

"Alicia still wanted to play with Madison?"

Nancy bit her lip.

"She wasn't afraid of her? Or angry?"

"She's a kid. They were friends. But we thought . . ."

I waited.

"We thought better safe than sorry."

"I would probably feel exactly the same way if I were in your position," I said, figuring Alicia for an only child, her mother not yet understanding that no matter what you did or didn't do, your kids would get hurt, the price you paid to be a human being, to be alive. "Still," I said, "I can't help feeling for Madison. She's so isolated."

"Ms. Alexander, did you come up here on her behalf, to see if Alicia could play with her? Because if you did . . ." She was shaking her head, out of words for the moment.

"No. Well, yes and no. I didn't come to see if Alicia could play with Madison. But I did come on Madison's behalf. As I mentioned, Leon's hired me to try to find Sally. He thinks if I can, Madison might talk again."

Nancy sighed, took a long look at Dashiell and stepped out of the way. "Come in," she said, the weight of what she was about to tell me almost too much for her to bear. "Sam is out with Alicia getting bagels and lox. We can talk until they come back."

I followed her into the living room, a large sunny room with lots of plants and pictures of the family all over the walls. The room was done in a pale green, the rug a slightly darker shade, as if Ms. Peach had been their decorator.

Nancy sat on the edge of the couch. I took a chair facing it and sat there, signaling Dashiell to lie down.

"Were you friends, you and Sally?"

"No, I wouldn't say we were. The girls played, usually here. Sally was in school and time to study was precious to her. I didn't mind having them both here, as long as they got along."

"And they did?"

"At first, yes. Madison always seemed very happy to stay here. Sometimes she'd ask to stay for dinner or ask to sleep over. She was . . ." Nancy bit her lip and turned away. "One time when she was here, she told me she was hungry. I offered her a cut-up raw carrot, Alicia's favorite snack. She said, 'Oh, a raw carrot. *Thank* you,' as if I'd slid a pan of hot chocolate chip cookies out of the oven and told her she could eat as many as she wanted, then take the rest home." She shook her head. "She was a very needy little girl, even before Sally left, disappeared. Leon's, well, vague. There's something insubstantial about him, do you know what I mean?"

. I shrugged. I wasn't here to share what I thought about Leon with her.

"And Sally, she had her nose in a book most of the time."

"Studying?" I asked.

"Or just reading. Even when I'd run into her at the playground, Madison would be on the slide or in the sandbox and Sally would be reading, not paying attention to Madison at all. And if Madison came up to her, she'd hold up one finger, you know, to tell her to wait until she'd finished the sentence she was reading or the paragraph she was underlining."

"What about Leon? Did he pay attention to Madison?" I asked, picturing the empty refrigerator, wondering when Madison's sheets were changed last, or if she and her father ever went to the movies or sat on a bench by the river and watched the boats go by.

"Oh, Leon's Leon," she said. "He's a perfectly nice man, I suppose, and I'm sure he wouldn't hurt a fly, but his head is in the clouds. After Sally left, before . . ."

"The accident?"

Nancy nodded. "I sent my maid down. I told him, 'Leon, every other week. You've got to do it.' The place was falling apart. If not for Annie, oh, I just can't imagine."

"But he must care for Madison. He hired me to . . ."

"He's very protective. I'm sure he cares a lot, in his own way. He just doesn't have very good parenting skills."

"And neither did Sally?"

"I hate to speak ill of . . ."

"We don't know that," I said.

She nodded. "Right. But where could she be all these years?"

"That's what I'm hoping to find out. That's why I'm here."

"Here? But what could I possibly tell you? What could I know?"

"You're helping a lot. I'm wondering, besides school, what Sally was interested in? What else did she like to do?"

Nancy shrugged. "Read," she said. "She just wanted to get lost in her books."

I heard the door open. A man's voice said, "Show Mommy what you got her." And a young girl, taller and heavier than Madison, appeared in the archway to the living room with a bouquet of flowers. She stopped when she saw me, or perhaps it was seeing Dashiell that made her pause.

I stood. Dashiell stood, too, wondering if this was another little girl he was supposed to befriend. But then Sam put his hands on Alicia's shoulders, ready to snatch her out of harm's way, so I dropped my palm in front of Dashiell's face, signaling him to stay where he was.

Nancy got up to see me out. "I'll explain later," she said to Sam as we passed him.

At the door, I thanked her for her help. She wished me luck. I was grateful. I thought luck was exactly what I needed, as much of it as I could get.

I took the stairs down to the third floor and rang Nina Reich's bell, but there was no answer. So I wrote a note on one of my cards and slipped it under her door. I took the stairs again, to the first floor and the apartment under Leon's. Ted was home, but apparently I woke him up. I apologized, told him who I was, why I was there, and offered to come back later. He turned around, padding back toward the kitchen.

"You drink coffee?" he asked without turning or stopping. He looked lost in his striped velour robe, Jacob's coat of many colors, a small, slim man with tousled hair and sleepy eyes.

"Tea," I said, wondering how I had the nerve to be so demanding when I'd just woken up a perfect stranger.

"Caf or decaf?" He turned around this time. "I was hoping he'd do something," he said. "*Something*. He sure took his good old time. Go sit down, Rachel. I'm going to take a sec and get dressed while the water boils."

"You're sure? I can come back later."

"Sit, sit," he said. "I'll only be a minute."

It was funny to be in Ted's apartment after being in Leon's. The layout was the same, the style another story. Where Leon's cluttered dining room began, Ted had a carousel horse facing the entrance, head down, mouth open, a foreleg bent and raised. The body of the horse was white, the leather saddle trimmed in gold. Beyond the horse was a round marble table, white, with leather chairs, a chandelier overhead. Ted's living room was white, white carpet, white sofa, white drapes. White, in New York City. How did he keep it so clean?

The walls were covered with pictures, too, but unlike Leon's, these pictures were all personal. They were all of Ted. Ted, it appeared, was an actor, so I got to see Ted in a hat, Ted in *Cats* (though with all the makeup, I couldn't tell which one he was), Ted as the master of ceremonies in *Cabaret*—so that was why he looked slightly familiar; he was a Joel Grey look-alike, at least in makeup. I was looking at that poster, the one for the road show of *Cabaret*, when Ted appeared, now wearing an ecru linen shirt with pale blue linen slacks. He'd obviously taken the time to put his head under the faucet and apply a ton of product to his hair. It did the trick, too. Not only was his hair slicked back, but he looked awake now, lively, as if this weren't a visit about a missing neighbor, but rather showtime.

"I was his understudy on Broadway," glancing at the poster, then back at me. "The man never so much as caught a cold." He shook his head. "So talk to me. Do you think the kid did it?"

"Do you?" Thinking about her fingerprints on the needle.

"She's angry, sullen, peculiar, pouty, exasperating, let's see, what else? Oh, yes, she's becoming an adolescent. Did you notice? Or was she wearing one of Sally's shirts? I bet Leon hasn't noticed. Did I mention angry? Or didn't you get to see the eyes she hides behind those dark glasses?" He shivered dramatically. "And then there's her father, so totally lost without Sally, he's barely alive. Why *wouldn't* the kid want to commit murder?"

I looked at the sofa, then back at Ted, communicating the way Dashiell does.

"I already told you to sit, missy. Do you want it engraved?" A moment later, from the kitchen, "What do you take in your tea?"

"Nothing," I said, anxious to hear what he had to say. "What makes you so sure?" I asked. "About Madison?"

He poked his head around the corner. "I'm not. So if you don't find Sally, then what? It doesn't look like a very promising gig for you, does it, what with Sally gone so long and the kid not talking?"

"I'm not ready to give up on it," I told him.

He walked back into the living room, glanced at a poster in which he was standing sideways, hat low over his brow, pelvis tipped back, arms at odd angles. "Theo Fowler is Fosse," it said. And under that it said "October 1–22, 1994, Miracle Theater, St. Paul, Minnesota."

"If she's still alive," he said, "you won't find her. Not unless she wants to be found."

"And what makes you so sure of that?" I asked. Dashiell was still checking out the room, poking his nose under things, around things, having a good sniff.

Ted turned and left again, coming back a moment later with a tray which he put down on the glass-topped coffee table, coffee, tea, biscotti, linen napkins, sugar, lemon, cream, spoons. How had he done all that so quickly?

He sat on one of the white leather chairs that faced the sofa, the coffee table between us. "She could come back, you know, even after all these years. He'd take her back. There's no question in my mind."

"And you think she will, when she's ready? You think until that time, should that time ever come, I won't be able to find her?"

"Are you good?"

"I work hard," I said.

He looked at Dashiell, maybe for the first time, then back at me. "What do you have so far?"

"A way she might have gotten out of town without money and without using her credit cards. Even with Roy."

Ted leaned closer. "How?"

"I'm not saying this happened. I'm only saying it could have happened. I tried it myself last night."

"What? What did you try last night?" He reached for his coffee, then changed his mind. "I'm all ears. Don't leave out any of the sordid details."

"Hitchhiking."

He sat back. "You're kidding."

"No, I'm not. I went out the same time Sally did, more or less dressed the way she was dressed. I even took Dashiell with me. No cars stopped for me, but then I walked over to the meat market and it was a whole other story."

"The long-distance truckers?"

I nodded.

"I could have gone to Kansas, Ohio, North Carolina. I had my pick. And Sally, well, Sally was twenty-three, blonde . . ."

"Unhappy." He finally picked up his cup and took a sip. "Okay. Leon did something right. You're good. But . . ."

"You don't think she's alive, do you?"

"In here," pointing to his perfect slicked-back hair, "no. In here," now pointing to his chest, "I hold out hope, but only once in a while, those times when I miss her the most."

"You were close?"

"I don't think Sally got close to anyone, but we might have had the closest thing to a friendship she ever had."

"Why do you think that was?"

"I never asked anything of her she wasn't capable of giving. I wasn't her husband or her kid. I didn't count on her emotionally. We just hung out sometimes. The truth is," both of us leaning forward this time, "she came down here a lot, to be by herself."

"When you weren't home?"

"Either way. But even when I was home, we'd talk a little, then she'd pick up her book, wiggle it at me and go into the bedroom and close the door."

"That seems . . ."

"Odd?"

He nodded. "You know how friendships are, Rachel. Whatever works you stick with. I liked having Sally around. Sally liked to read."

"Because she was going to school?"

"The other way around. She went to school because she liked to read. It wasn't possible upstairs. Leon wasn't a problem. But Madison was a real chatterbox and Sally was always telling her to be quiet. It was just easier here."

"Where did Leon think she was?"

"Oh, he knew." He shrugged. "She had to study, and anyway, Leon would have done anything to make her happy. He just wasn't able to."

I opened my mouth but Ted continued.

"It's not the usual story, that he was the wrong man, that she loved someone else. It wasn't that at all. If anything, Leon was the right man for Sally, the perfect man. He adored her and he didn't ask much of her."

"Just that she stay."

"Just that," he said.

I finally picked up the tea. It was in a bone china cup like the kind my mother had collected.

"Perhaps she didn't leave him," he said. "At least not intentionally."

"There's always that." I took a sip of tea. For a while neither of us spoke.

I could picture Sally here, curled up on the white couch or lying on Ted's bed, using his apartment as a sanctuary whenever she could. I bet it happened quickly, their friendship, or, more accurately, their arrangement. Maybe it was because of his occupation and the easy intimacy of theater people. Whatever it was, it had worked for Sally. For both of them.

"What else did she like to do besides reading?" I asked.

"Not much. Not that I know of. Once she started school, she didn't have much time for anything other than her studies and that," pointing to the ceiling.

"She cooked?"

"Never. They ordered in. Or Leon made eggs. Or spaghetti with sauce from a jar," grimacing at the thought.

"She cleaned?"

Ted blew some air out of his nose.

"She spent time with Madison?"

Ted rubbed his forehead. "Yes and no. She wasn't much of a take-the-kid-to-the-zoo type of mom. But she'd do things for her and she worried about her. Before the . . ." He made an eye twitch. "She told me Madison seemed very tense. That's when she painted her room like that."

"Sally did that?"

"Sure. What? You thought maybe Leon did it?"

"I thought Madison had done it."

Ted shook his head. "Sally thought it would relax Madison, all that blue, the fish, the coral. She thought it would make her feel better."

"But it didn't."

"Not one little bit. She liked it. She was very excited by it. I can't say how much of that was because it was so cool or how much of it was that her mother was doing something for her. But Madison needed more than fancy walls to fix what ailed her. She needed . . ." He stopped, picked up his cup, put it down again. "She needed more traditional parenting than she was getting."

"What would you say she was getting?" I asked.

"Benign neglect."

"I used to be a dog trainer," I told him. "You could tell the whole story by the way someone touched their dog."

"Or didn't."

"True, but very few didn't touch them at all. Of the rest, the majority, only a few touched the dogs as if they were theirs."

Ted stared at me for a moment before speaking. When he did speak, his voice was small, the opposite of a stage whisper. Even sitting this close, I could barely hear him. "You're right. That's what the story is upstairs. Leon keeps a camera between himself and the rest of the world."

"Including his daughter?" I asked. But I already knew the answer. I'd seen the space between them the very first day, space I thought Sally used to fill or might fill again if I could find her. But maybe that wasn't so. One way or another, Leon seemed to keep those he loved at bay. Perhaps that was why he'd wanted Roy. Dogs often filled the gaps between people, space they couldn't bridge on their own. Perhaps Roy was supposed to be the mortar that held them all together.

"Leon's not a toucher," Ted said.

"And Sally? Was she?"

He shook his head. "Didn't like it."

"No hugs good-bye?"

He shook his head again. "Tough on the kid," he said. "Tough on me, too."

"I've always thought that we're more like animals than we like to admit."

"That people need physical contact, too?"

I nodded.

He took a sip of coffee.

"None of this tells us where Sally is," I said, "if she's alive or dead."

"Nor if Madison killed her doctor?"

"You think?"

Ted rubbed his chin, his hand covering his mouth, then shook his head. "I've been wondering about the first question for five years, the second one since I heard. I can't help you rule it out, Rachel. I wish I could."

"You have helped me. You are helping me. You're the first person I spoke to who gave me any kind of sense of Sally. But—"

He waved his hand in the air, as if to erase what I was about to say.

"I had a client once. She was engaged and living with her boyfriend, but he was reluctant to commit to a wedding date. She'd pick one, he'd agree, then he'd change his mind, suggest a later date. One day she says, 'Harvey, I'm not getting enough love here. I'm getting a dog.' "

"You're thinking Roy? But he was Leon's dog, Rachel. Leon was the one who wanted Roy."

"I know."

Ted nodded. "He took him everywhere, starting from when he was this big." He held his free hand a foot or so above the floor. "In the beginning, he carried him in his jacket when he went out to shoot. The last month or so, Roy would just follow him, sit and wait while he took pictures, get up and walk when Leon did. He was doing this series about the amount of filming done in New York, movies and TV. I had a small part in *Law and Order* at the time. I was the nosy, chatty next-door neighbor who told the detectives about the person who'd been killed, what a slut she was. I know what you're thinking," holding up one hand.

"I wasn't thinking anything."

"Right. Typecasting. Well, so what. It's a living, meager, but a living."

"You were telling me about Leon and Roy and the shoot he was doing."

"The dog couldn't have been five months old and Leon's on the periphery of the set, kneeling down, climbing up on things, taking all these shots, and the pup, he was like a professional. He kept his yap shut. He watched Leon work, never took his eyes off him. Leon might have told him to stay sometimes because sometimes he trailed after him, but sometimes he waited. If Leon wanted someone to pay attention to him, Roy was his man, so to speak."

"But Sally took him. Didn't that strike you as weird?"

"Weird? You've met Leon and Madison and Emil/Emily and you think it was weird that Sally took Roy for a walk?"

"What do you think? An excuse to get out of the house?"

He shrugged.

"And then," I lifted one hand, "poof."

"One way or another," he said. "I hear him sometimes when I'm up late."

"Leon?"

He nodded. "He paces."

I nodded. "I'd pace, too."

"He needs to know what happened."

"One way or another," I said. "Thanks for the tea and sympathy. Mind if I come back again?"

I expected him to smile. Instead, his eyes teared up. For a moment, he couldn't look at me.

"I should have known," he said.

"Known what?"

"That Sally was going to take off."

"How could you have?"

"Something she said the week she disappeared." He put one hand over his eyes. His shoulders shuddered once. "I've never told this to anyone," he said, looking at me now. "She'd taken Madison to see Dr. Bechman that afternoon, and after dinner, she came down. She looked awful, pale and out of it in a way. She sat there, where you are now, and she leaned back, her head on the cushions so that she wasn't looking at me, and in this dreamy voice she said that Bechman's receptionist had told Madison she was leaving." He stopped and shook his head.

"And?"

"Then Sally said, 'Can you imagine a more perfect job? You'd have unlimited access to all those drug samples doctors always have by the drawerful. You could take something anytime you needed to. You'd never, ever have to feel pain. You could just float away into a world of nothingness.' "

He covered his face again. "Maybe if I'd said something, if I'd done something, maybe she wouldn't have gone."

"You don't know she went on her own volition. Besides, if she was that unhappy, what could you have done?"

Ted got up, walked over to a small white lacquer desk with drawers down one side, opened the top drawer and took out a card. He handed it to me as he walked me to the door. As I was about to thank him again, he put his arms around me.

"Yes," he said. "Come back. Let me know what's happening. Or if you need anything. Anything at all. Or bring a book. You can curl up on the bed and read. Bring him, too."

He had tears in his eyes when he stepped back. I could still smell the gel he used to keep his hair slicked down as I walked through the lobby and out into the street.

I looked up at Leon's apartment, wondering in the end what I'd have to tell this man, and there was Madison, looking down from the corner window. I lifted my hand and waved, but as soon as I did, she let the curtain fall back, and she disappeared.

CHAPTER 12

I was going to go home, make some notes, check and see if there was any further response from Classmates.com. There was some research I wanted to do, too, some thinking as well. I wanted to look up Madison's disorder and see what drugs were used to control it, see if there was anything else available that might help her. I knew I was being silly, or perhaps overly hopeful. What chance was there that I could find something the doctor hadn't considered?

Something about this case was different. I'd think of what I wanted to do, or what I should be doing, then half the time I'd head off in another direction and do something else. It was as if someone was holding on to me, pulling at me, telling me, no, not that, this. Is that what had happened to Sally, too? Had she gone out for a breath of fresh air, maybe to get away from Madison's chattering or Leon's silence? Had someone or something taken hold of her, pulling her away from what she wanted to do, what she thought she should do?

It would be easy to suppose that it had been a who that took hold of Sally, literally took hold of her. But what if it wasn't a who? What if it had been a what instead, like whatever it was that had taken hold of me?

What if, I kept thinking, but I couldn't finish the question. I was still standing there, across the street from Madison's apartment, thinking of it that way now, Madison's building, Madison's apartment, the kid pulling on my consciousness, filling it up, thinking of her mother, Sally, escaping to Ted Fowler's serene apartment so that she could read in peace.

I crossed the street and kept on going, back to where there'd been a C. Abele that had turned out to be Charles, not Celia. There were so few Abeles in the city, I was thinking as I approached the building. It wouldn't be too big a stretch to think some of them knew each other, or maybe were related. I crossed the street, found a step to sit on and took out my cell phone, calling information and getting the numbers of the two Abeles I'd found in Brooklyn, one in Queens, six in Manhattan, including the one who lived across the street from where I was sitting. Late Sunday morning, chances are I'd find some of them home.

Claire Abele never heard of a Celia Abele but she was very nice about my having called. Richard Abele was home, too. "Wrong number," he said, and hung up on me. I couldn't blame him either. There were so many calls lately you wanted to hang up on, people who wanted, one way or another, to get some of the money in your bank account into theirs.

Harrison and J. might have been out to brunch or at the gym. Harrison had an answering machine so I left a message. J. didn't, so I didn't. Louise had clearly been sleeping but she didn't seem at all angry at me for waking her up. Unfortunately, she didn't know any Celia Abele. I was almost ready to give up when Philip Abele answered his phone.

"She's my brother's ex," he said. "Only . . ." And then he clammed up. Who the hell was I to be asking personal questions, he might have been thinking. I would have. "What do you want with her?" he said. Protective? Or just another cranky New Yorker?

"It's about her old job," I told him. "I'm working for a family whose little girl went to Dr. Bechman and I need to talk to Celia about—"

"No," he interrupted. "No. No. No. I can't help you out here."

"Well, do you think Charles might?" I asked, making an assumption based on proximity and the fact that he was all I had left at the moment.

"That would be up to him," he said. And the line went dead.

I could have just dialed Charles's number. If there was a polite way to disturb a stranger, I suspect that would have been it. But I didn't call. I got up and walked across the street, finding the bell that said "C. Abele" and ringing it. But when the intercom crackled and he asked who was there, I wasn't sure I'd get anything more this way than I would have on the phone.

"I'm looking for Celia," I said, "on an urgent matter."

My day was full of surprises. Charles Abele buzzed me in. I pushed the door open, held it with my foot and looked back at the bell. He was on the third floor. Dash and I took the stairs.

He was standing in the doorway when we got there, his curly hair a bit messy, his shirt a washed-out-looking plaid in blues and grays, his pants baggy corduroys, looking as if he'd slept in them. Though, on second thought, I doubted that Charles Abele was sleeping any better than Leon Spector did.

"I'm sorry for disturbing your Sunday," I said.

He stepped back, making room for me and Dashiell, closing the door behind us, walking over to a light green couch, soft pillows nestled in the corners, a glass coffee table in front of it covered with sections of the *Times*. There were two black leather chairs facing the couch. I sat in one of those, Dashiell sliding down to smell the nubby pale wall-to-wall.

"What now?" he asked, a man as weary as my client but who seemed to be, unfortunately for him, far more connected to his own pain.

"I'm not sure I understand what you mean," I said, hoping he might tell me what had already occurred that made him look as if the bones in his body could barely hold him erect.

"What is it you want with Celia? What's the urgent matter?"

"You've had enough of those," I said, trying again.

But Charles Abele wasn't having any. He sat up straighter and looked me over. "Can we get to the point, Miss . . . ?"

"Alexander," I told him. "Rachel. I was hired by the father of a little girl who was a patient of the doctor Celia used to work for."

"Madison Spector?"

I nodded. "I wanted to talk to Celia about Madison because she knew her before she stopped talking."

He nodded. He knew that part, too.

"She lives two blocks away," he said.

"You're the only Abele listed in the neighborhood. Is she unlisted?"

"She went back to using her maiden name," he said. "Daniels. They live on West Eleventh Street."

"They?"

"Celia and JoAnn."

I'd already been too nosy. I had no legal status and this man owed me nothing. But I did tilt my head, the way Dashiell does, to show him that my interest hadn't waned.

"The baby."

"Mr. Abele," I said, "every time I ask you a personal question, I feel my mother turning over in her grave. I wasn't brought up to be, well, I know I'm being very intrusive. But there's a little girl suspected of murdering her doctor and she won't speak. She won't tell anyone that she didn't do that. Or that she did. And I'm trying, despite some awful odds, to . . ."

"I understand what you're trying to do, Miss Alexander. What happened to Madison is heartbreaking. Anyone would want to help."

"Then you know about it? It wasn't in the paper."

"Celia was very fond of her."

"That's the first I heard of that."

"Of what?"

"Anyone being fond of Madison."

"People are fond of all sorts of people," he said, "even people they shouldn't be fond of."

I nodded. "I'm so sorry," I said.

"She said she was quitting her job. Just like that. No discussion." He pointed to himself and then to me, as if I were Celia telling him the bad news. "The thing is, my writing hasn't taken off." He laughed. Perhaps more of an expulsion of breath than a laugh. "I have three novels out, but I haven't made it to mid-list yet. What I'm saying is that we couldn't live on my advances. We needed Celia's income and she'd agreed to give me five years, well, five more years. Unless . . ."

I waited, but Dashiell didn't. He got up and went over to Charles Abele, dumping his big blocky head in Charles's lap, the well-honed habit of an experienced therapy dog, helping when help was needed.

"But we hadn't gotten pregnant, so . . ." He waved a hand in the air, let it alight on Dashiell's head. "He's a very nice dog," he said.

"Thanks. Did she say why she was quitting so suddenly?"

"She did. She's very forthcoming, my wife." He laughed. I didn't know what was funny but I neglected to say so. "At least she was that day. She said she was pregnant so she had to leave."

"But it's against the law to . . ."

"Not that she was asked to leave. Not that. That she had to leave because it was Dr. Bechman's baby and it would be very awkward for her to remain there, what with the doctor being married, too."

"Oh."

"No big thing her being honest, you know, because we already knew it couldn't have been my baby, and we hadn't been trying artificial insemination. It cost more than we could afford. So, one way or another, I would have figured out that the honeymoon was over, wouldn't you think?"

"I would," I said, understanding why he'd asked me "What now?" when I'd walked in, understanding the laugh, too.

"She said she was moving out."

"Did she say that she and Dr. Bechman . . ."

He shook his head. "The doctor had no intention of breaking up his family. Only mine." He sucked in his lower lip, stroked Dashiell's head, then continued. "I told her she didn't have to do that, that she didn't have to leave. I told her I'd raise the kid with her, I'd love the kid, I'd give the kid my name, I'd do whatever, if she would stop seeing Bechman. She said she couldn't do that. She said she wouldn't do that."

"So she moved out."

"Yes, she did." Big breath.

"And got another job?"

Charles Abele shook his head slowly from side to side. "Bechman paid the bills."

"Is that so?"

"It was." He sighed. "I don't imagine Mrs. Bechman will keep up the payments, do you?"

"Mrs. Bechman knows about this?"

"No, I was just being . . ."

I nodded. "And who could blame you?" I said. "Mr. Abele, a few minutes ago you said 'the baby.' But wasn't this about five years ago? Because my understanding is that Ms. Peach has been . . ."

"She's a little over four. Four and three months. JoAnn, that's what they named her. Eric only had boys. He was thrilled to pieces, she said, Celia said. He doted on her. I do, too."

"You see her?"

He bent his head, figuring out, I thought, how to explain this peculiar arrangement to me. But he needn't have bothered. I thought I understood it already. If people could love a dog that bit them repeatedly, why couldn't Charles Abele love the child his ex-wife had had with her lover? And perhaps the ex-wife as well.

"It could be viewed as merely a practical matter, free babysitting. But it wasn't that. It was more like a kindness, giving me something to make up for what was taken away."

"How did it start?" I asked.

He sighed. "I can't really say. Things came up during the pregnancy, financial matters, social matters. And then there was the insurance. It was, is, in both our names, and of course it was awkward for him to be at the birth—how could he explain an eleven-hour absence?"

"So you were there?"

"I was. I saw her come into the world. I held her when she was a minute old and carried her to her mother. I fell in love with Eric Bechman's daughter before he did."

"And continue to visit and see her?"

"And love her. I'm Uncle Charles," he said, his eyes shining, one tear falling. "I have the same visiting schedule a divorced dad would have. Plus extra time when Celia needs me to babysit."

"You do that for her?"

"I do it to be with JoAnn. And for Celia."

"So you and Celia get along?"

"Most of the time." He raised a hand, dropped it back onto Dashiell's neck. "We've even talked about me taking JoAnn during the day so that Celia can go back to work. She'll have to now. She has no choice."

"Do you think she'd talk to me, about Madison?"

He lifted a hand, holding up a pointer, picking up the phone and dialing. But then he slid out from under Dash's head, got up and walked out of the room before she answered, choosing to explain things in private.

Men killed over smaller issues than this, I thought. He seemed to be a very gentle man, a loving man, a forgiving man. He seemed to be a hopeful man, too, perhaps ridiculously so. Had he been thinking that if he were the perfect ex, the loving uncle, the man Celia could always count on, still, that one day her relationship with Bechman would fall apart, that one day he'd have not only the woman he loved, but the child as well?

Of course, appearances could be deceiving and what things looked like might not be the way things were. Hadn't my client said that the first time we'd met?

There was a wall of books, a desk nearby, a stack of papers on the desk, a laptop, a printer, a mug with pens and pencils, probably a pile of unpaid bills somewhere, too. Along the widest of the bookshelves, there were framed pictures of JoAnn as an infant, JoAnn sitting up, standing, walking, on a swing, JoAnn as a toddler, JoAnn at four and JoAnn with her mother, a pretty woman with straight blonde hair, like Madison's, and serious blue eyes. Forthcoming, he'd said. God save us all.

Charles Abele came back into the room, put the phone in the cradle and handed me a piece of paper with a phone number on it. "She said you could call her," he told me.

"She won't see me?" I asked.

"She will. But she wanted you to call first. She's . . ." He was still standing, his arms at his side, looking off to the side, toward the pictures of JoAnn, who, unlike Madison, smiled for the camera. "She's having a bad day. A bad . . ." His voice trailed off.

"That's understandable," I said. "I'll call her tomorrow." I got up. "You've been so gracious, so helpful. I can't thank you enough." I put out my hand to shake his, but instead he took it and tucked it against his side, walking me to the door as if we were old friends.

He let go of my hand and opened the door. "Do you think Madison did it?" he whispered.

"I couldn't say. I suppose it's possible."

He shook his head.

"Not possible?" I asked.

"I don't know. It's just that . . ." He'd been looking down. He met my eyes now. "Having a kid, it's not like buying a pair of shoes, they pinch, you return them or you throw them away. I don't understand bringing a child into the world and then abandoning her."

He might have meant Sally, but I had the strong feeling it was Bechman he was talking about, Bechman who'd stolen Charles's wife and the child that should have been his. And then what, visited once or twice a week? How much more time could he have spent with them when he had another family to care for in Larchmont, his *real* family?

I began to wonder if beneath the sadness there was a ful-minating rage, and if so, if that rage was on behalf of his "niece," or perhaps for himself, for the damage Bechman had done to him.

And what of Celia, living on her own with JoAnn, waiting for those crumbs of time Eric Bechman could spare for them? How angry had she been? And was the "bad day" she was having today nothing, perhaps, compared to the bad days she had when Bechman was still alive?

CHAPTER 13

We took the long way home, weaving in and out of my favorite Village blocks, then discovering one of the last street fairs of the season, mostly people selling things they no longer wanted, an old manual typewriter, used books, stuffed animals, some with a missing ear or tail, that had once belonged to kids who were now in college, a bicycle that looked as if it might be okay after a few days in the repair shop, shoes with run-down heels, vintage clothes and just plain used clothes, some embarrassingly worn. One person's junk, another person's treasure. That wasn't only true for porcelain statues, lamps without shades, the shawl your grandmother crocheted that was filled with terrible memories rather than warmth. It was true for dogs, an abandoned mutt at the shelter, at least one of the lucky few, becoming someone else's beloved companion, and for people, a lover one woman dumps becoming the perfect man for someone else.

I thought of the way some people would sit outside selling their chipped knickknacks for a buck or two apiece, or hoping to, and other people held on to everything, mismatched china, a nasty dog, a distracted mate. I thought about Leon and Madison, living as if they were roommates as much as parent and child. And I thought about Sally, wondering again if she'd left or if she'd been taken away.

When I got home, I fed Dashiell, then went upstairs and turned on the computer. First I Googled Sally's name, Sally Spector, and got nothing. Then I tried her maiden name, Sally Bruce. Still nothing. So I tried Sally Madison, Sally Roy, Roy Spector, Roy Bruce, Bruce Madison, even, thinking she might have a sense of humor, Sally Forth. Nothing. I thought about what Ted had said, that I wouldn't find her unless she wanted to be found. I hoped he was wrong.

I picked up the pages I'd printed on chronic tic disorder, read some more about the syndrome that had shaped Madison's life for the last five years and perhaps had helped shape her mother's life as well. The dopamine blockers that were used to treat the tics, I read, had a limited rate of success and a high level of side effects. Most of the sites I found said that the tics might last into adolescence for some children, or they might last indefinitely. Tics, it reminded me again, grew worse during emotional stress. Unfortunately, I had already seen firsthand that that was so. But when I read on, I found something odd, something that made me curious: the fact that the tics and trembling that characterized the disease were absent during sleep.

It was late, but not too late. I dialed Leon's number. When he answered, I asked if he could drop Madison off at my house around four the next day. He said he could. I gave him the address. I asked if he'd send a change of clothes, her pajamas and a toothbrush, too. There was a silence on the line, Leon thinking over what I'd said. Fair enough, I thought, waiting until he was ready to answer.

"You want her to stay over?" he asked.

"I do," I told him. There was another silence and then I heard Leon cough. "Emil/Emily, too?" he asked.

I don't know why it was the question about the turtle that

made my chest tighten the way it did. For a moment I felt so sad it was hard to breathe. I found myself pulling a Leon, nodding into the phone.

"Yes," I said when I could. "Whatever—or whomever—she wants to bring." And then, "If she's willing to come at all."

"She will be," he said.

"How do you know that?"

"The jacket you found, Sally's jacket? She slept in it last night."

When I hung up I needed some air. I needed to be moving. I grabbed the keys to the Siegal house, and barefoot, Dashiell running ahead and barking, I crossed the garden and entered the town house via the back door, running up the stairs to close the window I'd left open. Then I went back to my own house and up to my office.

I studied the file cards full of notes I'd tacked up over the desk, adding some new ones, holding Celia Abele's card for a moment and then deciding not to wait, to call her right away, to try to see her in the morning. It was after ten, late to call a stranger, but I didn't think Celia would be asleep, and hearing Leon's voice a moment before, sounding as if he himself was the child I was supposed to save, I couldn't wait another moment.

I reached for the phone and then hesitated. Perhaps it wasn't Leon who needed saving. Perhaps it was someone else. When Leon had mentioned Emil/Emily, for a moment I was back in my mother's kitchen the day she said she was leaving.

Was that why this case pulled on me so, because when I looked at Madison, I saw myself as a little girl? My mother had come home, but not to me. From that time on, I knew I was alone, or if I wasn't, I could be at any moment. Isn't that what Madison knew? Isn't that why she clung so hard to Emil/Emily, someone that couldn't run away and leave her?

Celia answered on the first ring. She agreed to meet me for breakfast the next morning, after she dropped JoAnn off at school. When I asked where she wanted to meet, she gave me her address.

It was late and I was cold and wanted to go to bed. I decided to check my e-mail before shutting down the computer, to see if there was anything else from Classmates.com. And there was, just one letter. It was from one of the people who had written before, the one who hadn't bothered with a last name.

"Your not Sally," it said. "Who are you?" It was signed "Jim."

CHAPTER 14

Eric Bechman, Charles Abele had told me, was thrilled to have a daughter, but not thrilled enough, it seemed to me, to put little JoAnn and her mother, the late doctor's lover, into a building with an elevator or perhaps on the garden floor of a lovely old town house. By the time I'd climbed to the tiny top-floor apartment where Celia Daniels Abele lived with her daughter, I was thinking that perhaps the doctor hadn't been quite as thrilled as he let on. But that was no secret to Celia, Bechman's wife up in Larchmont having her teeth capped or doing Pilates with a private trainer or whatever it was you did in Larchmont, while she, Celia, had to carry her groceries, her baby and the stroller up all these stairs. Dashiell might have been the only one who found the trip to apartment 4B a total joy. He ran ahead, waiting for me at each landing with a manic smile, his mouth open, his tongue lolling out to one side, his eyes ablaze. Was he hoping for another flight to climb, then another still?

"JoAnn would love a puppy," Celia said, greeting me at the door with the teakettle in her hand. "But with all these stairs . . ."

As if I hadn't noticed.

She headed back to her kitchen. Dashiell was already inside. I followed him into the small, sunny living room and sat down on the couch. While Celia was making tea and heating the croissants, I slid off my jacket, letting it just fall behind me. The living room had an exposed brick wall and a small, nonworking fireplace. The couch I was sitting on opened up to a bed. The thickness of the seat told me that. And with two apartments to a floor, there could only have been one bedroom in Celia's apartment, the one that faced back, south, over the garden below and the one from the town house on the next block, back-to-back, like married couples who had stayed together but had nothing on earth to say to each other.

There was carpeting on the floor, nubby and in shades of oatmeal, very much like the one in the apartment she'd moved out of, and the furniture was decent. Had he paid for everything, I wondered, the blue vase on the windowsill with the single rose in it, long past its prime, the round coffee table in front of the couch, the two chairs facing the couch, one with a stain on it that might have come from a bottle of milk that spilled sometime back or a sippy cup with a loose top more recently, the bookshelves, the small color TV set, the primitive wooden carving of a bird of some kind? In this neighborhood, even a small walk-up would have a hefty rent, $1,800 a month, maybe more. If Celia hadn't been working all these years, how had Bechman come up with all this money without anyone knowing about it? That was the real question.

She came in with a tray and set it down on the coffee table, her blonde hair, cut to chin length, falling forward as she bent, covering her pretty face, her pale freckled skin, her large, sad eyes.

"She was never what you'd call a happy child," she said, as if I'd asked her to tell me about Madison a minute ago rather than the night before on the phone. "She was odd, very bright, her own little person, you might say. Even all those years ago, you knew there was something different about her, something out of the ordinary."

"In a nice way?" Her ex had said she'd liked Madison, but I didn't want to bring him into the conversation just yet, if at all.

"Oh, yes, for me, at least. I found her, well, compelling. You could have a conversation with her, at seven. Imagine that. And she'd notice things none of the other kids would notice, the fact that one of the doorways was raised, you'd have to step up to get into one of the offices or the fact that a light would blink when the phone rang. She had just as much reason to be scared as all of Eric's other patients, but she never seemed scared. She just seemed, well, curious, interested."

"Did she socialize with the other kids?"

Celia thought. "No. Not really. Only with adults. Sometimes she'd get into a conversation with me, sometimes with one of the parents, almost never with the kids. Or she'd take a book and read aloud to one of the toys, as if it were real."

"Did she bring the turtle?"

"I heard about that." She shook her head, a slight smile on her lips but not in her eyes. "The turtle came later, after."

"After her diagnosis? Or after her mother disappeared?"

"Both. And also after I had left my job."

"Had she stopped talking while you were still there?"

Celia nodded. "Poor thing," she said. "Poor girl. Yes, she had. The last two times I saw her, she wouldn't speak. She let me hug her, though, the last time I saw her."

"Did she know it was the last time she'd see you? Did she know you were leaving?"

Celia nodded. "Eric, Dr. Bechman, said not to tell her. He said she was in the middle of . . ." She stopped, looked off to the side, wiped her eyes with her fingertips. She wasn't wearing any makeup, no nail polish, no wedding ring either, I noticed. "A crisis," she said. "And that my telling her I was leaving wouldn't be a good idea. But I disagreed. I didn't like the idea of just disappearing from the life of a troubled child without any explanation. Little did I know what was coming," she said. "Poor kid."

"So you told her that last time?"

"No. I told her as soon as it was decided. I told her I'd only see her three more times."

"Then Sally was there when you told Madison you were leaving?"

"She was." Her face darkened. "That was the last time I saw her. As it turned out, she walked out of Madison's life before I did."

"What about the other kids? Did you say good-bye to them?"

"No. It didn't matter one way or another with the other kids. Some were friendly, some not, but none of them . . ." She raised one hand, trolling for the right word. "None of them related to me the way she did. None of them were affectionate."

"She was?"

"Very. She'd bring me presents and then tell me a story about each one. One was a rock named Gilbert." A real smile this time.

Celia got up and walked over to the bookshelves. At first I thought she was going to pick up the picture of JoAnn sitting on a swing, being pushed by her mother. Did that mean her father had taken the photo, that he'd gone out in public with his daughter? Perhaps not. Perhaps it was Uncle Charles who took the picture, JoAnn laughing, too young to know she shouldn't be as happy as it seemed she was. But it wasn't the photo Celia picked up. It was a smooth stone, the size of her fist, that had been on the shelf next to the picture of her daughter. She brought it back to where we were sitting, turning it over in her hand.

"Gilbert?"

She nodded. " 'Gilbert was a very special stone,' she told me. 'Why?' I'd asked her. So she held him up to my ear. 'Listen,' she said. And I did. 'Can you hear it? He's singing. He always sings when he's sad.' Then standing there, leaning on the desk, right next to my chair, she sang a little song she made up, 'Gilbert's song.' None of the other children did that either."

"Gave you singing stones?"

"No. Came around to my side of the desk. It was as if I were the teacher and they were in the classroom, as if they were a little afraid of me."

"How odd."

Celia shook her head again. "Not really. Have you ever gone to the other side of the receptionist's desk at a doctor's office?"

"I guess not," I told her, the stone, Gilbert, still cupped in her hand.

"Do you think she did it?"

Celia put the stone down on the coffee table and rubbed her palms against her skirt. She scowled, picked up her cup of tea, put it back down, almost tipping it over. "I've wondered about it."

I nodded. "And?"

"If she didn't," she said, "who did?"

I stayed where I was, but it took a lot of effort. I wanted to stand, to loom over her, to grab her by the throat and shake her. Was that the way people thought, I wondered, that Madison had committed the crime because they didn't know who else might have? If that was the way a friend of Madison's thought, what chance did this kid have with the cops?

"Just because we don't know who else may have done it doesn't mean Madison did," I said.

Celia opened her mouth, but I put a hand up, telling her no, telling her I wasn't finished yet. I reached for the stone, cradling it in one hand, touching the smooth surface with my other hand. Then I lifted Gilbert to my ear and cocked my head as if I were listening.

"Gilbert has a question," I told her.

She leaned forward, expecting something light, perhaps something funny to change the tone, to make things more bearable. But that wasn't at all what I had in mind.

"How did he pay for all this without his wife knowing? Is she that much in the dark about his finances?"

There was a slight gasp, her breath whistling as she inhaled, and that quickly, Celia Daniels standing suddenly, brushing some hair off her face, picking up the tray and heading for her kitchen, letting me know the interview was over.

I got up and followed her.

"Well?" I said.

"Why is that your business?" she demanded, the delicate skin of her face flushed, as if she'd just climbed all those stairs, her daughter pulling on one hand, a heavy bag from D'Agostino's in the other.

"You have no right," she said, her small, thin body visibly trembling. "It was between us. We weren't hurting anyone else."

"Is that right?"

No answer.

"Not your ex-husband? Not Mrs. Bechman? Not your daughter?"

"What happened between Charles and me, that's over. That's ancient history. And Mrs. Bechman didn't know."

"Which makes it okay?"

"Look," she said, getting angry now, "we didn't plan this. What happened happened and we were making the best of it, doing what was best for JoAnn and . . ." She took a big breath, let it out. "And none of this is any of your business."

Her back was to the counter. There was nowhere to go, and she knew it. There was nowhere to go in another way, too, because if I didn't get the answers I wanted from her, she knew I'd get them some other way, and that whatever that other way was, it would be worse, it would be public. Who was she protecting at this point? Her lover's reputation, his widow, her daughter? And if she was protecting JoAnn, who was protecting Madison?

"It *is* my business," I said quietly, nearly whispering it. "I'm here to speak for a little girl who's accused of murder and who refuses to speak for herself."

"What does one thing have to do with another?" she asked.

"That's one of the things I have to find out, don't I? So what was it, all told, five thousand a month? What about health insurance? He couldn't still carry you at the office, could he, not with two partners looking at the books? So how did he do it? With health insurance," I shook my head, contemplating the late doctor's monthly nut, "it would have been a considerable amount."

"He was a consultant," she said. "It's no big deal, it's done all the time, except . . ." Her eyes were wide now, and I could smell her fear.

"Except?"

Dashiell had gotten up when I did. He put his paws up on the sink now, asking for water.

"Well, it was separate from his practice, of course," shrugging, playing the little woman who didn't fully understand her man's business now. "It was hard, you know, putting in extra hours, but he had to do something so that he could . . ." Her hand made a small circle and then dropped to her side.

"Afford to take care of you?" I asked.

There was a bowl in the drainer. I filled it with cold water without asking and put it down on the blue vinyl tile kitchen floor for Dash, waiting for him to drink before continuing, wanting to make sure Celia heard every word.

"And this additional work he took on," I said, "it paid him in cash?"

Celia frowned.

"It was off the books?"

"I, well, I guess so. It would have had to have been. It would have been awkward if it showed up on his taxes."

"Very."

"I know what you're thinking. I worried about it, too. Doctors' incomes are scrutinized so carefully by the IRS, but he said it was safe and it wasn't all that much money." She bent and picked up the empty bowl, placing it in the sink. "He didn't want to hurt her. He didn't want to hurt his sons. It wasn't the way you think it was. He wasn't a bad person."

I lifted one hand, let it drop. "What else could he do? What other choice did he have?"

"Exactly," she said, so happy I understood their situation at last.

Celia smiled. I smiled back.

"And who was it he did this consulting work for," I asked, "to keep you and JoAnn in groceries?"

"Drug companies," she said, her voice even lower than mine had been.

"Drug companies?"

"For their advertising divisions. They do these focus groups, you know, asking people questions about new drugs they want to market, and they need experts to lead them. They pay very well."

"What sort of questions?" wondering why they needed a doctor to ask them. Were they technical questions perhaps?

"For instance," Celia said, "he'd ask them if they'd be more likely to choose a pill that was pink or one that was blue."

"I see."

"And he'd ask them about the wording of the ads, which words appealed to them, which would make them trust the product."

"And they needed a doctor, a specialist, to do this because . . ."

"Oh, it gave people the sense the drug company was really concerned about the needs and preferences of the patients."

I nodded.

"But I did worry about it. About the fact that it was . . ."

"Illegal?"

She made one of those little gasps again. "Oh, no, not illegal."

"Off the books isn't illegal now?"

"Well, yes, but . . ."

"He had no choice."

She nodded.

I watched her for a moment, neither of us talking, Celia not wanting to say where the money came from, not wanting to talk about the fact that her lover had not only cheated on his wife, he cheated on his taxes as well, me wondering if this was the whole truth and nothing but the truth, wondering, too, if the stories of extra work were an excuse not to be with her, with Celia. Perhaps the money he gave her wasn't that big a deal to him. Perhaps five or six thousand a month was chump change to the good doctor. Perhaps he took care of the family finances and his wife had no real idea what he earned and where the money went. That wouldn't be uncommon. Perhaps there was some way he was able to fiddle around with the books at work, have the business pay Celia's rent, claim it as something else. Who knew what was possible when there was powerful motivation matched with the need for secrecy? Who knew what people could and would do when they felt entitled to everything their beady little hearts desired?

Perhaps Bechman was cheating on Celia, too? Perhaps there was another girlfriend, another child stashed in yet another apartment? Did Celia ever wonder about that, all those nights she waited for him and he never came?

My mother always said I had an active imagination. But, still, it was possible, wasn't it? It was as possible that Bechman was killed for philandering as he was for screwing up a shot of Botox. At least that's what I was hoping at the moment.

I turned around and went back to the living room to pick up my jacket. I'd come to ask about Madison and I had. As for the rest, perhaps my mother was right. Perhaps I was just wishing that what I'd heard today might help with what I was hired for. But how? So what if Bechman wasn't as lily white as Ms. Peach would like everyone to think. Big deal. Who was? How would the fact that he had hidden income from his wife and his government get Madison off the hook? Because that was the point, wasn't it?

Celia was standing in the doorway between the kitchen and the living room.

"What now?" I asked her.

"I'm looking for a job. Charles said he could pick up JoAnn from school and take care of her until I got home."

"Every day?"

She nodded.

"You're a very lucky woman."

"I guess so. I just don't feel so lucky right now. It's going to be hard," she said. She looked small and vulnerable standing against the doorway, her arms folded across her chest as if she was trying her best to hold herself together. "I knew it would be hard when I decided to keep her." She shook her head. "No, that wasn't a decision. That was a given." Tears in her eyes now.

"Was there talk of not keeping her?"

She shook her head, shook my question away. What difference could it make at this late date?

"It's a mess, I know. It's been a mess from the beginning. We tried to do this without hurting anyone." She bit her lip, cocked her head. "But you can't. We couldn't. It wasn't possible. I know that now."

I turned to go and then turned back to her.

"Do you remember the song?" I asked.

"Gilbert's song?" She smiled, a weary smile. "I do."

"I'd like to hear it sometime."

She nodded.

"What will happen to Madison?" she asked as I reached for the doorknob.

I shook my head without turning around. When all was said and done, that was the real question, and I was nowhere near a real answer.

CHAPTER 15

Ms. Peach, I thought when I left Celia's apartment. And then again walking down all those stairs. Exactly what did Ms. Peach know?

I checked my watch. It was only ten-thirty. I could be at the office before she got there, or even better, after she got there but before office hours. We headed for Washington Square Park, the smells of ethnic cooking wafting out from the open doors of restaurants getting ready for lunch, pan-Asian on one corner, Indian in the middle of another street. An enormous slab of unwrapped salmon, cream-colored stripes of fat running through the orange flesh, was arced over a small man's shoulder as he carried it into a Japanese place. A brown paper bag of baguettes sat on the stone step outside a small French bistro, not yet open.

Dashiell sneezed as we passed the open doorways making room for the odors of cumin, soy sauce, ginger and the sweet, yeasty smell of the warm bread. But when we got nearer to the park, he began to walk faster, the dog run on his mind. We could hear the dogs barking when we turned the other way, Dashiell looking up at me wondering why I was betraying him.

"Soon," I told him. We had hours before Madison was due at my house, and at least one of those belonged to him.

I could see the lights on inside Dr. Bechman's office. Ms. Peach was already at her post. Perhaps she'd come in early to catch up on her paperwork. Good for her, even better for me. Because on the way over, I'd realized that the silly story she'd told me wasn't true. She hadn't come back for her book, not from West Sixty-eighth Street where the phone book said she lived. She'd come back because Celia had called her to find out why Eric Bechman hadn't shown up for dinner with his paramour and their daughter. It was Celia, it had to have been. Had she tried to page him and gotten no answer? Or was she afraid he'd forgotten and gone home? Was she afraid she'd have to tell JoAnn again that Daddy was too busy to join them that evening?

I rang the bell, and Ms. Peach came to the door, frowning at first because it was too early for patients to start coming, then even more so when she saw it was me.

She waved her hand from side to side, as if she were erasing a blackboard, as if erasing me. "I can't talk to you now," she said through the glass.

"It'll only take a minute," I said back.

"It's against our insurance regulations," she lied, as if I hadn't heard that one before, the excuse for everything nowadays. "No patients in the office before business hours."

"I'm not a patient," I said.

Ms. Peach stood firm, shaking her head from side to side.

"I only have one question," I told her.

When she saw I wasn't about to go away, her chest heaved once. She reached for the lock, twisted it, opened the door and then filled the doorway so that I would say what I had to say standing in that little alcove under the stairs and not think she was letting me in.

"I just met Celia," I said.

Her lips thinned out, her nose becoming pinched as she inhaled, and stood aside, making room for me and Dashiell.

He went first. I followed. Ms. Peach, Louise, the phone book had said, bringing up the rear.

I went into the waiting room and sat on one of the easy-to-clean faux leather couches. Dashiell lay down next to a stuffed animal that was lying on the rug on the far side of the coffee table, a wooden rectangle covered with coloring books and games.

"Celia suspects there's a third family somewhere, east of here perhaps?" I pointed toward NYU, in that direction.

"There most certainly is not." Sitting across from me, her cheeks trembling.

I smiled. "Only the two, then?"

Louise Peach flushed from the neck of her white wash-and-wear uniform right to her hairline, but she didn't speak.

"Tell me the story about the book again," I said, "the one you came back to get. Must have been a thriller, something you couldn't put down, something that couldn't wait another day while you took a night off to watch *Who Wants to Marry My Dad*?"

"*She* called. Or did she tell you that already? Why are you even here if you know everything there is to know?" Arms crossed over her bosom.

"I came to ask about the money, the off-the-books side business that paid the rent and sundries for Celia and JoAnn."

"There was no . . ."

"A consulting job? That paid cash? Surely . . ." And then I stopped in mid-sentence. The way Ms. Peach furrowed her brow, I wondered if it was possible she didn't know, that only Bechman, his employer and Celia knew. And since Celia hadn't mentioned the name of the company, perhaps even she didn't know that much. The less said, the safer. It was, after all, against the law.

"I can't talk to you about this," she said. "It's—"

"Illegal?"

Ms. Peach looked around, as if there was someone else in the office who might hear us. Perhaps there was. Perhaps one of the doctors had come in early to catch up on paperwork. I listened carefully but didn't hear a sound.

"He was doing the responsible thing," she whispered.

"How so?" I whispered back, steeling myself for whatever was to come. Whatever it was, it was going to be amusing, to say the least, the way people could rationalize any kind of behavior, transforming a self-interested sinner into a self-sacrificing saint.

"He didn't want to destroy his family and he wouldn't abandon her, Celia, or JoAnn either." She shrugged. "What choice did he have?"

"You mean he *had* to do the off-the-books consulting work?"

"Exactly." She sat back, her arms on her lap now, glancing at the clock on the wall across from us. "I have so much—"

I nodded. "So what was the name of the company he consulted with? And when did he do this, after work, early mornings, between hospital rounds and office hours?"

She was shaking her head. "I'm not at liberty to discuss this with you and you know that."

"And the money, you say he was paid in cash? So where did he keep it, here in the office?" And then it occurred to me, if he did, couldn't someone have come in to take it, killing him in the process?

She pursed her lips, shook her head. "I wasn't privy to any of this. I wasn't involved in his private life."

"Except for calls from Celia, trying to find out where he was."

"Sometimes."

"Even at home."

"Sometimes."

"You're a very devoted person, Louise." She blinked when I said her name. "The doctor was a lucky man to have you working for him."

She bent her head, looking at her hands, which were clutching her thighs.

"You can keep a secret, too, can't you?"

"It's part of . . ."

I interrupted her. "Even from the police."

"Well, I . . ."

"They don't know any of this, do they? They don't know there's another family. They don't know why you really came back that night. They don't know about the money. It doesn't show up anywhere, does it?"

She shook her head. "I guess he gave it right to her, to Celia."

"Or perhaps there was a safe-deposit box?"

"I wouldn't know." Looking at the clock again.

"Or an office safe? Is there a safe here, Louise, one of those little wall ones hidden behind a painting, a place to stow cash until it was needed?"

"Patients will start arriving at any moment," she said, standing now. "You'll have to go. *Please.*"

I stood, too, and so did Dashiell. He left the waiting room and headed for the door, his tail wagging. His turn at last. I walked to the door. When I looked back, she was standing near her desk, waiting for me to leave.

"None of this has anything to do with your case," she said. "None of this clears Madison or helps locate her mother. And that's what you want, isn't it?"

I turned and left without giving her an answer, the sound of her voice staying with me, stabbing me, as I headed to the dog run with Dashiell.

CHAPTER 16

Madison, wearing Sally's jean jacket, a backpack that looked bigger than she did hanging precariously down her back and the plastic purse with Emil/Emily in it swinging gently from her right hand, headed through the tunnel without seeming to notice me and without any gesture of good-bye to her father. Leon, bags under his eyes, his jacket buttoned a button off so that the ends didn't match, stood outside the gate as if waiting for me to tell him what to do next. I reached out and touched his arm.

"We'll be fine," I said, wishing I could believe it myself.

Leon nodded, reaching into his pocket, pulling out a mess of bills. "For whatever," he said, holding the money toward me, "dinner, a movie." He shrugged. "I don't know what you plan to do with her."

"Neither do I," I told him, pushing away the hand with the money. "I'll bill you," I told him, smiling, hoping he would know I was kidding.

Leon was still standing there. I turned around to see where Madison had gone and saw the rear half of my dog, his tail beating from side to side. Was he checking out Emil/Emily? Or was it Madison he was interested in?

"I might take her shopping," I said, facing her worried father again. "If that's okay with you?"

"Shopping?"

"I think she might need a starter bra," I said. "Maybe a haircut, if she's willing."

"Sally used to cut her hair," he said. He reached for his head, forgetting he had a baseball cap on. "Mine, too."

"That was a long time ago, Leon. She must have gotten her hair cut since then."

He scratched behind one ear, looked uncomfortable. "I tried it once."

"And?"

He shook his head. I figured it must have turned out like his jacket, one side shorter than the other.

"I think she cuts it herself."

"You're not sure?"

"I . . ." Leon lifted one hand, let it come to rest on top of his camera. "Sometimes there's hair on the bathroom floor, in front of the sink."

"It's not a problem, Leon. We'll figure something out. The girl stuff, I mean. If she's willing."

"You'll play it by ear?"

"My specialty."

He looked as if he wanted to go, but he didn't.

"Leon? Is there something you wanted to say?" I asked him.

"About Sally?" he said, a minuscule amount of hope showing for a bare second. "Is there anything yet?"

"I found out that she could have gotten out of the city with no money and even with Roy, but," I sighed, "that doesn't mean that's what she did. It only means it's what she might have done. I told you this would be hard, next to impossible."

"You did."

"Do you want me to continue with it? I can stop if you want me to."

He shook his head. "How?" he asked. "How could she have . . . ?"

"Hitchhiking. Not a car. The truckers in the meat market. I tried it with Dashiell. They're so lonely, most of the drivers, they even stopped for someone with a pit bull."

"And then?"

I shrugged. "I don't have a lot to go on, Leon. She's been gone five years," as if I had to tell *him* that. "But I am trying."

He nodded, head down like a dog who'd just been caught in the act, as if everything was his fault, Sally's disappearance, Bechman's death, the horrifying decline of moral integrity in the so-called civilized world, global warming, terrorism, the whole nine yards.

"Don't get your hopes too high," I said, wondering if he could even do that at this point. "But don't give up either." Then I felt like a complete idiot, talking to him in bumper-sticker slogans, as if anything I said would change the way he felt. "I'll call you in the morning."

Leon opened his mouth, then closed it again. I closed and locked the gate and headed down the tunnel toward the sound of barking. The backpack still on her, the purse with the turtle still in her hand, Madison was running in a circle around the large oak in the middle of the garden, Dashiell at her heels, cognizant of the unwritten rules and letting her stay ahead, though since they were going in a circle, maybe it was the other way around. I'd never seen Madison do anything normal, and watching them made me smile, but then I wondered if what she was doing could be considered normal, given the fact that she was doing it while carrying a turtle in a see-through lunch box.

"This way, gang," I said, "there's work to be done."

Dashiell got to the door first. I thought showing off might pay off big in the near future, that it might help convince this kid I had *something* to offer, get her to trust me a bit, so I asked Dashiell to open the door. Out of the corner of my eye, I saw Madison shoot a look at me, then quickly turn back to Dash. He took the doorknob in his mouth and twisted his head. I could hear the small click as the tongue of the un-locked door released. Then he let go of the knob, backed up one step and reared up, like a horse, hitting the door with his front paws and knocking it open. Madison was enthralled. Or at least attentive—it was hard to tell. And I began to think of the evening ahead as one long pet-therapy session. Where it would get me, I had no idea, but that seemed to be the hall-mark of this case, a fact I didn't even want to think about for now.

I'd made up my mind that connecting with the kid might help me find the mother. In the fading light of the fall gar-den, it seemed a ridiculous notion, given the fact that Madi-son was barely seven when her mother left and given the fact that she may have even been *why* the mother left. But it was all I could come up with at the moment, and I was sticking to it, with, I hoped, a lot of help from Dashiell.

Madison walked inside, looked around, wiggled out of the backpack and dropped it on one of the kitchen chairs. Then she carefully placed the purse in the center of the table, bending down and checking to make sure Emil/Emily was okay.

I went into the kitchen, got a big bowl, filled it partway with water and brought it out to the table.

"A swim before dinner?" I asked, not waiting for an an-swer. I'd be as likely to get one from Emil/Emily as I would from Madison. She opened the purse, picked up Emil/Emily and put him/her in the bowl, then stood bent over with her elbows on the table and watched the little turtle swim.

I walked back into the kitchen and took a piece of organic lettuce out of the crisper. I also had some chopped beef I was going to give Dashiell. I took a small piece out, rolling it in my palms to make a tiny ball. I put both on a plate and brought those out to the table.

Madison took the turtle out of the water and put it on the edge of the plate. I watched along with her as the turtle moved toward the little ball of beef, taking a surprisingly large bite, but then I thought of something my mother always said when we'd visit my aunt Ceil in Sea Gate, where all I wanted to do was stay in the water all day long.

"Do you think turtles are supposed to wait an hour after eating before they swim?" I asked Madison.

She looked up at me, her face blank. I could see a distorted image of myself in her oversize dark glasses, nothing more.

Maybe mothers didn't tell that to their kids nowadays. Maybe they did, but no one had bothered to tell Madison.

"We need to make Dashiell's dinner now," I announced. And when she didn't respond right away, perhaps waiting for me to take out a bag of kibble or a can of Alpo, I went back to the kitchen, pulled out the cutting board, set it on the counter and asked her if she'd rather grind or chop.

I didn't get the impression that Madison had to do anything at home, not set the table or help with the dinner, such as it was, or fold the laundry, anything that might make her feel she was helping to keep the family afloat. I knew dogs needed work and I thought kids did, too, for some of the same reasons. Doing something constructive was a great way to use your mind and your energy. And being a useful part of the pack is what made one feel secure, no matter what species the pack was. Besides that, I was out of homemade food for Dashiell, and if he was going to spend the evening seducing Madison, he'd need a hearty meal.

Madison came into my tiny kitchen and picked up the sharp knife I had put on the cutting board along with the carrot tops that needed chopping. Holding the knife, she looked up at me, perhaps wondering what on earth I could be thinking.

"Do you know how to chop greens?" I asked. "I can show you."

Madison put the knife back, picking up a carrot, studying the grinder, a little hand one I'd had forever. Then she held the carrot so that it would slide behind the cone and began to crank the handle. She did the sweet potato and the zucchini, too, and when the cone kept falling off, she looked at it carefully, figuring out how to get it back on so that she could continue, watching the colorful gratings pile up in the big bowl I'd put under the cone, orange, green and then the pale flesh of the sweet potato on top.

After she finished, I dumped the rest of the beef into the bowl and handed her the wooden spoon. Madison mixed, stopping each time I had something else to add. When I asked if she wanted to put in the raw egg yolks, she took the eggs from my hand, cracking one on the side of the counter, spilling half the white and the yolk onto the floor. For a moment, she froze. I expected her arms to start shaking, one cheek to jump and flicker.

"Not to worry," I said, whistling for Dashiell and pointing to the egg. Madison watched as he licked up the spill. Had she never cracked a raw egg before?

I pointed to the rim of the bowl and she cracked the second egg there. I mimed pouring the egg back and forth between each half of the shell and then held a glass under her hands to catch the white, praising her success when she plopped the yoke on top of the mixture, then smashed it with the wooden spoon. When we finished the food, stowing most of it in plastic containers and giving Dash his portion in the mixing bowl, I asked her what she wanted for dinner. I didn't know how Leon did this. How do you find out what a kid might want to eat if the kid won't tell you? Had I thought tonight would be any different, I would have been disappointed. Madison acted as if she hadn't even heard me.

I decided to order pizza. Madison was sitting with Dashiell on the living room floor and looked up when I made the order. I can't say she looked happy about it. I can't say she looked unhappy either. Maybe it was the dark glasses. You couldn't see much of anything, which, I suppose, was the point.

"You don't need those here," I said, tapping the air in front of my own eyes as if I were touching sunglasses. "He couldn't care less and neither could I." I didn't wait for a response. I didn't wait for her to remove her glasses, put them on the coffee table, feel all was okay with the world. I knew from doing pet therapy that things sunk in, or didn't, in their own good time.

I cleaned up the counter and the floor where Dashiell had licked up most of the spilled egg. When I looked back into the living room, Madison was nose to nose with Dashiell, her glasses still on.

When the pizza came, I asked Madison to get us some drinks. She brought two Cokes. Then she went back to the kitchen for Dash's water bowl and set that down next to the pizza box. We sat on the living room rug eating the pizza right out of the box, tossing Dashiell bits of crust, which he caught in midair.

After dinner, I ran a bubble bath and handed her the shampoo, miming washing my hair as if I didn't speak either. She held the door open for Dashiell, closing it behind him, and that was all I saw of either of them for quite a long time.

When she came out of the bathroom, wearing my terry

robe, all bunched up over the belt so that she wouldn't trip, I took a stool into the bathroom, put a dry towel around her shoulders and showed her the scissors and comb. As if we'd done this a thousand times, Madison pulled the towel tight and turned to face the full-length mirror on the inside of the bathroom door.

I combed her hair, then pointed to a length and waited. She seemed to be studying herself in the mirror, assessing my suggestion, the dark glasses still on. I could cut the back that way, but not the sides and not the bangs. So I began in the back, combing her silky blonde hair straight down and trimming across the end of the comb, the fine hair falling everywhere.

When I moved her around to face me, I just waited, scissors and comb poised. Madison slipped off her glasses, looking up at me for a moment and then closing her eyes. The droopy lid was still droopy, long after the effects of the Botox were supposed to wear off. But the other eyelid wasn't twitching. Still, sitting and waiting for me to finish her haircut, she looked so vulnerable it made me want to cry.

I trimmed the bangs and then ran my fingers through her hair, checking by feel to make sure everything was even and straight. Then I picked up the glasses from her lap and slipped them back on her.

"What do you think," I asked, "nails next?"

I still had some blue-black polish from when I went undercover as a transvestite hooker. Don't ask. We took turns doing each other's fingers and toes. Then we sat on the living room rug and played jacks, Dashiell retrieving the ball when either of us missed it.

"I thought we might go shopping tomorrow," I told her at bedtime, Dashiell running ahead of us up the stairs. I picked up her backpack from where she'd left it in the bathroom and handed it to her. The purse with Emil/Emily in it was in her other hand. "I'll be in here," I said when we passed the office, the door closed, "and you get to sleep in my bed."

But instead of passing by the office, she pushed the door open. There in front of us was my desk, and over it the bulletin board with all my notes about the case, notes only I was supposed to read. I'd planned to turn them all around after she'd gone to bed so that if she came to wake me in the morning, she'd only see their backs, blank cards and empty scraps of paper.

She stood still, her head moving slightly as she read. Then she turned and looked at me.

"Your father told you what I was doing," I said. "This is how I work," my voice as even as if I were still showing her how to prepare homemade food for a dog rather than talking about the search for her missing mother. "Every time I learn something new, no matter how trivial, I make a note and tack it up. Sometimes a pattern emerges. Or more questions. But even the smallest detail can turn out to be the thing that leads me to the path I need to be taking, to the solution. Most of what I learn will turn out to be useless. But I keep trying. I don't give up. Giving up is not part of the plan. It's not acceptable. Not for me. And not for him," pointing to Dashiell, who was standing next to her in the doorway.

Madison turned and looked up at me. I didn't need to hear the question.

"He's my partner," I said, letting that sit in the air between us for a moment. "He can do things I can't." Her face still turned toward mine, listening.

I pointed to my nose. "You know dogs can analyze odors in a way humans can't, right?" Was I expecting her to answer me? "Well, suppose I find Sally. How would I know her? I only have an old picture of her, from when she was a fifteen-year-old kid." I took a step into the office and picked up the yearbook and opened it to the page where the Post-it was, the page with Sally's picture on it. I thought Madison might react, take the book, make a sound, start to cry. But she didn't. She looked at the picture of her mother, then back at me. "But if I had something of hers with me, like the coat I found in the back of the closet on Saturday, Dashiell would know her scent, and he could tell me if the person I thought was Sally really was."

I closed the book and put it back on the desk.

"It's a long shot, finding her." I put my hands on Madison's shoulders. "But that's not a reason not to try, is it?"

For a moment, we stayed like that, Madison facing me, my hands on her skinny shoulders, feeling the small bones under her skin. Then she turned and continued down the hall to my room. She put the purse with Emil/Emily in it on top of my dresser, dropped her backpack on the floor and slid into bed.

I pulled up the covers and shut off the light. I wanted to kiss her, to sit on the bed and hug her, but I wasn't sure it was a good idea, and I didn't want to spoil what seemed like the beginning of trust. Then, in order to make sure she didn't get scared, I ended up doing it anyway.

"If you wake up and I'm not here, it means I'll be walking Dashiell around the block and that I'll be right back."

She still had her glasses on, but it didn't matter. There was no way to hide what was happening. The twitching began immediately, quickly followed by that jumping in her cheeks, both this time. Her mouth opened as if she was going to say something, but she didn't. Even in the dark, I could see that her lips were trembling.

Not the notes over my desk, not the discussion of how Dashiell might help identify Sally, not the photo of her mother at sixteen and pregnant. What terrified her was the thought of me going out to walk the dog and disappearing off the face of the earth, the way her mother had.

She sat up against the pillows. I sat on the bed. Dashiell jumped up and stood at the foot of the bed, then walked up and lay down across her feet.

"Would it make you feel better if you got dressed and came with me?"

There was no response, of course. Madison stayed where she was, under the covers, not making any attempt to get up, her face turned away from me.

I put my hand on her leg, near where Dashiell was lying. "Eventually, you're going to have to make up your mind to let a lot of this stuff go," I said.

She turned and looked at me.

"Terrible things happen to people, all kinds of things, and some people seem to get more of them than others. You, for instance. But the awful things that happened to you, they're not your fault. You do know that, don't you?"

That's when the first tear fell.

"So at some point," I whispered, leaning a little closer to her, "maybe not today, maybe not until you're fourteen, say, or even a grown-up, but at some point, you have to decide to live your life despite the bad stuff. You have to say to yourself, Madison Spector, it's your life and you have a choice in how you want to live it, in what you want it to be. You already know you can't control everything. But there are things you can control," reaching out to touch her hand. Then whispering, "Despite *everything,* you can have a life."

She was still looking at me, not moving.

"It's true," I said. "You can. You're strong and you're smart and you're beautiful. You're a fabulous kid. If you don't believe me . . ."

I turned and looked at Dashiell, as if he would chime in now, help me convince Madison that our higher opinion of her worth was the one she should embrace as well. She reached out and put her hand over my mouth, her fingers warm against my lips. Then she slid down under the covers, turning away from me. She'd had enough, and who could blame her?

Or was it something else? Was she thinking what had just occurred to me, that one of the bad things might indeed be her fault and what kind of a life she might have if she'd indeed killed Dr. Bechman?

I suddenly felt terrified for her. Was that how Leon felt, too? I wanted to grab her and pull her close and make her listen to me. I wanted to tell her that if she didn't kill Bechman, she better speak up fast, she better talk and keep talking until she was believed. But if she did it, if she did stab him in the heart with the Botox injection, she better not talk to anyone, not now and not for a very long time. Instead, I sat there quietly for another minute or so before getting up, Dashiell jumping off the bed and following me. I closed the door most of the way, leaving the light on in the hall, the way her mother might have done. Then I went into my office and turned on the computer.

Luckily I hadn't printed any of the letters I'd written or received via Classmates.com. I wouldn't have wanted Madison to see letters I'd written pretending to be her mother, signing her mother's name. What she'd seen was more than enough, too much for a young girl to have to deal with.

I checked my mail to see if Jim had written back. "Your not Sally," he'd written after my first post. "Who are you?"

"You're right," I'd written back, "I'm not Sally. Sally went missing five years ago when her little girl was seven. Now her daughter is in trouble and needs her mother. I've been hired to try to find her but the trail's ice cold—in fact, there is no trail. I was hoping to find someone who knew her before and might be able to tell me something about her, anything at all, that might give me a clue where she might have gone. I would be most grateful if you'd talk to me." I'd given him my name and both phone numbers, landline and cell, but hadn't heard back. Nor was there anything now.

How interested could anyone be after all these years? Curious, maybe, but beyond that? After all, Sally had abandoned all her friends. According to Leon, they'd gone to Delaware and moved to Manhattan, without a word to anyone.

There were two new letters to Sally, both from girls. I wrote back, but it was difficult to feel hopeful.

I decided to let Dashiell out in the garden instead of walking him. When he ran to the gate, I called him back, sitting on the cold steps and waiting while he made his rounds, and left some notes that only he would get to read.

Back inside, I opened the door to my bedroom enough that I could see Madison. Her glasses were on the nightstand and she'd turned onto her back, the covers pushed partway down, one leg sticking out on the side. Her face was smooth and calm in sleep. And with her eyes closed, you couldn't tell that one lid drooped when they were open. She looked like a normal little girl, peacefully asleep.

Lying in the bed in my office, Dashiell squeezed under the covers at the foot of the bed, I couldn't sleep for wondering what would happen to Madison. I didn't hear her at first, bare feet on the wooden floor, but the old boards in the hallway squeaked and then the door to the office opened, and she was silhouetted in the doorway, her dark glasses back on.

I figured she was looking for Dashiell, so I held up the covers to show her where he was, to let her wake him and spirit him away, but she misunderstood my gesture, taking it as an invitation. She slipped into bed beside me, her cold feet touching me for a second and then coming to rest against Dashiell's warm back. Then she rolled toward me, as if by accident, until she was leaning on me as well. I could smell the sweet almond scent of my shampoo in her hair. I let the cover drop, my arm with it so that both covered her. I felt her arm move as she reached for her glasses, slipping them off and letting them drop to the floor. And lying like that, nestled together, we fell asleep.

CHAPTER 17

I woke up alone, to the smell of bacon. Or rather the smell of burnt bacon. When I got downstairs, there were two cans of Coke on the table, and Madison was making peanut butter and bacon sandwiches. There was an empty pan on the kitchen floor so I knew that Dashiell had been fed. And Emil/Emily was in the swimming bowl, which sat between the cans of Coke like a centerpiece, a rock in the bowl, meaning Madison and Dashiell had been out in the garden. She might have even walked him had she known where the key to the wrought iron gate was kept, but luckily she didn't. Had I awakened to find that Madison and Dashiell were gone, I would have been at least as scared as she'd have been were it the other way around.

"Hey," I said, sitting down on the chair nearer to the stairs. "This looks great."

I took a sip of the Coke and a bite of the sandwich. Trust was a two-way street, wasn't it? Besides, it wasn't nearly as awful as it looked.

Emil/Emily swam while we ate, then got up on the flat stone and peered at us, first Madison and then me. I noticed the red kiss marks on his or her cheeks, the stripes all leading toward the small, dark, inscrutable eyes and the bulldog mouth. I wondered how long these little turtles lived and whether Leon had ever found the thing dead when Madison was in school, and replaced it before she'd gotten home. To me anyway, one small green turtle looked pretty much like another, but I guess some people thought that about cocker spaniels and Border collies, too.

Not me. I wasn't sure I'd know Sally, having only seen a picture of her that was eleven years old, but I thought I'd know Roy.

"Here's my plan," I said across Emil/Emily's bowl. "The Guggenheim Museum, shopping at Bloomingdale's, lunch on the fly, and then I'll take you back home. Sound okay?"

No response.

How did Leon do this? Or didn't he?

Madison was already dressed. I took a quick shower and got dressed while she cleaned up after breakfast. I called Leon to let him know we'd survived the night and gave him a time when Madison would be home, and then decided to change the day's itinerary. I thought at first that Madison would take Emil/Emily along. She seemed to take the turtle everywhere. But the way things were going, I thought Dashiell should go as well. If Madison and I were getting along, it was because of him. He was the bridge between us. More than that, he was a reminder to me that you could understand someone else without benefit of words, though, more than ever, words were what I was still hoping for from Madison, words that would help me find her mother, words that would tell me she hadn't killed Dr. Bechman.

The Guggenheim wouldn't let Dashiell in, but Bloomingdale's would. I told Madison about the change, and she went right for Dashiell's leash, leaving the turtle on the rock in the bowl on the marble table.

Not taking Emil/Emily with us meant we'd have to come back to the cottage before Madison went home. I thought that might be why the turtle was not going to take what might have been his/her first cab ride, so that we could come back here. I didn't know how far this would go, but I was pleased. I was clearly doing better than I had my first time alone with Madison.

Getting a cab with Dashiell along wouldn't be too difficult in the Village, where there were more cabs than customers, but coming home would be another story. In midtown, the competition for taxis was fierce, something I figured we'd deal with when the time came. Madison's plan was to hold the leash, that was pretty clear even without words. It was okay with me as long as Dashiell stayed right at her side when we were in the store. Since Madison wasn't talking to him either, I showed her the hand signal that would get him to heel, and we managed to get to the kids' department without tripping any of the other shoppers.

I thought that Dashiell's presence probably helped Madison over her initial embarrassment, and by the time we were finished, she still had the leash and I had a huge shopping bag with bras, a short cotton nightgown, new jeans and a pair of pale green high-top sneakers that were so cool I would have liked a pair for myself.

We stopped on the main floor for some barrettes and found one in the shape of a turtle. I bought the barrette, but when we found a green plastic turtle pin with rhinestone eyes, Madison paid for it with the ten-dollar bill that had been in the pocket of Sally's old jean jacket.

From Bloomingdale's, we walked all the way to Central Park, Madison and Dashiell ahead, me carrying the shopping bag and following along behind. We bought hot dogs and sodas from a street vendor and sat on a bench eating them in companionable silence. I didn't at all mind not having a conversation while we ate. The leaves were turning red and gold and orange. Dashiell was sitting in front of Madison, hoping, I figured, that she'd break off a piece of her hot dog and give it to him. And it was nice just to sit there. But I had a job to do and I was still hoping that somehow Madison would be able to help.

More than that, there were things she needed to do to help herself. Even if she outgrew the tics, she'd never be part of the world again without talking. I turned to watch her chewing her hot dog, her open soda on the bench between us, in that gulf she usually left between herself and anyone else, except for last night. I picked the soda up and put it on my other side, sliding closer to her.

"I have a proposition for you," I said. Even without feedback one way or another, I wasn't worried about the vocabulary I used since I'd seen that Madison was reading adult books. "If you've got anything to say," I said, talking in a whisper even though no one else was close by, waiting while she turned to look at me, to pay attention to the odd thing I had started to say to her, "you know, to help me with the case or just something you want to say, you can do that. I won't expect it means you'll be talking all the time, or even ever again. And I won't tell a soul. That's a promise."

Madison screwed up her face, but her left eye wasn't twitching and her cheeks were remarkably smooth and without movement.

"You can decide case by case, mood by mood, this is worth saying, this isn't, this is worth answering, this isn't. You follow? So you can talk to me today, for example, but not tomorrow, not ever again if that's what you want. Talking today would not oblige you to talk again tomorrow. It would be entirely up to you and totally between us."

I broke what was left of my hot dog in half, gave one piece to Dashiell and put the rest in my mouth.

"Don't say anything now," I said, my mouth still full of food, "just think about it."

She was looking at me as if I were out of my mind.

"I mean, I wouldn't want you to make a rash decision or anything. These things take consideration and time."

I was looking toward Fifth Avenue now, a playground between us and the street. We'd walked farther away from home, and it was getting late. I took a last swig of my soda and stood up.

"Ready?" I asked, expecting nothing. That was what I'd promised her, wasn't it, that I'd expect nothing?

I picked up the shopping bag, and Madison took the leash. We dropped our garbage in the nearest can and headed for the exit. Standing at the curb with my arm up for a cab, my cell phone rang. I figured it was probably Leon, getting nervous about where we were, though we still had over an hour before we were expected. But it wasn't Leon.

The caller ID showed an unfamiliar area code 718 phone number, meaning the call was coming from outside Manhattan. I wondered what someone was trying to sell this time and how the hell they got my cell phone number. I must have barked "Hello" because for a moment, no one said anything. I was ready to hang up when he finally spoke.

"Rachel?" Whispering. Not a telemarketer. A potential client? Because he sounded scared. No, worse than scared, desperate.

"This is she." Then waiting for him to tell me who he was, to see where this was going.

"I need to speak to you," he said, his voice so low I could barely hear him over the sound of the traffic.

"Who is this?" I asked.

Madison looked in my direction.

"Where are you?" he asked. Not answering my question, leaving it to me to figure out who was calling, who needed to talk to me so badly that he couldn't take the time to tell me who he was. "Your e-mail didn't say where you live."

A cab pulled toward the curb, saw Dashiell and pulled away.

"Jim?"

"Yes."

"New York City," I said, Madison still watching me.

"Can you get to Coney Island?"

"I can."

"There's a coffee shop on Mermaid Avenue and West Twenty-eighth Street, Dean's. I get off work at six-thirty. I can be there a quarter to seven."

With Madison right next to me, still paying attention, I couldn't ask the one question I wanted to.

"I'll be there," I said. "How will I know you?"

"Good," he said. "Thanks." And the line went dead.

CHAPTER 18

It took ten more minutes to get a cab, then another twenty to get down to the Village. Madison stared out the window on the left side of the cab, Dashiell leaning his chin on her shoulder. I looked out the right, thinking of the e-mail exchange I'd had with Jim, barely registering any of the passing scene.

By the time we got to the cottage, we only had time to pick up Emil/Emily and Madison's backpack if we were going to get her home on time. Madison ran up the stairs before I had a chance to do so myself. I stayed in the living room, waiting, thinking about the strange phone call from Jim, whatever he had to say it was so urgent he had to say it tonight and in person.

When Madison came bounding down the stairs, Dashiell right behind her, I picked up the shopping bag and handed her the plastic purse. But instead of taking it, she picked up the leash and clipped it onto Dashiell's collar.

Walking her home, she and Dashiell ahead of me, the way her head was moving, the way he kept turning his face to look at her, I'd swear she was talking to him, but I wasn't close enough to hear.

Leon was waiting out front. Madison handed me the

leash and took the shopping bag and the turtle, barely seeming to notice her father as she passed him and headed into the lobby. I guess she did have a key.

"How did it go?"

"Fine, really fine."

"What do I owe you for . . ."

I waved a hand at him. "I just bought her a few things, it's no big deal."

"What about the haircut?"

"I did it myself. She looks great, doesn't she?"

Leon nodded. He even smiled.

"I hope you don't mind about the nail polish," I said.

He turned toward the lobby, but Madison was inside already. When he turned back to me, he looked puzzled.

I showed him my nails. "I did hers. She did mine," I said, my mind elsewhere, Jim's whispered words ringing in my ears.

"What next?" he asked.

"I'll call you," I told him.

When I got to the corner, Leon was still standing out front. I walked home quickly, keeping Dashiell close at my side, leaving the door open to let some cool air into the house, to let Dashiell choose where he wanted to be. For a moment, the house seemed empty without Madison sprawled on the rug communing with Dashiell, without Emil/Emily swimming in his/her makeshift pond on the green marble table.

I dropped my jacket on the arm of the couch and headed up to the office. I wanted to look at those letters again, see if there was anything I'd forgotten, something telling that I'd missed in his letter or mine, but when I leaned over the desk to turn on the computer, something caught my eye. There was a small photograph sitting on the keyboard of my laptop, beaten up from having been handled so much, one of

the corners broken off, that edge rough and uneven. I picked
it up, turned on the lamp, holding it in the light, a pretty
young woman addressing the camera without a smile. She
had the same straight blonde hair as her daughter did, some
of which was still clinging to my terry robe and spread out
like tiny pickup sticks on the blue tile floor of the bathroom.
Her eyes, like her daughter's eyes, were blue, her skin pale
and clear, and her expression, too, was like her daughter's.
Or was it the other way around? Wasn't it the daughter who,
in her grief, had modeled herself after her missing mother,
her face neutral, almost serene, no hint of her inner life, her
feelings invisible? Except that hadn't worked for Madison.
Circumstances had pushed her over the top, out of control.

Out of control. That's what Leon had said that first day at
the dog run, that Madison was sometimes out of control. I
thought of Dr. Bechman's monochromatic office, pictured
him lying on the rug, his arms and legs askew, the needle
next to him. Had she been out of control that day?

And what of her mother? Perhaps Sally was better able to
hide her inner chaos, at least until five years ago.

I held the picture of Sally under the light for a long time.
Then I tacked it carefully onto the bulletin board, letting the
heads of the pins brace the edges of the photo so that when
I returned it to its owner it would have no holes in it. Sally
at twenty-two or twenty-three, I thought. Sally more the way
she might look today, enough so that if I found her, I'd know
who she was.

CHAPTER 19

I sat in a booth at the far end of Dean's Coffee Shop, facing the door. He would be around Sally's age if he knew her in high school, twenty-eight or twenty-nine, maybe thirty. He said he'd be coming from work, but he didn't say what he did, so I had no idea what he'd be wearing. Would I know him? Would he know me? Not a problem so far, I thought. There were three people eating at the counter, a Hispanic couple, a tall thin black man wearing a UPS jacket, all three decades too old to have gone to high school with Sally Bruce. There were two black girls in a booth near the door. They were probably Madison's age, drinking colas, poking each other and giggling. There was a young mother and a baby in the booth behind them, the mother looking too young to be a mother, just as Sally had been.

The man who'd waited on me could have been seventy or older, his skin pleated and sallow, his eyes faded. I'd ordered a ginger ale, not wanting to commit to anything more elaborate, not wanting to stay if Jim didn't show. It was five to seven and he wasn't here yet.

I looked out the window at the street. I was only a few blocks from my aunt Ceil's house in Sea Gate, but that neighborhood was a world away from this one with its proj-

ects, clusters of tall brick buildings that had replaced the
two- or four-story tenements that lined the blocks adjacent
to the ocean when I was a kid. There were rides on one end
of the island, what people thought of when they thought of
Coney Island, the Cyclone, Nathan's hot dogs, places where
you could buy a hot knish, other ethnic food now as well,
tacos, pizza, Thai or Chinese takeout. Walking here from the
subway, I'd smelled the food, but I'd also smelled the ocean,
just a block away.

Seven o'clock. Still no Jim. I took a sip of ginger ale,
checked my watch again, and then there he was. We might
have been in Grand Central Station, I'd still have known
him. It wasn't the dark hair, curls covering the top of his
shirt collar, some falling over his brow when he took off his
baseball cap. It wasn't his height, so tall that his shoulders
were rounded, as if he were trying to make himself seem
shorter. It wasn't his complexion either, because even
though he'd clearly attempted to clean up, there was so
much dirt on his face I couldn't see if he was fair or dark. It
wasn't even the pain on his face that made me know he had
to be the man who'd made the call. It was something else,
something that even before he got to the table, changed
everything I thought I knew, tilting the world so that for a
moment my stomach swirled so badly that I felt prophetic
for having ordered that ginger ale.

As he got closer, knowing me, too, I saw that what covered his face wasn't dirt. It was grease covering his skin and
his hands. He wiped one against his jeans and extended it
toward me, grease in the creases on his knuckles, grease
under his nails. A mechanic. When he slipped off his jacket,
his name was over the pocket of his dark blue shirt, dark
blue like the blue of his eyes, confusion in those eyes now,
not knowing how to do this. Jim, it said over his pocket, part
of the *m* missing.

He tossed the jacket onto the bench opposite me and slid into the seat, his hands flat on the table, looking around for Henry, his name over his pocket as well, ordering a Coke, no ice. I noted the wedding band on his left hand, scratched and worn looking. He apparently didn't take it off when he was working.

"Do you want anything else?" he asked. "The burgers are pretty good here. The BLT's not bad."

"Sure," I said. "Whatever you're having." Buying time more than feeling hungry.

He got up, leaned over the counter and spoke to the woman there, a net covering her bright red hair, her pink uniform stretched tight around her ample bosom, the buttons barely able to hold the stiff material closed. Then he was back, bringing the Coke with him, sitting across from me, hands around his glass, eyes down, having trouble getting started.

"When was the last time you saw her?" I asked.

"Sally?" As if I might mean someone else. He took one hand off the glass, lifted it, turned it over, then touched his forehead with two fingers. "High school, senior year."

"You were good friends?"

"Yeah, I guess you could say that." Then, "No, not exactly good friends." He picked up his glass, moved it off to the side. "I thought we were. Then I thought we weren't. Now," lifting his hands, "now I don't know what to think." He took the glass again, taking a long drink this time.

"Because?"

"She disappeared twice, you know."

I nodded. I did. "Five years ago, that would be the second time."

This time he nodded. "She took off back in high school, too. Same thing. She just disappeared. I tried like hell to find her, but there was no way, no way."

After that, he stopped talking. He checked the time, he tapped the table with his fingers, he bit his lower lip. "Maybe it was my fault. Who knows?" he said.

"What was your fault?"

"Her going away like that. The first time."

"How so?"

He looked away, then got up and went to the counter again. I saw the woman with the red hair nodding, no expression on her face, you want this, fine, you want that, fine, why would she give a rap, standing on her feet all day for coolie wages?

When he came back to the table, he picked up his glass, but he just moved it out of the way so that he could lean forward, elbows on the table, his face so close to mine I could feel his breath.

"I thought I could do this," whispering, "but I can't. I just can't."

"You're not telling me you asked me to come all the way to the ass end of Brooklyn and now you have nothing to say, are you? You're not—"

"No, no, that's not what I meant. I'm sorry. I meant I can't talk *here*. I asked for the sandwiches to go," he said, drumming his fingers on the table, looking at everything but me.

"Where do you want to go?" Wondering if he had a car outside, if he lived nearby, wondering how I should feel about either prospect.

"The beach. Won't be anyone there. Do you mind?"

I shook my head. With nothing but sand and ocean, not another human being around, maybe Jim would find himself able to talk. Why not, no one but a stranger willing to listen, the inky water, the dark sky?

Henry brought the sandwiches, grease already leaking out of the waxy paper they were wrapped in and onto the bag. Jim paid. Without talking we headed for the beach, walking under the boardwalk where you could barely see your hand in front of your face, nothing visible except the moonlit sand up ahead. We walked partway down the beach, far enough so that the sound of the ocean was loud enough to make my skin vibrate. Jim took off his jacket and spread it out for me to sit on, but I shook my head, sitting on the cold sand, slipping off my shoes and socks and burying my feet the way I did when I was a kid.

"One day she was there, the next day she was gone," he said, the grease-stained bag sitting on the sand in front of us, neither of us touching it. He shook his head. "No one knew where she went—or if they did, they wouldn't say. It's not that I didn't ask."

He looked at me, his eyes wet, as if to say it was my turn now, my job to tell him what I knew, where Sally had gone back then.

"You were lovers," I said, a statement, not a question.

He looked at me, a crease between his eyes, then back down at the sand, tracing a line with one finger. "Yeah, we were."

"How did it start?"

His hands lay flat on the sand now, his face turned away from me.

"I know she meant something to you, Jim. I think she meant a lot to you. Whatever it is you're feeling now, that's not what's important. Whatever happened back then, it doesn't really matter much anymore. What matters is this little girl, Sally's little girl. What matters is finding Sally, if that's even possible."

He turned to look at me. "What do you mean?"

"I mean we have no way of knowing if she's alive or dead."

"But—"

"I need you to tell me what led up to Sally going missing back then. I need you to tell me everything you can, because something you tell me, some little thing, might be the very thing I need to point me in the right direction." I touched his arm. "Will you do this for me?" I waited. "You did call me, Jim. You did ask me to come here. I know you want to talk about it. And I want nothing more than to listen. I didn't come here to judge you or Sally. I came here to find help."

"What good will it do now, to tell you about her, about us, back in high school? It was a million years ago. It can't have anything to do with what she did five years ago. It couldn't possibly help."

"Do you have kids, Jim?"

He looked surprised. "Yeah, I do."

"How many?"

"Three."

I nodded. "How old are they?"

"The boy is ten. The girls are six and four."

"This isn't about us, about my job or your feelings. It's about a little girl who's twelve, though frankly, when I first met her, I thought she was only nine or ten. She's small, like Sally. She looks just like her."

"She does?"

I nodded.

He looked away, toward the water. "I might've fallen in love with her the first time I saw her," he said. "There were all the girls in high school, and there was Sally."

"She was that beautiful?"

"She was. And all these years, I never once, I could never figure out what she saw in me. But she said she loved me, too. I used to run to meet her after one class, just to walk her to the next. Or we'd go to the library together. Never my house. Never hers. My father, he had a bit of a problem, well, an elephant of a problem with booze. You'd never know what you were going to find if you went to my house. And Sally's mother was a little crazy, I think. She sat in church half the day, every day. She scared the shit out of Sally not only about boys, but about everything. So we never went there. We never had much time at all. If Sally got home more than ten, fifteen minutes late, she'd have hell to pay. But then the senior class trip was coming up, to Lauderdale. We'd have time together. It seemed, it seemed like . . ."

"Sally's mother let her go?"

"She did. We couldn't believe it, but she did. She had this big thing about shame. Sally told her all the kids were going, she'd be the only one if she didn't, and there were three chaperones, she said, teachers. They'd be watching every minute. Her mother said she'd have to pay for half of it, out of her babysitting money, and Sally agreed, she said she would and her mother signed."

"So you both went? And what happened?"

"The teachers, the chaperones, they didn't much care what we did. They were doing their own thing. Anyway, we were seniors, a lot of us eighteen already, and in a few months we'd be out of the school and out of their lives. They just didn't pay a lot of attention."

"And?"

"We left, me and Sally. We just wanted to be alone. That's all we ever wanted, just to be together with no one else there. I'd been working weekends and sometimes after school, and she'd been babysitting. We had a little money with us. We took a bus and went down to the Keys and we found this motel along this strip of land, across the road from the water just south of Long Key, and we stayed there two days, two nights, just the two of us. It was a dumpy little place, just these little wooden cabins, no restaurant, no pool, not much of anything. But it was the most wonderful . . ."

Jim took off his work boots and stuffed his socks into his

shoes. He stood and offered a hand to help me up. I followed him to the hard, wet sand, and we stood there letting the foamy, ice-cold water rush around our bare feet, neither of us saying anything.

"And then what happened when you got back?"

"At first, it was just like it had been before. I'd walk her to her classes. We'd meet in study hall or the cafeteria. I'd wait for her after school and walk her partway home." He looked at me. "Not close enough for her mother to see us if she was looking out the window." He turned his face back toward the ocean. "Sometimes we came here, when the beach was empty. But it wasn't the same, not like it was down there."

"And then what happened?"

"She came and told me she was pregnant."

"And what did you say when she told you?"

"I was scared, more scared than I'd ever been in my whole entire life. I was living with my parents. I didn't have a dime. I had no way to make a living, to support her and a kid. And she was fifteen and a half. I could have gone to jail for what I did. I just wanted it to be not true. I wanted . . ." A whistling sound came from deep in Jim's chest, the noise an animal might make after the hunter found his mark. I reached for his hand and he let me take it. "God help me, I wanted her to go away, to disappear."

"So you questioned the baby's paternity?"

"I did. I asked her whose it was."

"It was a long time ago," I said. "You were, what, seventeen, eighteen? Just a kid. You were terrified. You made a mistake."

"She was . . . you should have seen her face when I said that. As soon as I did, I knew I'd done the stupidest thing I'd ever done in all my life, but the words were out there, and a minute later the bell rang and she was gone."

"And you were still scared?"

"Terrified. But I waited for her outside of the school, where we'd always met. I figured, we'd have to work it out somehow. Only she didn't show. I didn't know it yet, but it was already too late. She wasn't in school after that. She was gone."

"That fast?"

He nodded.

"You called her at home?"

He nodded again. "I waited until that weekend, hoping every day she'd be in school, or come and meet me afterwards. Then I called her house, but her mother never said a word. She just hung up on me. I went by her house, too, rang the bell. Her mother said, 'She's not here. She doesn't live here anymore.' I didn't know what to do. I never told a soul, not until now, and I didn't . . ."

His shoulders started to shake and then I heard the sobs. I stepped closer, putting my arms around him, letting him cry, tears he'd been wanting to cry for twelve years and counting. When he stopped crying, I stood back. He wiped his face with his hands, looking down, where the water was swirling around our feet, our feet sinking slowly into the wet sand, the bottoms of our pants cold and wet, pressing heavily against our ankles.

"She must have been every bit as scared as I was."

"More," I said. "She was the one who was going to have the baby."

"I always figured she must have had an abortion. When she didn't come back, I pretty much wrote the whole thing off, wrote her off, until . . ."

"Until you read my second letter."

He nodded. "Where did she go? What happened?"

"The reason you couldn't find her is that she got married," I said, watching his face, watching him take it in.

"They moved to the city. She was using another name, his name, so—"

He turned to face me, grabbing my arms.

"*Married?* You mean I was right? You mean the kid's *not* mine?"

He let go of me. He was nodding now, not the kind of nodding that says he agreed with what I was saying, the kind that said he was nervous, angry, the kind that said if he were a volcano, it would be time to step back, get the hell out of the way.

"All this time, all these years, because she disappeared and I couldn't talk to her again, I figured I really fucked up. I really hurt her. And now it turns out I was right all along. There *was* someone else. Man, she had me fooled. Man, I could have been played for the worst sucker on the face—"

I started shaking my head. It took him a moment or two to notice.

"What?"

"Not so," I said.

"The guy she married, he's not—"

"He's not the genetic father, Jim. You are."

"How can you possibly know that? You don't even know Sally. You never even met her."

"But I have met your daughter." I reached out, not for his hand this time. I reached out and touched his face, the cheek that was twitching. It had been his eye earlier, when he'd walked into Dean's, the eye that told me he was the man who'd called, the eye that told me why.

He brushed my hand away. "It happens when I'm nervous. It was much worse when I was a kid. Now it's only once in a . . ." Getting it, understanding how I knew.

"She's got it, too?"

"She does."

For what seemed like a long time, we stood there, Jim

staring at me, me staring back, both of us rewriting history
as we knew it, trying to get it right this time.

Then I just nodded. And he did, too.

"The man Sally married? He knew the baby wasn't his?"

"I'm sure he did."

"I don't get it."

"I don't either."

"Who is he? Who did she marry?"

"Leon Spector."

"Who . . . ?" He looked away, then back at me, his face
contorted. "Mr. Spector, the history teacher?"

I nodded.

"Mr. Spector married her. I . . . And they weren't having
an affair. Why would he?"

"Maybe he saw the same thing you did, this beautiful
creature sitting in his classroom every day, the most beautiful thing he'd ever seen. And now she was in trouble, bad
trouble, and he could help." He could be a hero, I thought.
But things never work out the way you think they will.

"So they got married?"

"In Delaware. Parental permission isn't needed there for
pregnant teens."

Jim nodded, trying to absorb it all.

"And Mr. Spector's got her, my daughter?"

I nodded.

"And Sally's gone?"

"That's right."

"You said she was in trouble, the kid?"

"Come on," I said, pulling on his sleeve. "Let's sit down."

We walked back to where Jim had left his jacket. Sitting
there on the sand, I told him about Madison, about her decision to stop talking, about the death of Dr. Bechman,
about trying to find Sally in the hope that Madison would
speak again. I told it all to him, everything I knew. When

I'd finished, we sat there not talking for a while. I was thinking about what he told me, how Sally had come to him, scared, to say she was pregnant, how he'd panicked and rejected her, how she'd disappeared back then, too. Leon said she'd cut herself off from her friends, moved to another borough, changed her name. No one at Lincoln could have possibly guessed that she had married Leon, even though he'd disappeared, too. No one would have put that particular two and two together and come up with four. It was too weird to contemplate. And no one would have been able to find Sally either, no matter how hard they tried.

Jim picked up his jacket and put it on. We brushed the sand off our feet as best we could, putting on our shoes and socks. Then, still without talking, he picked up the bag with the sandwiches and carried it to the nearest trash can. I'd never asked what he'd ordered. No matter. Neither of us was hungry now.

When we came out from under the boardwalk, he asked me how I'd come.

"Subway," I told him.

"I should've gone to the city to meet you," he said. "I'll drive you home."

I didn't argue. I thought he needed to do something. I thought there'd be more questions, that he'd need some time to formulate them, time to know what it was he wanted to know. But he didn't talk in the car. He drove silently along the Belt Parkway, through the Brooklyn Battery Tunnel, up along West Street until we got to the Village. I told him where I lived. He turned on all the right one-way streets until we were in front of the gate to the cottage.

"What's her name?" he finally asked me.

"Madison."

Jim's mouth opened, but nothing came out. He turned away, and when he turned back, he was crying again, this time silently, like his daughter.

"Madison," he repeated.

I nodded.

"If you think of anything else . . ." He had my phone numbers, but I gave him my card anyway.

He opened the glove compartment and took out a small pad, writing something on it and handing it to me. "It's my work number."

"I understand."

"There're two Jims there, so you have to ask for Jim Russell."

"Okay," I told him.

"Do you think you'll find her?"

I shrugged.

"Will you call me if you do?"

"I will."

I opened the car door but I didn't get out. "Did you and Sally swim when you were down in the Keys?" I asked, visions of Madison's room swirling in my head. "By any chance, did you go snorkeling?"

"Yeah, we did. There was a place where you could rent snorkels, masks and fins just down the road from the motel."

I leaned over and put my arms around him, holding him tight. Part of it was gratitude, part was that there was something about him that broke my heart the way his daughter did.

CHAPTER 20

The street lamps were already on, the light smoky and diffused. I stood on the sidewalk in front of the gate to my cottage watching Jim drive away. Then I went inside and got Dashiell, going back out with him for his nighttime walk. Barely paying attention to what was around me, I pulled out my cell phone, called Delta Airlines and made reservations to fly down to Miami late the following night. I needed to get ready, but I didn't want to wait a moment longer than I'd have to. I wanted to take Madison's medical records with me. And a picture of her, too, a recent one. I'd have to make arrangements for Dashiell, too. I stopped to wait for a car to pass, glancing down at Dashiell. He was looking up at me with a goofy smile on his puss. If he couldn't be with me, I knew exactly where he'd be happiest. The question was, if I wanted Madison to trust me, how far was I willing to go to trust her? And as soon as I formed the question, I knew the answer. I took out my phone again and called Leon, asking if he and Madison would be willing to take Dashiell for a few days, starting the following evening.

"Sure," he said. No questions asked. Quintessential Leon.

I was prepared to tell him about the way Dash and Madison had gotten along when she stayed over. I was going to say that if they spent some time together, it might help her open up, if no one rushed her, if we just let nature take its course. But he probably knew that already. He'd had a dog of his own, one he took everywhere. Anyway, he'd already said yes, so I didn't need to keep selling, did I?

"I need a couple of other things, too," I said. The car had passed, but Dashiell and I were still on that corner.

"What's that?" he asked.

"I need you to call Ms. Peach and request a complete copy of Madison's records. Everything in the file."

"Okay."

"I'm pretty sure she'll ask you to put it in writing, Leon."

"I'll take care of it."

"I need it tomorrow. I'll need to get it from you when I come to drop off Dashiell. If she says she can't do it that fast, you're going to have to insist she does. Is that a problem?"

"What are you looking for?"

"I'm not sure," I said. "Sometimes you don't know what you're looking for until you find it."

The truth was, I wasn't looking for anything at all. I was hoping I'd be able to give the envelope to Sally, to let Madison's medical records do some of the talking for me. But I didn't want to say that to Leon, not now, not before I knew what I was going to find when I got to Florida.

"There's one more thing, Leon. I need your approval to spend some money. The reason I've asked you to take Dashiell is that I'm going to be out of town for a few days doing some research."

"On the case?"

"It's a really old lead," I told him. "Not much chance I'll find anything helpful, but I figured you'd want me to . . ."

There was a silence on the line. I heard the phone hit the desk, as if it had been dropped. I waited, but nothing happened. I couldn't hear Leon walking away. He might have been wearing sneakers. Or socks, kicking off his shoes the minute he walked in the door the way I always did. Or he might have been standing right there, afraid to hear what else I might have to say, afraid not to hear it, too.

"What have you found out?" he asked.

"I know it's asking a lot, Leon, but I'm asking you not to ask. I'm asking you to trust me on this. Please. Just let me do my job and tell you things when I'm ready, when it's right to do so."

There was another silence. Then, "You found her?"

"No," I said. I crossed the street, turned left, Dashiell staying close. The last thing on earth I wanted was to tell him what I'd learned tonight, not yet anyway, maybe not ever. "I didn't find her. But I'm still working on it."

"Then . . ."

"The records, the trip, it's all part of the research I need to do. I can't say yet if anything will pan out. If the money's a problem, I'll—"

"No. It's not about the money. Spend whatever you have to. And tell me when you can. I've waited this long," he said, "I guess I can . . ." I waited for the end of the sentence but it didn't come.

"Thanks, Leon. I know this isn't easy." I was heading back to the cottage, no one else along the street I'd taken. "I'll come by with Dashiell at around six, if that's okay," thinking I'd have to leave from there to get to the airport on time. "If you have any trouble getting Madison's records . . ."

"There won't be any trouble."

"Swell. So I'll see you then. I'll have Dash and all his stuff with me. If it's okay, I'd like to talk to Madison about taking care of Dash. She knows how to prepare his food and she seemed to like doing it," thinking he ate better than she did, than most kids do, living on Happy Meals, sodas and processed food.

"Sounds good. We'll be here. I'll tell Madison you're coming and that Dashiell will be staying over. She'll be pleased."

I was back at the cottage. I thanked Leon again and ended the call. Then I unlocked the gate, walking into the tunnel, locking the gate behind me.

It was late and it was cold out, but instead of going inside, I sat on the stone steps while Dashiell investigated a pile of dead leaves in the far corner of the garden. Madison's room had been painted as if it were underwater, the fish circling her bed and desk and dresser the brightly colored ones you'd see if you were snorkeling, red and yellow and blue, nothing like anywhere else. Despite the chill in the air, I sat there a long time thinking about Madison's room, about her mother's past, about what I was hoping I might find in Florida.

Even when I went inside, sleep was out of the question for a long time. I packed a small bag, tucking Madison's picture of her mother carefully into the zippered pocket. I took my new digital camera, small enough to fit into my jacket pocket. I packed a bathing suit, too. If I found the place I was looking for, perhaps that shop would still be there and I'd be able to rent a snorkel, goggles and fins, the way Sally and Jim had. Maybe whoever owned the shop would recognize Sally from her picture. Maybe he'd say, "Yeah, sure, I know her. She comes by from time to time, lives in the area, lives right down the road." Maybe.

I zipped the bag closed, then opened it up again and tucked in the copy of the picture Madison had drawn, the one found on Bechman's desk right after his body was discovered. If I found Sally, if things were going well, she might want to see that, too.

Still wide awake, I got Dashiell's food packed, leaving the bag in the refrigerator. Then I made a fire in the fireplace and sat on the floor with my dog, watching the flames, feeling calmer than I'd been since I first took on this case.

Later, way later, fish swam through my dreams. There were fish with spots like friendly dogs, fish with undershot jaws, fish that swam in schools, all facing the same direction one moment, just hanging in the water as if suspended by invisible wires, then miraculously, the turn unseen, all looking another way. There were rocks in my dreams, too, coral, grasses waving gracefully one way and then another as the current moved them, huge turtles with powerful claws, creatures I couldn't name, not all of them real. The water seemed to be made of light. No matter how deep I went, I could see everything around me, everything, at last, was clear.

CHAPTER 21

There were pretty flowers for sale outside one of the ubiquitous Korean delis, one on every third corner. My mother always told me not to visit anyone empty-handed, and though I'd spent my life ignoring all the things she'd tried to teach me, I could see the wisdom of this particular piece of advice at this particular time. I bought a bunch of red roses, watched as they were rolled into the pretty wrapping paper, cone-shaped, a large opening at the top, a small one at the bottom. I asked for a little card, wrote Madison's name on the envelope and then stood there, unable to think of what to write. Despite the fact that after waking up late, I'd walked Dashiell all the way down to the tip of Manhattan and back, then spent an hour swimming laps at the Y, I couldn't clear my head enough to think about anything but my conversation with Jim, with Madison's father. The little man in the blue apron was waiting. Finally I just slipped the card into my pocket, paid for the roses and thanked him.

But a few blocks later, when I was almost at Madison's house, I thought of exactly what I wanted to say. I took out the card, wrote on it, tucked it back in the envelope and slipped that between the paper and the roses where it would fall out when Madison was ready to put the flowers in water.

Walking up the stairs after getting buzzed in, I unclipped the leash, turned the bouquet sideways and gave it to Dashiell to carry. Madison met us at the door, dropping to her knees, taking the bouquet, putting it down on the floor and throwing her arms around Dashiell's neck, pressing her face against his fur.

"So did your dad tell you? Dashiell's going to spend a couple of days here." Experience taught me not to wait for a response. "His food is in the shopping bag." I put it on the dining room table. I put my overnight bag next to it, just a big tote with a zipper on top, a couple of zippered compartments inside. I wouldn't need that much in Florida, a couple of T-shirts, a pair of shorts, a bathing suit and a pair of sandals. I was glad I didn't have to take Sally's old winter coat with me or fly with Dashiell, putting him in the hold.

"You can make the food all at once if you want to, the way we did at my house, then keep the rest in the refrigerator. He eats twice a day," I said, "but he's not fussy about the time." She pushed the pair of oversize old-fashioned-looking sunglasses higher on her nose, the white frames heart-shaped, a different pair for every mood, I guessed. "He goes out three times a day, as long and as far as you and your dad are willing to go. And at night, let's see . . ." I walked past her, down the hall, into her room. I heard Dashiell first, his nails ticking on the wooden floor, Madison, I was sure, her white socks drooping around her ankles, coming silently behind him. I figured Leon would stay where he was, maybe put the flowers in water, hoping that I could have a little time alone with Madison. But when I turned around, Madison was holding the flowers, standing in her doorway, watching me.

"I guess maybe he could sleep right here," I said, touching the bed, Dashiell sailing up there without further invitation.

"Coffee?" Leon called from the kitchen.

"No, thanks. I don't have time." Checking my watch, thinking about the traffic on the way to the airport, the road looking like a crowded parking lot unless you were on it at three in the morning.

I pulled Madison in and closed her door.

"Read the note," I said.

Madison carefully turned the bouquet around, looking for a little envelope stapled onto the wrapping paper, and then she turned it upside down and gave it one quick shake. The envelope with her name on it fluttered down to the floor. She bent and picked it up, putting the flowers under one arm as she opened it and pulled out the card. There was a picture of some flowers in one corner, white daisies with yellow centers, three of them. What I'd written was beneath that. She read what was on the card, then looked up at me.

"That's my cell phone number," I told her. "In case you have any questions, or think of something you want to tell me. You can call me anytime, day or night. I'll keep it on." Serious now. Madison, too. She wasn't talking, but she wasn't shutting down either. "Or if you don't feel like talking but for some reason you want to call anyway, that would be okay, too. I'll know it's you. I'll keep the line open until you hang up," I said. "Sometimes it's nice to know someone else is there, you know what I mean?" I smiled, but she didn't smile back.

She was holding the flowers in the crook of one arm, looking up at me. For a moment, we stayed like that, neither of us moving, the air between us sweet and rich with the smell of roses.

"Thank you for the loan of the picture," I whispered.

I reached out and put my hand on top of her head and let it stay there a second. "And thanks for this, for taking care of Dashiell for me." I walked over to the bed and put my hand on Dashiell's head. "You stay here and take good care of Madison," I told him, walking out and closing the door behind me.

Leon was waiting near the dining room table. There was so much I wished I could tell him, not about where I was going and what I was hoping to find there, but about Madison, about what we'd done and how it had worked out. I wanted to tell him that she needed some responsibilities so that she could feel essential, that she needed more time with him, quiet time, giggling time, all kinds of time. I wanted to tell him how she'd come into my office in the dark, how she'd crawled into bed with me, how hungry she was for a little affection. But I kept my mouth shut because it wasn't my place to tell him how to raise his kid. I was the detective; he was the parent. And because even if I did, who says I was right? And if I was, who says he could do it anyway? Who says he wasn't doing the best he could, like everyone else? Besides, I had a plane to catch.

I was standing near the dining room table, looking at the pictures of Madison. "Do you have anything recent?" I asked him.

"You want to see some?"

I nodded.

He pulled open the top drawer of one of the file cabinets and pulled out a thick folder, one of those hanging ones with pleats on the bottom. I began to look through the photos, picking out two five-by-seven pictures of her, walking over to his desk and looking at them under the light.

"May I borrow these?" I asked.

"Sure."

"Did you get the medical report?"

He turned and picked up the envelope from his desk.

"Any trouble?"

"None at all."

I unzipped my bag and slid the photos into the book I'd taken to read on the plane, putting the copy of Madison's medical records next to it. Then I turned around to yell something back to Madison, but there she was, Dashiell standing next to her, his tail wagging. She walked over to my bag and looked inside, reaching in and pulling out my bathing suit. Then she folded it carefully and put it back, slipping off her heart-shaped sunglasses and putting them into my bag, too, zipping it closed for me.

I nodded. "Thanks," I said. "They'll come in handy."

I picked up the bag, hoisted it onto one shoulder and headed for the door. Then I turned around one last time. Madison had her hand in Dashiell's collar, letting him know he was supposed to stay.

"Don't forget," I said, "if you have pizza, you have to let his slices cool before you give them to him."

Halfway down the stairs, though it was already dark out, I opened the bag and put on Madison's sunglasses. Then I walked quickly out to the street, stood at the curb, lifted my arm and, when a cab stopped, told him which airport I needed.

CHAPTER 22

By the time I got to Long Key, the sun was coming up, the Bay of Florida an emerald green, the ocean aqua. I reached into the tote bag, which was on the passenger seat of the rental car, a silver Mini, and pulled out Madison's sunglasses, the world way too bright without them. The right side of the road was lined with motels and restaurants, but as I kept driving, there was very little again, an occasional motel, small attached cabins in bright colors, a car parked in front of each one, a pool surrounded by a chain-link fence in the middle, then down the road, a convenience store, a bait shop, a gas station, lots of nothing in between.

I hadn't slept at all and decided to stop at the next motel, get some sleep, begin my search for a needle in a haystack when I woke up. The excitement of what Jim had told me had ebbed as I peered out of the plane window into the black night. Anxiety had taken its place. Why would Sally return to the place where she'd gotten pregnant, when her lover had rejected her, when she had rejected the child of that union? What made sense on the beach in Coney Island and then sitting in Jim's car in front of my cottage no longer did. But what in this case wasn't held together by the slimmest thread? I'd get some sleep and see what I could find out when I woke up.

About two miles past Long Key, I saw a vacancy sign, two rows of attached cabins badly in need of paint, a small, sad-looking swimming pool in the space between them, the ocean just steps across U.S. Highway One. Though I hadn't seen another car since I left Long Key, and only two there, both delivery trucks, I signaled, then turned in and parked the car outside the small office. The woman behind the counter, a cigarette dangling from her lipsticked mouth, had waitress eyes—been there, heard that, couldn't give a damn if she tried. She slid a small card across the counter toward me, a ballpoint pen with someone's tooth marks on the cap, and swiveled her chair so that she could pull a key off one of the hooks on the Peg-Board behind her back, twenty hooks, one for each of the beat-up-looking cabins.

"Ten," she said. "It's away from the road. Looks like you could use some sleep. Some sun, too," she added. "You're a northerner, right?"

I nodded.

"One night?" she asked. Not a place where people stayed longer.

"Two," I told her. There was a little plaque on the desk that said P. DeMille, Manager.

"You only have to pay for one now," she said. "Anyways, you might change your mind."

I handed her my credit card, watched her swipe it in the machine, wait for it to print the receipt.

"Is there a place nearby where I can get some flippers and a mask?" I asked her.

"Back to Long Key," she said. "Or just up the road a piece. You can walk it. Hank's. When he's there."

"He doesn't keep regular hours?"

She snorted some air through her small, wide nose. "Yeah, he does. But not at the shop."

I waited. Ms. DeMille picked up a crossword puzzle, a pencil, went back to what she'd been doing when I came.

I drove the car to cabin 10, parked in front, shut off the engine, picked up my tote bag and stepped up onto the communal porch, just a narrow deck with two wooden chairs out front. There were only two other cars parked in front of cabins, neither of them near mine.

The key had a long tag hanging from it with the name of the motel, Polly's Motor Park. I looked around behind me, the sun shining on the sad little cabins and on the water of the small pool. Not the place where Jim and Sally had stayed. No pool, he'd said.

Except for the triangular piece missing from the bottom right-hand corner of one of the shades, they pretty much kept the sun out. But since I'd been up all night, it really didn't matter. By the time I slipped under the scratchy sheet, I could have slept with klieg lights shining on me.

I dreamed about fish again, the fish on Madison's walls this time, the ones Sally had painted. They were moving in the dream, and the result was like what you see from a carousel, everything but the horses and riders a blur of colors. I felt dizzy in the dream, dizzy for a while when I woke up. I didn't remember the last meal I'd had. I thought it might be time to find some food, check out Hank's, maybe find him before he went to wherever it was he kept regular hours. I wondered if there'd be a sign on the store saying when he'd show, just in case he wasn't there. I wondered what he'd say if he was, if I showed him Sally's picture, asked if he'd seen her around lately. And what if he had, would he tell a pale visitor a local's business? Would it be like that here? Was that the way to do this, by asking around? Feeling suddenly like a fish out of water. I knew what to expect on my own turf. But here? If I asked about Sally, would Hank tell me, sure, I know her, or, never seen her, or would he give me a New York answer, "What's it your fucking business?"

I found a coffee shop where I could get greasy eggs and underdone toast, supermarket-brand tea in a mug with traces of someone's lipstick on it. Then I continued down the road on foot until I found Hank's shop. It was two o'clock. But Hank was out to lunch. Or so the sign said.

I walked back to Polly's Motor Park, changed to my suit and headed for the strip of white sand across the road, beyond it, the same ocean that had wet my bare feet when I stood on the beach with Jim. But of course it didn't look the same, dark, nearly a navy blue, in Coney Island after dark. Here, in the middle of the day, the sun so bright that even with Madison's glasses on I had to squint, the water was as pale as light, as if I'd be able to see the fish I'd dreamed of without having to dive.

Waiting for a couple of cars to pass, I thought I should have shown Sally's picture to Polly. A small place like this, wouldn't everyone know everyone? But I hadn't. Was I just too tired when I checked in? Or was it something else? What was I doing here if not looking for Sally? And then I felt it, the fear that all this would lead to a dead end, that I'd have to go back and tell Leon and Madison I'd failed.

There was no sign of life on the little beach. I dropped my towel on the sand and walked into the water, then dove in and began to swim. I swam straight out for a while, then took a deep breath and dove. Even without a snorkel, mask and flippers, I could dive deep enough to see some wonders I'd never seen before, the water clear enough to see some fish beneath me, the silver of their scales shining up through the water. I swam until my head was clear, until I felt strong again, until I couldn't swim any longer. I returned to the beach, put the towel around my shoulders and waited for three cars to pass before crossing the highway and going back to cabin 10. I showered quickly, changing into shorts and a T-shirt. I slipped the picture of Sally into my back pocket, the camera, cell phone and my money and credit cards into the front pockets and headed first for the office.

Polly wasn't there this time. There was a kid there instead, seventeen, maybe eighteen at most. Bare feet up on the counter, he was reading a comic book, an open can of Coke next to his big feet. His hair was gelled so that it stood straight up. When he looked up, I expected eyes as green as the bay, but they were brown, dark, shining and without a bit of curiosity in them. Except for a handful of whiskers sprouting unevenly on his chin, his face was smooth, nearly blank, too. He didn't ask what I wanted. Whatever it was, he must have figured I'd cough it up sooner or later, let him get it over with and get back to his reading.

"Hi," I said. Trying not to do this in a New York minute, trying not to stand out as a stranger in town despite my pallor.

"Hey," he said. "You need a cabin?"

"Got one," I told him. "I checked in early this morning."

He looked back at the comic, then back up at me.

"Everything okay?"

"Perfect," I told him.

He nodded.

I smiled.

"I'm trying to find an old friend of mine," I said, reaching into my pocket for Sally's picture. "I haven't seen her in years. This is actually from about five or six years ago. And the last phone number I have for her is stale."

His eyebrows went up.

"Out of date," I said. "Disconnected. She's not there anymore."

"Oh."

"I was wondering if she looks familiar to you, if you

might have seen her around, at the Piggly Wiggly or swimming or something," putting Sally's picture down on the counter where he could see it.

He leaned over the photo and squinted. "Pretty," he said.

I waited, but he just sat there, saying nothing, waiting, too.

"But you don't know her? She doesn't look familiar?"

He shook his head.

"Well, thanks. Might as well pay for one more day," I said, putting Sally's picture away and reaching for my credit card this time.

"Just one?"

"At a time," I said.

He ran my card. I signed the receipt. I wiggled my fingers at him, and he watched me go.

Five o'clock. Polly was sweeping off the long deck in front of the cabins nearest the road. I walked over.

"I see you got some color," she said.

"I didn't find Hank in, but I took a swim anyway."

"Everything to your liking?" Nodding toward my cabin at the end of the line.

"Fine. I just paid for another night."

"Checkout's noon," she said. Then she shrugged. "Don't mind if you need a late checkout, though. We're pretty empty and it always looks good to have as many cars parked here as possible. Place down the road? The Palmetto? You probably didn't come that way. You flew into Miami, right?"

I nodded.

"They're jammed. No Vacancy sign hardly ever turns off, name like that," shaking her head, "no pool, you never know what people want, do you?"

"I guess not," I said, figuring I should check out the Palmetto next. "By the way, I came down here to look for an old friend of mine. The picture's from when I last saw her, about six years ago, but I was wondering if maybe you saw her around. The last phone number she gave me, it was this area code," I shrugged, "but she might have moved or something. It's no longer working."

Polly leaned the broom against the railing, wiped her hands down the sides of her peach-colored shorts and took the picture, holding it close to her face.

"Pale, like you. She a relative?"

"Uh-uh. We were neighbors, then she moved down here."

"I don't get out much, dear, just into Long Key once a week for supplies. Bertie takes the desk days and I got a man comes in three nights a week, but this place don't make enough money for me to have a real staff. I'm not complaining, mind you. I wouldn't want to be anywhere else. It's quiet here, even in season. Suits me fine. But," handing me back the picture of Sally, "young girl like that, maybe she went to someplace bigger, someplace with a little more action."

"I guess."

I walked back past the coffee shop, wondering what they might be unable to ruin that I could eat for dinner, heading back to Hank's. "Bait," the sign said, and underneath that, "Masks, Snorkels, Tanks, Boat Excursions Arranged, Ask Within." I tried the knob, no dice. Then I held my hand over my eyes so that I could see in the window, but there was no one inside the small, cluttered shop. Hank, apparently, was still out to lunch.

I decided to keep walking. I thought maybe I'd find a better place to eat, come up with some other ideas. How was I figuring to find Sally? What had I been thinking?

Despite the heat, I began to walk faster, something to keep my mind off what looked like a failed effort. The Palmetto was just down the road, like Polly said, the green neon No Vacancy sign turned on. I walked into the office anyway, told my story, showed the picture, watched the clerk shake his head.

"You say she's here, at the Palmetto?"

"Guess not," I said. "But maybe you've seen her?"

"I'd remember," he told me, handing the picture back.

I kept going, trying to stay in the little bit of shade there was, once from a huge billboard, several times from a small grove of trees. And then I saw it, a group of tacky white cottages with tiny porches out front, palm trees at the periphery, the office off to the right and the neon sign, pink, the thing that caught my eye, on a tall pole so that it would be visible to approaching cars. The Madison. Below that, "Vacancy," the first c out, the y blinking. Is this where they'd stayed? Did this explain the look on Jim's face when I'd told him his daughter's name?

I walked into the office. The clerk looked up at me and smiled. His wizened face was the color of mocha ice cream. I couldn't see his eyes behind his small, round, dark glasses. Then I heard it, a dog's tail thumping against the wooden floor.

"Okay, Ellen, you can go say hello."

The yellow Lab was old, too, and walked slowly. She still had her leather harness on. Maybe he was the night man and he'd just come on duty and hadn't had the chance to take it off her. Maybe she kept it on while she was in the office, to let her know she might be working at any time. I bent and stroked her big head. Then walked up to the counter, where I'd intended to show Sally's picture.

"Can I help you?" he said, looking somewhere to the left of me.

"I was just wondering if there was someplace good to eat around here. I thought you might know."

"Why, sure I do. Anita's. Good home cooking, fried chicken, mashed potatoes, Key lime pie. You're not from around here, am I right? You got to try the Key lime pie before you leave. You promise?"

"I do. And thanks," I said.

I waited for a refrigerated truck to pass, then crossed the road to the small white beach across from the Madison. The beaches dotted the coastline, trees in between, not a place for much action, for socializing, just a convenient place to swim, if that was your thing.

The beach was empty, a 7UP can half buried in the sand to my right, a broken flip-flop near it. I stood watching the long, low waves come into the shore, then I headed down the road to find Anita's. At least there was one promise I could keep.

CHAPTER 23

For the next three days, I woke up with the first light, before six, put on my bathing suit with a pair of shorts over it, ate quickly at the coffee shop and headed out. I saw a lot of heads shake. I heard a lot of people exclaim that I must be down from New York. I ate a few more bad breakfasts and a couple of really good meals at Anita's. I even lost some of my northern pallor. But there was no sign of Sally Spector.

On Sunday morning, I finally found Hank. The door to his shop was ajar and Hank himself was outside sitting on an old wooden straight-backed chair, sipping coffee from a styrofoam cup.

"Too early to get some flippers?"

"Not around here it isn't. You signed up for the boat?"

"No, just swimming here," pointing across at the ocean.

"Good a place as any," he said. He was shorter than me, wider than me, much more muscular than me, older, too, probably at least sixty. His hair was a yellowy gray, but he had a full head of it and I wasn't sure if it was wet from an early morning shower or maybe an early morning swim because all he was wearing was a bathing suit and an old T-shirt, both wet.

He looked down at my feet. "Seven and a half, I'd say. That means you'd get an eight."

"I'll need a mask and a snorkel, too."

"Got those. No problem."

As in the little corner delis in New York, I couldn't believe the amount of stuff crammed into what was no more than a shed, the wooden door barely closing properly, the two small windows, one of which I'd peered through the day before, painted shut decades earlier.

I took out my credit card while Hank was putting my things into a paper bag, "Hank's" stamped on each item. Good advertising, I guessed. When he looked up, he began to shake his head.

"For your convenience, we take cash only."

I pulled out the cash. Then pulled out the picture of Sally and told him my story. Hank took it in his bent fingers, the tip of one pinkie missing, and held it flat to try to catch the light from the open door. I stepped out of his way.

"So what happened in between?" he asked, putting the picture down on the counter.

"In between?"

"In between when you took her picture and now?"

"You mean why did I wait all these years?"

"Ah-huh."

"Well, I didn't. We've been writing and calling, but, you know, not all that often. Then I called on her birthday and the number was disconnected."

"You from New York?"

My heart made a little hop. "Yes," I said. "Do you . . ."

"It's just the way you talk so fast," he said. "Hard for me to keep up with what you're saying."

"Oh. Sorry. It's a—"

"I know. It's why I live down here."

I picked up the photograph. "She's older now, of course. But—"

"Never seen her," he said. He picked up the bag, folded the top down and stapled the receipt onto it, an odd touch, odd that he even had a stapler in the shop. He handed me the bag. "I hope you have a good swim," he said. "You change your mind about the boat, you know where to find me. Seven days a week, at least when I'm in the mood."

I thanked him and turned to leave.

"You know to spit, don't you? Into the mask. It keeps it from fogging up. Don't feel I've done right by you big-city folks if I don't tell you a thing like that."

I crossed the road and walked along the ocean side, having to wait for traffic sometimes when there was a tree near the road, the trees that made the beach into separate little coves.

As the days had passed, Hank had become my best hope. The more frustrated I'd become, the more I'd pinned on Hank. Now all I had was another dead end and no other ideas, no trace of Sally, no hint of Sally, no nothing.

Getting lost was one thing. Staying lost was quite another. Staying lost meant cutting all your ties, and that's exactly what Sally had done. She'd left her husband, her child and her home. She'd dropped her education. She'd left her friends without a word to anyone. Hell, if there still *was* a Sally, if she'd left on her own, cutting ties was precisely what she'd wanted, as far as I could tell. It was the point of it all. So why did I think she'd be here, of all places?

My flight home was the following morning, and I was ready. No one in the area knew Sally. No one had remembered ever seeing her. It was time to go home.

But when I came around a huge palm tree to the small spit of land across from the Madison, the ocean beyond seemed not to be water but light, the way it was in my dreams, and there he was. He stood at the very edge of the sand where the water would barely wet his white feet. He stood watching the ocean, like a lonely wife waiting for her sailor's ship to appear on the horizon. He never turned when I walked onto the little beach, put the bag from Hank's down on the sand, squatting down next to it. Even when I slipped the camera from my pocket and took his picture, he never moved. He stood still, his attention riveted on the water, the waves just ripples rising up to the sand, nothing like the waves the ocean made at home.

I knew he knew I was there. I'd seen one ear turn briefly in my direction before facing back toward the sea. Squinting toward the bright ocean, I sat on the sand and kept the vigil with him.

And then there she was. I saw the tip of her snorkel, her blonde hair, her face, the mask covering her eyes and nose, but no matter. It was Sally. Her hair was lighter than Madison's, her skin darker, a result of where and how she lived. She was as slim as a young girl and beautiful enough to take anyone's breath away, beautiful enough to hitchhike down here, even with a dog, to have Hank and everyone else want to protect her from this fast-talking city woman, God knows what on her mind, and for her history teacher to marry her when she'd gotten pregnant with someone else's child, even when it meant giving up his career.

When she got in close enough to stand, she motioned to the dog to join her, and from complete and utter stillness, he burst forward, leaping into the water, sending it high like sparks spitting out of a new fire, and headed straight for her.

They swam together for about fifteen minutes before heading back to the beach. Then she stood, the water still up to her knees, the dog's feet not yet finding purchase, and she pulled off the mask, shaking water from her hair, bending to take off the flippers. I managed three shots while her face was turned away before slipping the camera back into my pocket. I stood as she stepped out of the water, the dog shaking right next to her.

She seemed to notice me for the first time, and though the sun was behind her, she lifted a hand to shield her eyes as if the light was too bright for her.

I said her name and took a step toward her.

CHAPTER 24

Sally's hand stayed where it was, an eave over her eyes.

"Leon sent me," I said.

She turned to face the ocean and sat, her back to me. I expected to see her shoulders shaking, her head drop into her hands. I expected fear, remorse perhaps. But when I walked up to where she was sitting, the sand sticking to her tanned wet skin, I didn't get either. I sat near her, Roy now at the water's edge fishing with his white paws the way Dashiell did.

"I've been waiting for this for five years," she said, "for someone to figure it out. How did you find me?"

"How isn't the issue," I said. "Why is the question."

Sally sighed. "Have you been looking all this time?"

"No," I said. "Just about a week."

She turned to look at me, her face as still and blank as it was in the two pictures I'd seen. "Why now? Why after all these years?"

"Because Madison's in trouble," I told her. And sitting there on the sand, I told some of what I knew, about Madison's tics, about the Botox, about Dr. Bechman's murder. She stopped me there.

"She did that?" she asked.

"I don't know."

"Well, what did she say? Did she say she did it? Did she deny it?"

"Madison doesn't speak, Sally. She stopped talking shortly after you left."

"Not at all?"

I shook my head. And then we sat for a while without speaking either.

"There's nothing physical? It's not part of the tic disease?" Sally asked after a while.

"No, a decision, they think."

"Does she write notes? Does she nod, shake her head? Does she try to . . . ?"

I shook my head again.

"She's a great kid," I said, barely loud enough for her to hear me, even sitting just a foot apart. "But . . ."

Sally waved a hand back and forth to stop me. "You can't think that I'm going to go back." She turned away, toward Roy, toward the ocean, shaking her head. "If you met them, if you met my husband and my daughter, you know that I can't be anyone's wife, anyone's mother. You know I never was. Not ever. I don't —"

"Tell me how you got here, will you? Tell me what happened that night, the night you left home."

"Home," she said. "If only." She stood and walked toward the water's edge, the way Jim had when the conversation had gotten more painful. I followed her, and we stood with our feet in the water, Roy off to the right hauling a frond he'd found around the sand.

"You felt at home in school," I offered.

She shook her head. "Not really. It was reading I was after, losing myself in books."

And now here, I thought, looking out at the ocean.

"But even that was hard, with Madison always wanting your attention," I said. Sally didn't respond, but Roy came back to stand near her, looking up at her face. "The night you left, had you planned it, had you planned to leave?"

She shook her head. "I was feeling as if I was suffocating, a way I almost always felt then. I thought I'd die if I didn't get outside and get some air." She looked me right in the eye. "If I didn't get away from them."

"Both of them?"

She nodded. "Both of them. Leon is the sweetest man alive. What he did for me, what he tried to do, what he's doing now . . ."

"I met Jim," I told her.

"You are thorough." Her foot stirred the water. "So there's that, too. He's raising her and she's not even his."

She's his now, I thought, saying nothing. Whatever his faults, he was committed to Madison, to his daughter, you had to give him that.

"So you took Roy, so that you could go out for a walk?"

Sally nodded. "Yes, because he'd ask if I'd just gone out."

"Where you were going?"

"Why I was going. Like my mother. I was on a tight leash."

"But you were going to school," I said. "I thought he—"

"He encouraged that. Don't get me wrong. He was . . ." Sally shook her head. "It's just that he . . ." She looked at me again, and I could see the pain in her eyes. "He loved me too much," she whispered, and I could feel the trap, a kid so young with a kid of her own who needed her attention, a husband who was the same way, pulling on her to give them something she just didn't have.

"I'd be reading and I'd look up and both of them would be watching me."

"So that night . . ."

"I took Roy as an excuse." The dog cocked his head when he heard his name. "I only planned to get some air, a few minutes to myself."

"And?"

"Leon used to walk him in the meat market. The side streets are pretty deserted, so he was able to take the leash off, let Roy run. He'd find things in the street, an old work glove, a sock, a plastic soda bottle, human detritus that would be a treasure for a dog, and he'd toss his prize and run after it."

"Leon told you this?"

She shook her head. "He took pictures. I knew it from the pictures."

"He didn't talk much?"

"No, he's not a big talker. I would have thought he would be, because of his teaching, but he was a pretty quiet guy."

More so now, I thought.

"But you had the story, in pictures." The way Madison communicated, when she did at all.

"So that's the way I turned when I got out of the house. It's the way Roy turned, where he wanted to go. He went around the corner and down to Washington Street and then north. I guess that's the way he went with Leon a lot of the time. I didn't give it any thought. I was so glad to be out. I just followed him. And then this trucker stopped." She turned to look at me as if for the first time realizing how bizarre what she'd done was. I saw her hands were shaking, her lower lip, too. "He asked if I needed a lift. He said he was going to North Carolina, he could use a little company. I said no. I thought it was funny at first, then scary. And then we walked up Little West Twelfth Street and Roy found a sock. I let him off leash and he was running with it, growling at it, dumping it back on the ground, crouching as if it were a sheep, then grabbing it again, and I kept thinking about the ride I'd been offered and it just pulled at me. It just kept after me, the way Madison used to.

"I tried to go back home. I really did. I got as far as Horatio Street and then I stopped and I walked back to the market, to where the trucks were. Another one stopped on Gansevoort Street, the hookers giving me the eye, like was I taking their jobs away from them. I was going to walk away but then the driver opened the passenger door and asked if I needed help. I told him I did. It was strange, hearing myself say that. It was as if someone else had answered for me. But the moment it was out, I knew it was true, perhaps the truest thing I'd ever said."

"What did he say?"

"Nothing. He leaned across the seat and reached for my hand." Sally sighed and looked at the ocean for a moment. "Roy jumped in first," she said, her face still toward the water. "And then I got in. The driver leaned across me and pulled the door closed. 'Where to?' he said. And I said, 'Where are you going?' And that's how it started."

"Did you come here right away?"

"I didn't know this was where I was headed. I was headed away, not toward, if you know what I mean." Checking to see if I did, if I was on the same page.

"I do," I told her. And I did.

"He went as far as Georgia. He gave me bus fare to get here. Paul. That was his name. He never told me his last name."

"Did you tell him yours?"

"My first name only. But I remember thinking Russell, Sally Russell. So someplace inside, I must have known I was coming back here. We'd signed the register 'Mr. and Mrs. J. Russell.' " She looked out at the water, then down at the sand. "I doubt we fooled anyone. I was fifteen. Now that I'm in the business, I know it doesn't matter." She shrugged. "No one cares."

"But why did you come here, after what happened?"

"This is the only place on earth I've ever been happy."

"Are you happy now?" I asked her.

She looked down at Roy, then out at the water.

"I am," she said, "as happy as I think is possible for me."

"Do you live here?" Nodding back toward the Madison.

"I run the place. I have a cabin in the back with a small kitchen and a modest salary. I don't need much."

The sun was overhead now, the air still and hot. I suddenly wanted to swim, to swim with Sally. I walked back to where I'd left the bag from Hank's, tore it open and pulled out the snorkel and the flippers, nodding this time toward the ocean. Sally smiled, the first and last one I'd see.

I pulled off my shorts and put on the flippers. When I took out the mask, she said, "Don't forget to spit in it."

"Thanks," I told her. And I did.

Water could wash away forensic evidence, dirt, even stress. It could reshape rocks, smooth glass, and sometimes, perhaps for Sally, it could wash away memories or at least the pain that came with them. Perhaps it would wash away the pain I was feeling, pain for a little girl back in New York, because though I'd found Sally, she wouldn't be coming back with me. With my heart feeling broken, I followed Sally into the ocean, hoping that would glue it back together, hoping for some of the magic Sally had found here, not once but twice.

CHAPTER 25

Once again I dreamed of fish, striped, dotted, patterned, pied fish, tiny fish that swam together as one being, solitary fish with undershot jaws, fish that looked as if they'd eat you as soon as look at you, New York fish, street-corner fish, gangsta fish, only this time I was wide awake. This time I was following Sally into a small cove, grasses swaying as if they were at the end of a long dance marathon, schools of brightly colored fish suspended as if in midair, Sally, clearly in her element, moving gracefully, easily through the water ahead of me, as if she were one of them.

Afterwards we sat on the warm sand, Roy between us, Madison and Leon between us, too.

"I have Madison's medical records with me," I said, knowing it was too late for all that, years and years too late, but still feeling I had to try.

She waved a hand in the air.

"I have a couple of pictures."

"I can't," she said. "I don't expect you to understand, but I just can't."

I nodded, and for a while we sat there quietly looking at the ocean, neither of us able to think of anything to say.

"How did it happen," I finally thought to ask, "you and Leon?"

"Me and Leon," she said, "some pair. It was the day I'd told Jim that I was pregnant." Turning to look at me now. "Did he tell you about it?"

I nodded.

"What he said to me, he told you that?"

"He did."

"I can't think of words to describe how I felt, Jim's sneering disbelief on one side, my mother's fanatical intolerance of anything less than perfection on the other, and me fifteen years old. I was even too afraid to cut class—so I went."

"Leon's class?"

"I actually sat through another class first. Creative writing. Then Leon's honor history. Last period. When the bell rang, I couldn't move. It was as if I was telling my body to stand and it didn't hear me.

"He didn't do anything at first. He was packing up his briefcase, putting some books in it, erasing the board. Then he saw that I was still sitting there and not doing anything. I must have looked like hell. He must have known something was really wrong because before he came over to talk to me, he walked over and closed the door. Then he sat at the desk next to mine and he said, 'Something the matter?'

"I still remember the way the tears welled up and out of my eyes, remember how they felt running down my cheeks, how helpless I was to stop them, how helpless I was, period."

"So you told him?"

She nodded. "Everything but who."

"And where."

Sally looked at me, a line between her eyes.

"He didn't know about this place, right? He didn't know the circumstances. Nor how you'd chosen your daughter's name. Is that right?"

She nodded, sighed, put a hand on Roy's back.

"But he knew the boy knew?"

"Yes."

"And that you had your back against the wall?"

"Yes, he knew that."

"And then what?"

Sally turned to look at me, her eyes shining. "He said, 'Marry me.' He said, 'I'll take care of you. I'll raise the baby as if it were mine.' "

"Did you agree right away?"

"I didn't say anything. I couldn't. I was so overwhelmed by the whole thing, by fear, by grief, by anger, by gratitude, I couldn't speak. So Leon took charge. He worked it out. He figured it out on the spot, what we'd do, how we'd do it, everything. He was so sure."

"That you became sure."

She nodded. "Without thinking."

"There's that," I said. And now this, I thought.

"What about your mother?" I asked. "How did that . . . ?" I stopped in mid-sentence, lifting a hand, letting it fall back to the warm sand between us. I knew the answer, didn't I? So why ask?

"Leon asked how she'd handle it, and all I could manage was more tears. So he said I shouldn't worry about it at all, I should leave everything to him, if that was okay with me. I'm saved, I thought. He was talking, and I remember sitting there thinking, I'm saved. That's all I could manage. It was like falling off a building, and at the last minute you saw there was a net, you weren't going to die."

Or you saw Superman coming to scoop you up in his powerful arms moments before you hit the ground.

"So he took the heat on this, too, the blame?" I asked.

"He did."

"Then how did it end up he wasn't in trouble with the

law? Did your mother relent? Because he said there were no charges pressed. A teacher and a fifteen-year-old student . . . ?"

Sally was shaking her head. "My mother went insane. She never forgave me. Nor Leon."

"But?"

"When he went to the precinct, and to the Board of Education, he had proof that he wasn't the one who'd gotten me pregnant."

"I don't understand. What sort of proof?"

"Leon didn't tell you?"

"Tell me what?"

She shook her head. "He's still protecting me. Even now." She smoothed the sand in front of her, making lines afterwards with one finger. "Leon never wanted to have kids." Not looking at me. "He'd had a vasectomy when he was twenty-eight."

We sat for a long time after that. She told me more about the night she'd left, how she'd sat saying nothing in the truck for hours, just listening to Paul go on and on and on, sometimes only pretending to listen, or pretending to sleep, sitting there terrified, not understanding what she was doing, what she'd done. They'd stopped at a diner, the parking lot filled with semis, even in the middle of the night. She didn't know where they were, not even what state they were in. She didn't know the time. She didn't care either.

She told Paul she wasn't hungry, but he insisted. He told her not to worry about the money, how often did he get the chance to eat with someone when he was working, and anyway, he told her, they were in the South, cheap living, this was New York, he might think twice. He'd meant it as a joke, to lighten things up, but Sally hadn't laughed. She just got down from the cab, and as she was closing the door, he asked about the dog, didn't he have to eat, too? And Sally was confused because in New York you couldn't take your dog into a restaurant, and anyway, Leon had always fed Roy. She'd never had to think about it, about feeding him, walking him, about anything else he might need. What had she done? she wondered. Why had she taken him along? Now there was Paul making her worry about Roy when all she wanted to do was never worry about anyone again for the rest of her life. She looked toward the diner across the sandy parking lot, then back at Roy. She'd never been anyplace where you could take a dog into a restaurant but she'd read once you could in Paris, only this wasn't France, this was the middle of nowhere, or maybe the edge of nowhere.

But Paul had taken the leash, had whistled the dog down from the truck, and they'd gone into the diner, Maud's, she told me. She still remembered the name. She still remembered a lot about that night, the night her life changed, the night she became a free person. The night her husband's life changed, I thought but didn't say, the night Madison's life changed as well. The night their worst nightmare came true.

Roy had gone under the table, all on his own, and Sally said she thought maybe Leon did that with him when they were out on a shoot and it got to be lunchtime, maybe he just walked in someplace with the dog and no one said boo, and Roy went under the table where no one would see him, and then Leon might feed him from his hand. That was what Paul did, first asking the old man who waited on them for a bowl of water, to put it in a take-out container if anyone was going to be fussy about eating from a bowl that a dog ate from, and the guy had laughed and told them, you going to be fussy, you're not stopping at Maud's, the old bat wouldn't spend a nickel she didn't have to. Have the fried chicken, he'd told them, it's the only thing we can't seem to ruin here. Some folks say it's not half bad. When he laughed, you could see he had a tooth missing, one of his upper canines, maybe a result of eating at Maud's. They ordered the chicken, Paul taking the meat off the thigh and the leg of his half, putting it on the palm of his hand for the dog to take. And then he'd asked her, what made you take the dog with you? And that's when she told him, spilled it all, every single bit of it. It was the first time, too, the first time she'd ever said any of it out loud, and it felt like a cement block was being lifted off her chest, and that's when she thought about the Keys, where she'd been happy for two days, where she felt what that was for the first and only time in her entire life.

Paul wasn't only a good talker. He was a good listener. He nodded a lot. He didn't seem to judge her. And then when they got to Georgia, he'd given her money. This is for a bus ticket, he'd told her, folding her hand around the money with his, leaving it there for a second. You pick the direction. You pick the place. It's up to you.

He gave a hundred dollars on top of it, but when she'd asked for his last name and his address so that she could pay him back one day, he'd said no, that that wasn't part of the deal. He didn't want to know her last name, he didn't want that responsibility, and he wouldn't tell her his.

"Sally, had there been any talk of abortion? Did Jim suggest it? Or Leon?"

She shook her head. "No. And I couldn't have." Looking away again. "I know it makes no sense, but I just couldn't have."

We took one last swim, Roy, too, to rinse off the sand. Then we stood at the edge of the beach, Sally holding her mask, flippers and snorkel, mine in the bag from Hank's.

"You're sure?" I asked.

"I am," she told me.

I nodded. I thanked her for being up front with me. I didn't suggest she come back for just a week or so, see if Madison would start talking. For her to do that and then leave again, I couldn't think of anything worse.

"If Leon wants to come down here . . ." She shook her head. "You tell him . . ."

"I will," I said, knowing she'd be gone anyway. Knowing she'd be someplace else, someone else, before I got off the plane in New York. Even staying in one spot, she'd been traveling light for over five years. She knew how to do it. I imagined there wouldn't be more than a couple of bags to pack, more than likely, no car. No bank account either. My guess was that Sally Russell didn't exist the way the rest of us did, that she didn't pay taxes, serve jury duty, have a phone, a library card, get junk mail. I'd passed a used book store on the way down. I bet they knew Sally there, the way Hank did. I bet if I'd shown her picture there, whoever was behind the desk would have shaken their head, no, no, pretty girl, never saw her. Something about her made you want to protect her. By the time I was in a cab on my way back to the Village, I was sure Sally Russell would be swallowed up by the Keys again, paying cash, living free. It was something everyone thought about from time to time, disappearing without a word to anyone. Standing there, my last minutes with her, part of me was rooting for her to get away with it.

She clipped a short rope onto Roy's collar and turned to go. Then she looked at me one last time.

"I used to have a pair of glasses just like yours." She looked sad for a moment, but only for a moment. "But that was a long time ago."

CHAPTER 26

There was an airport in Marathon. I could have returned the car there, flown to Miami, and tried to get an earlier flight home. But I decided to drive back to Miami. Heading toward the mainland, the Bay of Florida on one side, the Atlantic Ocean on the other, visible because of a full moon, I'd have time to think, time I needed because I had no idea what I was going to tell Leon and Madison about this trip. What, I wondered, were my choices? Leon was my client. I'd come here to try to do what he'd asked me to. I'd come here on Leon's dime. So what would I tell him, that against all odds, I'd found his missing wife, but what might seem like a combination of incredible genius, some great second-guessing and a ton of good luck hadn't turned out all that great after all, that said missing wife had refused to come back with me, had declined the opportunity to even look at photographs of her daughter or to examine Dr. Bechman's records of the treatment, if you could call it that, of Madison's disease? Would I tell him, too, that while I was driving to Miami to catch my plane home, I was sure Sally was packing her few belongings and moving elsewhere, that even before he heard what I had to say, she'd be missing again, this time for good?

And what of Madison, hearing all of this? What of Madison? Of course, I could talk to Leon privately. Then what? Would he lie to Madison and say I'd failed to find Sally? Would I do that, too? Would she be better off thinking Sally was still out there someplace, not wanting to come home, not wanting her, or that she was dead? And where in myself could I possibly find an answer to these questions?

I'd taken a turn someplace past the one to the Everglades to stop for something to eat, something to wake me up. There'd been only three other vehicles at the all-night diner, all delivery trucks. On the way back to the highway, I heard the mournful sound of a train whistle, but I didn't see the railroad crossing or the train. Still, the whistle kept blowing, warning people that something big and fast and unforgiving was heading their way. Watch out, it said, watch out, watch out. Why couldn't we have something like that in our lives, some warning sound to indicate that danger was barreling down on us, something to tell us to jump out of the way? Leon and Madison would be hearing the warning now. Rachel's coming, Rachel's coming, get out of the way.

By the time I'd turned in the rental car and spent four hours in the Miami airport, waiting to board my plane, I'd changed my focus. Finding Sally, that was done. It was over. Whether Leon would be better off knowing she was alive but wouldn't return, that wasn't the issue for me. Madison was the issue. Saving Madison was the issue. And in order to do that, I had to see if there was any way I could help her on the assumption that she *had* killed Bechman. As I boarded the plane, that was my new bottom line, no longer thinking about a series of mistakes a young girl had made, now thinking about her daughter and about the issues of malice, premeditation, and deliberation.

The detectives were trying to get the court to allow them to see the records of all the children Bechman had treated, to determine Madison's *mens rea*, her guilty mind, trying to prove Madison was a bad seed, with a little help from Ms. Peach, it seemed. But even if Madison had committed the crime, it seems to me it would have been in a moment of uncontrollable frustration and rage, her doctor not understanding that the kid was already hanging on by a thread, that the droopy eyelid had polished off any remaining positive sense of self she had. The needle was filled with Botox and ready. She'd handed him the drawing. Had he merely put it down on the desk without really looking at it?

Mens rea holds the belief that people should be punished only when they understand that their actions will cause harm, when they are morally blameworthy. Did the detectives believe that Madison had researched Botox on her computer, as I had on mine, and that she fully understood what it could do if the needle were plunged into her doctor's heart? Acting out of control was one thing. A cold-blooded, deliberate homicide was something else entirely. To accuse Madison of murder necessitated both the act, *actus reus,* and intent, *mens rea.* But how could we know what was in the mind of a child who didn't speak?

What if Madison had been impaired in some way due to medication? Wouldn't that change everything? Wasn't that why the detectives wanted Bechman's records, to see what, if anything, he'd given Madison and what the side effects might be, and to compare the effect of those drugs on his other patients, to see, for example, if several of the children taking dopamine blockers such as pimozide or risperidone to reduce tics suffered fits of violence?

Leon had said Madison hadn't been taking any drugs. Had he told the detectives that as well? Had they, in fact, given up on getting the children's records released?

Suppose Bechman had given Madison the drugs by injection? Madison didn't speak. She couldn't have gone home and told Leon. Would Bechman have bothered to call and tell him, a father who didn't even show up with his child when she came for treatment, a father who seemed to be sleepwalking through life?

I unzipped my bag and pulled out the envelope Ms. Peach had given Leon, the envelope Sally wanted no part of. It was sealed, and I slit it open, pulling out the folded sheets, opening them on my lap. There were all Dr. Bechman's notations, the first visit five and a half years ago, the mother and father both there, the doctor's perceptive note about a stressful home environment, the parents "loosely connected," in his words, the child wearing socks that didn't match, a button undone at the back of her dress. Notes for the next visit were on the next line, the second visit just three days after the first. There were two visits before the diagnosis, chronic motor tic disorder, and three more before Sally's disappearance, and then a note with a box drawn around it saying that the patient now declines to speak both at home and at the office.

The plane was finally boarding. I put away the notes, pulled out my ticket and walked to the end of the line, people queuing up even before the announcement to do so. Once seated, I took out the copy of Madison's medical treatment again, reading the sometimes elaborate paragraphs now separated by whiteness, space to indicate the passage of time between appointments, to separate one visit from another. I checked the dates. The change in the way the notes were written happened after Ms. Peach had been hired, perhaps part of her overhaul of office procedures, her redecorating intruding into the patient files. The notes were easier to read this way. If the change had been the result of Ms. Peach's suggestion, you had to give her that.

I read all the notes, the recommendation of an ear, nose and throat specialist, a child psychiatrist, relaxation exercises, biofeedback, increasing the amount of exercise Madison did, including the recommendation that she be taken swimming. But no drugs had been prescribed. Until the first and only Botox shot, there was no mention at all of medication.

Leon had to be with her for the first few years. She wouldn't have been old enough to walk to the doctor's office on her own, but the records didn't say whether he was there or not, what he'd been told and what he hadn't been told. Either way, there were no medications used at all until the Botox, and there was a note prior to the use of Botox that Leon had been "informed" and had signed the appropriate forms giving permission for the procedure.

When I got to the last page, I was surprised to find a note written the day Bechman had been killed. Often doctors take notes while they talk to you, ask you questions about your health, your habits, your complaints if any. But Madison didn't talk. So he must have stopped after examining her to make his notes before attempting to give her the shot.

Is that when she drew the picture, when he told her he wanted to give her Botox on the other side, that he was willing to take the chance that both her eyelids would droop and make her feel like a total freak?

Notes the last day. And then nothing, of course.

I put the pages back inside the envelope and closed my eyes, thinking of the drawing. Would that seal Madison's *mens rea*? A threat would surely show intent, would surely demonstrate malice, premeditation and deliberation, wouldn't it?

And no meds. I'd been hoping for something that would lead to a lesser charge, but it wasn't there. I'd looked up the side effects of Botox, hoping that might explain Madison's actions, and to my surprise, dysphasia, the inability to speak or understand words, was at the top of the list. But Madison could understand words without any difficulty, and no one, not her father, her former doctor, the throat specialist, the child psychiatrist, none of them thought that Madison couldn't speak, only that she *wouldn't* speak.

None of the other side effects could mitigate *mens rea;* nausea, neck pain, an asymmetry if the Botox were injected into the wrong muscle, ptosis or drooping of the upper eyelid, the side effect we know Madison had, bruising at the injection site, headache, upper respiratory infection and, of course, the intended effect of Botox, paralysis of the muscles in the area of the injection.

How could anyone think an extremely bright twelve-year-old couldn't figure out what Botox could do to the human heart, her own paralyzed for so long?

Homicide was at an all-time low in the city, but still, no one liked the idea of a murderer on the loose, even one who was only twelve. The cops weren't going to let this go. They were going to keep at it, no matter what it took. Well, so would I.

I closed my eyes and must have fallen asleep because the next thing I remember was the sound of the landing gear descending, then clicking into position, and the announcement alerting passengers to fasten their seat belts and return their trays to the upright position. The envelope with Madison's medical records was still on my tray. I tucked it into my tote bag, zipping it closed, then waited for the plane to land, taxi up to the terminal and let us go on our way.

I was walking toward the exit where the taxis lined up when my phone rang, the number familiar but only vaguely so.

"Alexander."

"Rachel? It's Charles Abele. I've been trying you at home and when you didn't return my call . . ."

I wasn't sure if I'd lost the signal or if Charles had temporarily lost his voice. I reached the door and stepped outside, but still I heard nothing.

"Charles?"

"I'm sorry," he said. "I can't . . ."

"What happened?"

A cabdriver opened the rear door for me but I stood on the sidewalk, not wanting to lose the signal.

"It's Celia," he said. "She's dead."

"Oh my god. How?"

"They're saying it was suicide, but it can't be. It just can't. She never would have left JoAnn."

"Where are you?" I asked.

"At home."

I got into the cab and gave the driver his address.

"I'm at the airport. I'll be there in thirty minutes."

CHAPTER 27

"Where's JoAnn?" I asked when Charles opened the door.

But he just stepped aside to let me pass. I did, walking over and sitting on the sofa, waiting for him to sit down and tell me more.

For a moment, he just stood in the doorway, his face pale, his hands shaking. I went into the kitchen and got some water for him. When I came back into the living room, he was sitting on one of the chairs that faced the couch, his mouth moving as if he might be biting the inside of his cheek.

"They said she was despondent over Bechman's death," talking too loud. "They said that's why she did it, that she couldn't cope. That's not Celia." Shaking his head, his hands curled into fists now. "If there was one thing Celia could do, she could cope."

"How did it happen?"

"She went out the window."

"And where was JoAnn?"

"Asleep in her bed." Shaking his head again. "Even supposing it were true, that she just couldn't live without that bastard, she never would have left JoAnn unprotected like that. Never."

"When did it happen, Charles?"

"Thursday night."

The night I left for Florida.

"Eleven forty-five," he said.

"How do they know the exact time? Broken watch?" Thinking unless there was a witness, they wouldn't know. There'd be a range of time during which it probably had happened.

"The woman on the ground floor in the back, Ida Berman, she actually heard Celia land. Can you imagine?" He squeezed his eyes shut. "It seems she hit the outdoor table. Ida looked out the window, then called the police right away."

"So JoAnn, she was taken care of, she didn't wake up to find herself alone?"

He shook his head. "No. She was still asleep when the detectives got there."

"When did you hear?"

"Around two. Ida told the police that JoAnn was with me a lot. The ex, she called me. She didn't know my name but they found it in Celia's address book and called. They didn't tell me what had happened at first. They asked me to come down to the precinct. I had no idea what it was about. 'At this hour?' I asked the detective, and he said, 'It's important, sir, it's about JoAnn.' "

"So you did, you went?"

"They said there was an open bottle of wine on the coffee table and one glass but the glass was unused, and they didn't find any alcohol in her system. That's what they said. 'Her system.' "

"So she hadn't had too much to drink?"

"She hadn't had anything to drink."

"And they don't think it was an accident, that she fell?"

"No, they said it was deliberate, not an accident."

"Was there a note?"

He nodded.

Why hadn't he mentioned it right away? "What did it say?" I asked, leaning closer, talking softly.

He shook his head.

"They didn't show it to you?" Wondering how I might get to see it.

"No, they did. It was addressed to me."

I waited, watching his face.

"It said '*Dear Charles, Please take care of JoAnn. Celia.*' "

"So they're sure, because of the note? It was definitely her handwriting?"

He looked surprised at my question, then he nodded. "It's her handwriting. There's no doubt about it. And the door was double-locked."

"I guess she took it pretty hard."

"Bechman's death?"

I nodded.

"She . . ." But then Charles just shook his head. "They asked me a bunch of questions and then they gave me JoAnn," he said.

"Because of the note?"

"No. She didn't tell you?"

"Tell me what?"

"They weren't married, of course, so it would have been awkward for Eric to have his name on the birth certificate."

"You're saying that *your* name is there?"

He nodded. "I'm the father of record. As far as the law is concerned, she's my daughter. As far as I'm concerned, that's true as well."

He stood and walked over to the windows, his back to me. "She wouldn't have written it like that."

"Like what?" Trying to keep up as he leaped from one thing to another.

"I had this nickname for her, you know, something just between the two of us. She would have used it. She never called herself Celia to me. I hated the name and so did she."

"Even after everything? Even after Bechman, the split, JoAnn, even so?"

He turned and walked over to his desk, opening the top right-hand drawer, prime space being used for whatever it was he wanted to show me. He picked up a sheaf of notes held together by a paper clip, came over to the couch and handed it to me. I read the top one.

Charlie,

> *Many, many thanks for your offer. You're as stand-up as they come.*

> *Betty*

"Betty?"

"It was from when we decided to get married. I'd told her I'd always wanted to marry a Betty and she'd said, 'Then that's what you should do.' "

I began to look through the rest of the notes, some on pale cream notepaper, some on scraps of paper torn off a paper bag or written in the white space around a crossword puzzle. She always called him Charlie. She always signed the notes Betty.

"You told the police this?"

"I did."

"You showed them these?"

He nodded.

"And?"

"One of the detectives put his hand on my shoulder. 'Mr. Abele,' he said, 'no one wants to believe that someone they,' he hesitated, you know, because we were divorced. Then he said, 'someone they were fond of would do a thing like this.' "

"So they don't think this means anything?"

Charles shrugged. "The detective said that people don't act like themselves at a time like this, when they're so desperate. They act out of character. He said I should understand that when someone is this despondent, enough to want to end their life, they do things to cut off their feelings for the people they're leaving behind. If they didn't do that, he told me, they wouldn't be able to . . ." He just lifted one hand, twisting it so that the palm faced up, then dropped it again. "They said she had no plans."

"No plans?"

" 'No investment in the future,' one detective said. He had her appointment calendar in his hand. He said there were no dates with friends, no dental appointments, no theater tickets. They said there wasn't much food in the house, that the yogurt was out of date, that the hamper was full. The detective said these were signs of depression. But there could be reasonable explanations for all those things, couldn't there?"

"Then you don't agree with the detective? You think she was coerced," wondering who but not how. How someone had gotten her to write the note, probably dictated, with JoAnn asleep in the next room was a no-brainer.

He nodded. "What I want, the reason I called, I want to hire you. I have to know who did this to Celia."

"Me, too," I said, "because whoever did this to her also murdered Eric Bechman."

CHAPTER 28

I could hear Dashiell barking as I climbed the stairs to Madison's apartment, and then the door opened and he came barreling out at me, his whole body wiggling with delight. Madison and Leon were both standing in the doorway waiting. Something about it was like coming home after being away a long, long time. Except that it wasn't home and what I'd come to tell them was going to break their hearts.

And then something happened. I followed Dashiell into the apartment. Leon asked me to sit and asked if I wanted anything to eat. I heard myself telling him no, that I hadn't slept at all, that I needed to take Dashiell and go right home, my voice sounding as if it were coming not from me but from someone else, someone standing across the room.

Madison took a step back, a step away from me. Was it because I wasn't staying or because Dashiell would be leaving? I opened my bag, gave her back the heart-shaped glasses, telling her I wore them all the time, thanking her, but she just put them down on the coffee table.

"We've had a great time with Dashiell," Leon said, as if that was all there'd been to it. He looked at Madison, then back at me. Was he waiting for her to tell me more?

"We were at the dog run yesterday and the day before," he said, picking up a pile of contact sheets from his desk and handing them to me. "Take these with you," he said. "After you sleep, or whenever, see if there are any you'd like to have."

I slipped the contact sheets into the open tote bag, slipping them in next to the folded copy of the picture that had been found on Bechman's desk the day he was killed.

Leon was still talking about their adventures with Dashiell, me only half listening, Madison, I thought, not listening at all. "We walked along the river," he said, "all the way down to the tip of Manhattan. Every time we passed those metal grates dogs hate to walk on, Dashiell pulled to go that way. He's fearless and he likes to prove it, doesn't he?" The question addressed to Madison, as if she'd answer him, nod and react in some way. Then back to me. "We'll be sad to see him go."

Madison went to her room and came back with a rawhide bone, one knot chewed off. She put it into my open bag and then leaned back against the table.

"How did your trip go?" Leon finally asked, as if it were a vacation he was asking about, a trip to Disney World, a week in Paris, a cruise to the Galápagos.

I caught his eye and shook my head. I wanted to check my watch, to say I had an appointment, or just to break and run. I needed time to think without Madison staring at me, without Leon's unspoken hopes.

Leon didn't ask anything further. He must have understood that if he wanted to know more, it wasn't going to happen with Madison in the room. That conversation, the one I was dreading, would have to wait until later because I didn't want to tell him what had happened and just leave it at that. I wanted to offer him something more, something hopeful. And in order to do that, I had to get out of there.

Fifteen minutes earlier, sitting on someone's stoop after I'd left Charles's apartment, I'd gone over what he'd told me, that Celia wouldn't have written the note that way, which meant she'd been murdered, and that it had happened late on the day Leon had asked for Madison's records. I didn't think that could be a coincidence. I'd taken out the records again, and this time what seemed to jump off the pages were those white spaces, spaces not indicating the passage of time as I'd previously thought, but showing that information had been removed, whited out on the first Xerox and then copied once more, information that Leon and I were not supposed to see. It had to be something Celia could explain, that Celia knew about, everything now pointing in the same direction. Even the locked door could be explained. After all, Bechman had the keys to Celia's apartment, and he wouldn't have kept them on his key ring. He would have kept them at his office.

The keys wouldn't be there anymore. Not now. But I still needed to get into Bechman's office again. I needed to see the originals of Madison's records, to see what was written where the copy I had only showed blank space.

But not before I tried to clarify something urgent. For that I needed Madison, Madison who was now standing a foot away from me with her arms folded across her chest, her lips a tight little line. Who did I think I was fooling with my research trip? Not Madison. That much was clear.

"I need to talk to Madison for a minute, if that's okay," I said to Leon, not the way I usually did things, but the way I thought I might get what I needed this time. Without asking Madison, without waiting for anyone's approval, I grabbed my tote bag and headed for Madison's room. I put the tote on the end of her bed and pulled out the copy of the drawing that had been found on Eric Bechman's desk the day he was killed.

When I turned around, Madison and Dashiell were standing in front of me, the door closed.

"I need your help again," I said.

Madison looked down at Dashiell.

"No, not with Dashiell this time. It's about what happened to Dr. Bechman. It's about what people think you did."

There was a little flicker in one cheek, the one under the droopy eyelid, the same kind her father had when he got tense.

"There was a drawing found on his desk. The police were told you did it and that it was a threat, that the meaning of the drawing was that you wanted to stab Dr. Bechman in the heart for what he did to you."

She seemed to notice the folded piece of paper now. She looked back at me and waited.

"I need to know two things. I need to know if you drew this picture. I need to know what you meant to say when you drew it. And I need to know if you left this drawing on Dr. Bechman's desk the day he was killed."

For what seemed like forever, Madison stood staring up at me. Then she took the drawing from my hand, unfolded it and studied it for another eon. Finally she held up one hand, the thumb, pointer and middle fingers pointing toward the ceiling, the ring finger and pinkie folded against her palm.

"You're right," I said. "Three things. My mistake."

While some stars died and new ones were born, Madison Spector stood in front of me just staring. Then she turned and walked over to her desk, picked up a pencil and wrote something on the sheet of paper I'd given her, folding it carefully when she had finished, walking back to the bed and slipping it into my tote.

Standing at the foot of her bed, I looked at the walls Sally had painted, the gigantic fish, the turtle, the coral, rocks, sea grasses, and wondered, when the time came, how much I'd tell Madison and what she would do when I did.

I zipped the tote bag and sat on the end of the bed for a moment.

"This is temporary," I said, "my not talking. There are a couple more things I need to check out and then I'll be back."

She came and sat next to me.

"So you figure that when I get home and look at what you wrote, I'll have the answers I was after?"

Madison just slid one of her hands into one of mine. She looked so much like her mother that it was almost spooky, but it was her father's hand she'd put in mine, wide, almost square, the fingers blunt, the nails, with most of the black polish chipped off by now, flat with tiny ridges running from side to side, giving them the delicate texture of a seashell. We sat there for a minute or two, neither of us speaking. Then I thanked her for taking care of Dashiell. And for her faith in me.

"Back at you, kid," I told her. "I trust you completely." I meant it, too.

I didn't tell her anything about my trip, about seeing Roy waiting on the beach, about my talk with Sally. I never mentioned a word about the death of Celia Abele nor the evening I spent sitting on the cool sand in Coney Island talking to her genetic father. Even before I thanked Leon and Madison again and told them I'd call him very soon, I was already thinking about another little girl, one who slept peacefully in her bed while in the next room her mother did what she had to in order to save her baby's life.

CHAPTER 29

I didn't wait until I got home to see what Madison had written on the drawing. I sat on the steps in front of her building, opened the tote and slipped out the folded piece of paper right there, smoothing it open on my lap. There were no words. Madison had merely continued the wavy line. Now it went all the way through the heart, dividing it in two. It was no longer a stabbed heart, no longer a threat. It was a broken heart. She'd simply been telling Bechman how she felt.

Had he stopped her before she'd finished it, telling her he understood, explaining again that the droop was temporary, that it would go away. Had he told her they could wait and see before trying the Botox again? Is that why the needle had been left on the desk or on the counter behind him? He'd had it ready but changed his mind when he saw how upset Madison was. And had she picked it up after he'd put it down, the way she picked up everything? Bechman would have been wearing latex gloves. Madison's hands would have been bare.

"How's my favorite research person coming along?"

When I turned, startled, there was Ted. You used to hear people coming, but no more now that everyone and his grandmother wore running shoes. He sat next to me. In daylight, he looked older than he had in the apartment. Given his profession, I didn't think the flattering lighting in his apartment was a coincidence.

"Not bad," I told him. "And you?"

"Fabulous. My agent just called. He has a lead on a commercial I'd be perfect for. If I'm lucky, I'll get to play the guy with diarrhea. Or maybe it's acid reflux. I forget. The important thing is the *cachet* I get putting this on my résumé." He rolled his eyes. "And how goes your work life?"

"Plugging along," I told him.

"Any leads to Miss Sally?"

I shook my head. The last thing I wanted to do was tell the gossipy neighbor something my client didn't yet know.

"Oh. The tan could have fooled me. I thought perhaps you'd tracked her to Belize. Or Costa Rica. Isn't that where people go when they want to disappear?"

"Yup. Rich people. People with assets to hide. Sally didn't have any of those. She didn't even have a credit card with her when she left. She didn't have a watch."

"Just house keys and Leon's dog."

"That sounds about right."

"Too bad. I thought perhaps you'd found the trucker who'd spirited her away."

"I wish," I told him.

"But you're still working on it, aren't you? Please don't tell me you've given up. I do miss her so." He waited a beat, stood, then tossed his striped scarf over one shoulder. "I'm off. Did I mention that I have to *audition* to play the guy with psoriasis? Plum roles like this don't just get handed out. One has to work for them."

He started to walk away. "Don't forget to keep me posted," he said, his back to me, wiggling the fingers of his right hand in the air. I was about to get up when I heard another voice, the stoop turning into Grand Central Station.

"Rachel?"

"Yes?"

"Nina. You left your card under my door. I'm sorry I didn't get a chance to call you. Things just kept coming up."

She sat down next to me, a tall, horse-faced woman with big teeth and bad skin.

"I knew it was you because of him. I saw Leon walking him last night and so I said, 'Oh, you got another dog,' and he said he hadn't, that the dog was yours. When he mentioned your name I had this gigantic guilt attack that I hadn't called, but Leon said you were away so of course I waited."

"I was hoping you could tell me something about Sally." It was stale by now, no longer needed, but again, I didn't want to say so. It would make more sense to listen for a couple of minutes than to reveal the truth.

"Why is he doing this?" A conspiratorial whisper. "She's dead."

"What makes you say that?" Glad she hadn't called before I'd gone to Florida.

"It's the only thing that makes sense," she said, taking out a cigarette, holding the pack out to me, then lighting hers, blowing a stream of smoke straight out in front of her. "She had everything, a guy who adored her, the freedom not to work but to go to school, an adorable kid." Nina shrugged. "Why would she have left of her own volition?"

"You're saying she was happy? She never complained about anything?"

"Happy? Who's happy? You tell me who you know that's happy." Angry now. "That's a reason to toss away a good deal like Leon? The man would have killed for her, he was that devoted."

"But—"

"Me, I wouldn't look a gift horse in the mouth." She took another puff of her cigarette and tossed it toward the gutter.

"A lot of people would be happy with what she had. Shit, with less than she had."

"Did you tell her that?"

Nina sighed and ran her hands through her aubergine hair. "She expected too much from people, too much from life."

"You told her that, too?"

She adjusted herself on the step, then changed her mind and stood.

"She took offense?"

"I couldn't say. I got a new job around then and Sally decided to take an extra course."

"So you were both short on time?"

"Exactly."

"Was this around the time Sally disappeared?"

"You're not—"

"No, no, no. Of course not."

"I was only trying to help her see how lucky she was. Isn't that what friends do?"

I nodded and thanked her for her help.

"How long will you keep trying?" she asked. "The police . . ." She didn't finish, just stood there shaking her head, her lips pruned up, a line between her eyes.

"Until Leon tells me to stop," I told her.

"Are you married?" she asked, bending toward me and whispering.

"No," I said.

Pointing at me now. "See. Exactly my point."

It was two o'clock. Bechman's office would be open already, the waiting room full of children. I wanted to get there later, after the kids had left but while Ms. Peach was still there. I folded the copy of Madison's drawing, tucked it back into my tote and headed home to formulate a plan for getting what I was after.

But on the way, as I was passing the Bleecker Street playground, a little kid coming down the slide on his belly, going face-first into the sand, too stunned to cry once he landed, it occurred to me that not every idea was a good one. Ms. Peach? What did I think she would do, let me see the original files, see if the doctor had changed his note-taking style, see if perhaps there were notes removed before Leon was given the copy of Madison's records I now had in my bag? I had no legal standing, not even a PI license. But what good would that do in this case? Even if I were related to Madison, all I'd be entitled to is exactly what I had—a copy of Madison's medical records, not a look-see at the original file.

I could take Dashiell with me. I could bully my way in, have Dashiell keep her in one place, find the file and check it out. I could take a gun, too, a baseball bat, a meat cleaver. What was I thinking? I couldn't threaten Ms. Peach on the slim chance she had doctored the doctor's notes. Because if she hadn't, or even if she had, threatening her could land me in jail, and that was not going to help Madison at all. Helping Madison was the point. It had been the point from day one, I thought, passing Mama Buddha, smelling black bean sauce as I passed the open kitchen door, a small man in an apron, his foot against the wall, catching a smoke in the crisp fall air. There had to be another way to get what I was after. There had to be a better way.

There was always Hyram Willet, the doctor who seemed to own the practice, or if not the practice, at least the building that housed it. And while there was no way short of dynamite that I could get into the medical office from the street, check the records in privacy and get back out undetected, Dr. Willet, I was sure, could get there from his apartment. If I told him my theory, would Dr. Willet invite me into his house, take me down to the office, give me free run of the files, Dr. Willet who was fighting tooth and nail to prevent the detectives from doing the very same thing? I didn't think so.

There was one other doctor at the practice, Laura Edelstein, a pediatrician. In fact, I thought I'd seen her name on the copy of Madison's records. I was around the corner from home. I checked the time—not quite two-thirty. If the office was open at all, that meant that either Dr. Willet or Dr. Edelstein was working. Standing outside the gate to my cottage, I dialed the office, getting even luckier than I'd hoped I would. Ms. Peach was taking or making a call. My call went through to voice mail, but before I was invited to leave a message, I got to hear their message, giving me the office hours for both Willet and Edelstein. Dr. Laura, it said after the general message, was in Monday through Thursday afternoons from one to five.

For the moment, as I unlocked the gate and unclipped Dashiell's leash, all my hopes were on Dr. Laura.

CHAPTER 30

I stood across the street from Dr. Bech-
man's office waiting for the last patient to leave, a little boy
holding some sort of robot, refusing to let his mother take
his free hand.

"You know you have to hold a grown-up's hand to cross
the street, Jeffrey," she said as I crossed the street. Then,
"What do you suggest?"

I could see Ms. Peach in the waiting room, picking up
toys and books and putting them back where they belonged,
bringing order back to her world. Dr. Edelstein would be returning phone calls. I decided to go into the park on the odd
chance that Ms. Peach would be leaving the office first.

I sat on a bench facing north, Dashiell up on the bench
next to me. I could see the brownstone that housed the doctors' offices, the gate closed, no one coming out yet. Back at
home, I'd pulled out Madison's records again, checking
them carefully, line by line. I had seen Laura Edelstein's
name there, but only on the top of the letterhead, all three
names still there. No one had thought to have new stationery
made. Perhaps they were waiting for someone to buy Bechman's practice. Perhaps they were trying to keep expenses
down, avoid the cost of interim stationery. Whatever the rea-

son, Ms. Peach had used the old letterhead. Some people did that with Christmas cards after one spouse dies inconveniently close to the holidays, crossing out the dead person's name and sending the cards anyway. Merry Christmas!

I was hoping that it was Dr. Edelstein who had referred Madison to Dr. Bechman. If not, there'd be less of a chance I could persuade her to help me. But then I thought of another possible connection, perhaps an even stronger one. I pulled out my cell phone and made a call, got my answer, then waited some more.

Dr. Edelstein was at the gate now, opening the latch, closing it carefully behind her, a plain-looking woman with a long nose, pale skin, dark brown hair pulled back in a ponytail. She was a big woman, taller than average and with a weight that fell somewhere on the high side of normal on those charts doctors always had in their offices, which meant by New York standards, she was on the heavy side. Hell, by New York standards, where sizes 4 and 6 were considered a medium, Olive Oyl was on the heavy side.

She headed east, and I did so as well, walking inside the park until I got to an exit. For a while, I stayed on the opposite side of the street, but when we came to Fifth Avenue and she turned left, I left the park, crossed the street and caught up with her.

"Dr. Edelstein?"

She turned, looked at me, then looked down at Dashiell. "Yes."

"I understand you were at the medical practice around the corner when Celia Abele worked there."

She stepped back. "What is this about?"

"And that you are JoAnn's pediatrician, but you see her at your other office, at the hospital. Is that correct?"

"Who are you? What is it you . . . ?"

"You heard about Celia, of course."

Dr. Edelstein blinked. I didn't wait for more.

"Charles doesn't think that Celia committed suicide, Doctor, and neither do I. I think her death is connected to the death of Eric Bechman."

"Of course it is."

I shook my head. "Not in the way you think. It wasn't grief that killed Celia."

I watched the information play across her face, waited as she took another step back, another step away from me.

"If you could only give me ten minutes to explain."

"Who are you? What is your connection to Celia and Eric?"

"My name is Rachel Alexander," I told her. "I'm a private investigator, hired by Leon Spector, whose daughter, Madison—"

She began to shake her head. "I can't talk to you. I can't help you with this."

"Madison didn't kill Dr. Bechman. If we can sit down somewhere, I can explain. I can show you—"

"I have to get home. I'm expected . . ." Making a point of checking her watch.

"Do you have children, Dr. Edelstein?" Knowing she did, a girl of six. Ellie. When I saw the look on Dr. Edelstein's face, I lifted one hand. "I'm not here to threaten you, Doctor. Far from it. It's just that since you have a child, too, a daughter, you must understand how Charles Abele feels, how Leon Spector feels."

"Of course I understand. What does that have to do with anything?"

"I have good reason to believe that Madison didn't murder her doctor. And she surely didn't murder Celia. If I'm right, and let's assume for the moment that I am, someone else did. Someone else killed them both."

She had finally stopped walking. She was standing there, holding her jacket tight around her body, just staring at me, wondering what the hell was happening to her orderly life. Well, who hadn't ever worried about that? No one I knew. And wasn't that the point I was trying to make, that Leon's and Charles's lives had been torn to shreds, not just once either. If she was going to help me, she'd have to understand that, no matter what it took.

"Who?" she said.

"I don't know yet. That's why I need your help."

"You said you could show me something," she said. "Show me what?"

I had Madison's drawing in my jacket pocket, the copy of her medical records as well. I took the drawing out first, unfolding it, handing it to Dr. Edelstein. "This is a copy of the drawing that was found on Dr. Bechman's desk a few hours after he was murdered."

She began to shake her head.

"I know it looks different. As you know, Madison doesn't speak. She stopped speaking shortly after her mother disappeared. I was hired to find her mother—and I did."

Dr. Edelstein's mouth opened, but I held up my hand before she had the chance to speak.

"Mr. Spector thought if I could find his missing wife and bring her home, that if she had her mother back, Madison would speak again, that she would tell us whether or not she had committed this terrible crime. But her mother won't come back." I shook my head. "Wishes won't change that. She won't."

Try as I did to stop it, I felt my eyes getting wet. I felt a tear fall.

"I've been trying, with Dashiell's help," looking down at him, then back at her, streams of people passing us going both ways, the world leaving work and going home for the evening,

"I've been trying to get through to her, to Madison, to connect with her, to show her that she could trust me, and I think I did, somewhat, because she was willing, just today, to tell me what this drawing meant by finishing it."

Dr. Edelstein looked down at the drawing in her hand, then back up at me.

"You saw the original, didn't you?"

"Yes, of course."

"So you can see the difference."

"Yes, I can, but what does it mean?"

"The drawing wasn't a threat. Madison was telling Dr. Bechman that the effects of the Botox had broken her heart. He must have understood. He must have stopped her before she finished it, to tell her that, to say she didn't have to have the second injection."

"What is it you want from me, Ms. Alexander?"

"If whoever murdered Dr. Bechman also murdered Celia, the likelihood is that Celia was killed because she knew something, something someone didn't want me to find out." There were benches in the entranceway of Two Fifth Avenue, low bushes behind them, a place to wait for a friend who was coming down. "Can we sit a moment?" I asked her. "There's something else I'd like to show you."

Dr. Edelstein hesitated, then walked to the closest bench and sat. I sat near her, turning so that I could face her, pulling the copy of Madison's records out of my jacket pocket.

"I asked Mr. Spector to obtain a copy of Madison's medical records for me, something I could show her mother if I located her."

"Even with that . . . ?"

"She wouldn't look at them. But I'm hoping you will."

"She wouldn't look at them? At her own daughter's—"

"That's done and gone, Doctor. There's no use discussing

it because all the talk in the world is not going to make Sally come back," picturing her cabin, empty now, perhaps Roy's water bowl forgotten in the corner, a single shoe lying on its side in the closet.

She reached for the papers. "Of course I'm aware of her condition because of the—"

"It's not the diagnosis I want you to see. It's the form in which the notes are written."

"The form? You mean you can't read his handwriting?"

"No. It's not that. It's the spaces." I handed her the sheets. "As if something had been removed, whited out, and then the copy recopied."

"You mean a problem with the copying machine, part of the records missing?"

"Yes and no. I believe parts of the records are missing, but I don't think it's a problem with the copying machine."

"And what is it you think I can do for you, Ms. Alexander? Surely you don't think I can give a private investigator access to the medical records of one of the children who come to our practice." Stopping, shaking her head, one hand on her shoulder bag as if she suddenly thought I was planning to snatch it, that that's what this was all about.

"I'm aware that you can't do that. It would be against the law. But *you* could look at them, couldn't you? You could see if they've been altered."

Laura Edelstein held my eyes for what seemed like a very long time. Then she reached for the envelope with Madison's records in it, pulling the sheets out, opening them on her lap and beginning to read.

When she'd finished reading Madison's records, she folded them and put them back in the envelope. "If you'll just give me a moment to call home, we can go back to the office." Her face grim.

"No, we can't. I'm afraid that's not a good idea. The office—someone might be watching the office. I don't want to put you in danger."

"Then what do you have in mind?"

"Is there any way you can look at them tomorrow, by going in early or by somehow getting Ms. Peach out of the way?"

"Are you saying Louise Peach has something to do with Dr. Bechman's murder?"

"All I know is that Ms. Peach gave the records you have in your hand to Madison's father when he asked for a complete copy of her medical history with Dr. Bechman. Perhaps I'm wrong, Doctor. Perhaps they're accurate. But if they aren't . . ."

She shook her head. "I'm in the hospital before office hours, so I can't get there early. But I can get rid of Louise. I can send her out to fill a prescription for me. She won't be happy, but she'll go."

"Would that be an unusual thing to do, sending her out on an errand?"

"No, not really."

"And wouldn't you have the medication you need in the office? I thought doctors get free samples of everything."

"I'll be sure to come up with something we don't have on hand. I'm sure I can figure that out. Meanwhile, can I hold on to this?" Holding up the envelope I'd given her.

"Of course." I took out a business card and added my cell phone number. "You'll call me as soon as you know?"

"I will."

"Doctor, can you make a private call from the office, one no one else can listen in on?"

She stood but she didn't walk away. "I can," she said. "I can use my cell phone." Serious as a bad diagnosis, something you never want to hear, even for your worst enemy. "What if the files are identical? What if Louise Xeroxed what was in the file, as it was in the file, then what?"

I shook my head. "I tracked down Celia. I was hoping for another view of Madison. I was hoping for something more sympathetic, which is what I got. But I also got more than I'd bargained for. I got this cock-and-bull story of how Dr. Bechman was supporting his second family. You do know . . ."

"Yes," she said. "Of course. I didn't think what they did was right, but—"

"Not the point, Doctor. We all judge, but that's not the issue here. And all beside the point now. The issue is that he needed enough money to take care of Celia and JoAnn without it showing up on his taxes, forms his wife would be signing, too. Even if she's one of those unconscious women who has no idea what's going on financially in her own family, just having that information available in black and white was a poor idea. For example, had they ever split up, had a lawyer ever gotten hold of his tax forms," shaking my head, "that wasn't a trail he wanted to leave. If his wife did find out, he'd be finished in every way you can think of."

Dr. Edelstein sat down again.

"Celia said that Eric has this gig with an advertising company where he ran focus groups for them to determine things in advance about new drugs before they went on the market, what kind of wording would make people feel most confident, what color the pills should be, that kind of stuff. She said they paid him off the books, that they paid him in cash."

I could see by the expression on her face that she didn't buy the story either.

"Unlikely," I said. "That's what I thought, too. Oh, I'm sure the drug companies hire advertising firms and I'm sure those firms run focus groups and do everything they can to sell us, the public, on their new products, even in those circumstances where the need for such a product didn't previously exist. They're very good at that and the American public is endlessly gullible. But to pay enough money to support a family and do that off the books?" I shook my head. "That I can't imagine. And even if I could, Doctor, just the same way when you hear a few symptoms, you can list the rest of them, just the same way the traffic cop shakes his head when you tell him you were only speeding because you were going downhill, that's the way I can tell when someone's spinning out a story, making it up as they go along. The voice goes up in register, ever so slightly, but I can hear it. Eye contact diminishes. And most people talk faster, even louder, once they're on a roll, particularly if they think you're buying what they're selling."

"Is that why you think she was killed, because she knew the truth and she might tell it one day?"

I nodded.

"And you think the truth, whatever Eric was doing to raise the money he needed, you think that is connected to what may have been removed from Madison's records?"

"I do, Doctor."

"Some kind of insurance fraud?"

"I can't answer your question until you call me tomorrow."

She stood. Again she didn't leave. I stood, too, and reached for her free hand.

"Please be careful, Doctor. Someone was willing to let a child take the fall for stabbing her doctor in the heart. Someone killed a second time to keep a secret."

"Then you don't know?"

"Know what?"

"The needle used to inject Botox into the muscles just beneath the surface of the skin is barely an inch long."

"So it couldn't reach the heart?"

"There's more than one way to reach the heart, Ms. Alexander."

"I read that Botox could prove fatal if it paralyzed the respiratory muscles. Is that what happened?"

She shook her head. "He died too quickly for it to have been any sort of paralysis from the Botox."

"Anaphylactic shock?"

She nodded. "His body shut down in a matter of seconds."

"Did he know about the allergy?"

"I have no reason to think he did."

"But then whoever killed him couldn't have known either."

"We can assume that."

"Which means his death was an accident?"

"Of sorts," she said. She took the copy of Madison's medical records and slipped them into the outside pocket of her purse, handing me the finished drawing, a heart broken in two.

"But Celia's death wasn't," I said. "And it wasn't suicide. It was murder." I folded Madison's drawing and put it into my pocket. "We may never know what was in the heart of the killer the first time, Doctor. We may never know his or her intent. It might have been, as the police suggest, something that happened in the heat of the moment, a mindless explosion of rage that left Bechman dead for a reason no one could have guessed. But what happened to Celia was another story. That death was clearly premeditated, coldly planned and heartlessly executed."

"And it left that poor little girl without a mother," she said. "Things like that shouldn't happen, not ever."

"I couldn't agree more," I said, thinking about two little girls, not one. "I'll wait for your call."

She reached out and touched my arm, then turned away and headed home.

I avoided the park on the way home. I was mostly thinking about what Dr. Edelstein was going to find. It was hard to think about anything else. But something else was trying to get my attention, something I had seen that had invaded my subconscious. Walking along the dark side streets of the Village, I tried to play it out of hiding, the way you would tease a cat out from under the bed with a feather on the end of a string. But whatever it was, it stayed beyond reach, safely hidden in the dark.

CHAPTER 31

There was no use waiting around the house all morning for a call that wouldn't come until afternoon. I took Dashiell for a long walk, then headed for the Y to swim. Would I ever stop thinking of Madison's room when I was swimming, of the way Sally had painted the walls in the hope that the underwater scene would calm her daughter, as if that were all it took, all the kid needed? She did it for Madison, that's what I'd been told. Perhaps that wasn't so. Perhaps she'd painted her daughter's room that way in an effort to stay, as a way of trying to bring the world she needed to the place where she was. And then like a siren, all that blue called to her, pulling her away from Madison and Leon, drawing her to a more comfortable place, a world of fish and coral and rocks, a world without people, like the one on her daughter's walls.

My head in the water, my arms reaching out in front of me, then driving the water back, I was in that world, too. No matter that there was someone swimming laps in the next lane, that in other parts of the Y people were walking on treadmills, riding stationary bicycles, doing yoga, step aerobics, ballet. All I could see was the pale blue of the pool's water as if I were alone in the world.

Was that what Sally was after? Was that what she had achieved? No emotional attachments, a job where strangers came and went, no one staying long enough to make things personal. And when she wasn't working, a world away, apart, a cool, quiet place where she never had to tell a needy child to be quiet, a lonely husband that she had to study, where she never had to tell her family that she didn't love them, at least not enough, that she never had and never would.

Where had she gone? I wondered. Someplace else where she could slip under the radar, work off the books, spend her time reading and swimming. I thought of the dog, Roy, waiting on the shore, a demanding breed, but nothing compared to the demands of family, nothing compared to the demands Madison must have made on her. Sally could meet Roy's demands, a walk in the morning, a swim in the afternoon, a game of fetch when the air cooled down at night. Perhaps he slept on the foot of the bed, too, and that might have been all she needed, all she wanted, all she could handle.

Floating on my back at the end of my time in the pool, I thought about the people Dashiell and I did pet therapy with. Some of them had come not to trust another human. But they trusted Dashiell. They trusted a dog's nonjudgmental attitude. They felt safe with him. And for some, that safety allowed them, over time, rapport with the person who had brought the dog. Sally had stopped, it seemed with Roy, Roy who would never ask a question that would tear her to shreds, Roy who would never ask for more than she could give.

I picked up lunch on the way home. Then, sitting at my desk, sharing my sushi with Dashiell, I began to go over all my notes again, knowing that sometimes what you were looking for ended up being right under your nose all along.

I had started a time line for Sally's disappearance, at least for the one when Paul spirited her away from the meat market in his truck. I put that in a folder. It was no longer the point. I put the notes from the meeting with Jim there as well, and the printouts of the other letters I'd gotten by posting Sally's name on Classmates.com.

I had notes from speaking to neighbors in Leon and Madison's building, Nancy Goodman and Ted Fowler. I hadn't made notes after talking to Nina. I didn't think anything she had to say would help me help Madison. I put all those notes away, too.

That's when I noticed the contact sheets Leon had given me, pictures of Dashiell from the time I was away. I checked the time. I wouldn't hear from Dr. Edelstein for at least another hour, probably much longer, so I took out my loupe and started to look at pictures of Dash, Dash at the waterfront, Dash at the dog run, Dash with Madison. I guess Madison was learning how to use his camera, too, because there were even shots of Dash with Leon. I thought by now the whole world had gone digital, but not Leon. Leon was out of step. He probably always was. Leon and Sally. What a pair.

I went downstairs to make a cup of tea, thinking about the pictures, thinking that Dash had given Leon and Madison something to do together, thinking that that was a good thing; it was exactly what they needed.

As I waited for the kettle to boil something occurred to me, that when Ms. Peach went out, I might be invited in, that if Dr. Edelstein found something telling, she might want me to see it, too. Or she might ask me to come in for just a moment to pick up a real copy of Madison's records. After all, the letter from Leon was in the file, and he had given me the first set, the set where I thought things were missing. Why not just give me the corrected version? We hadn't planned that part. But why not be on hand, just in case?

I shut off the stove, grabbed my jacket and picked up Dashiell's leash. If I was at the dog run when I got the doctor's call, I could be at the office in a minute, gone just as quickly, long before Ms. Peach got back. But if I was home when she called, I wouldn't be able to get in and out without the chance that Ms. Peach would see me. In fact, something else occurred to me. Binoculars might look funny at the dog run, but a camera wouldn't. I'd gone digital, too, but I still had my old Nikon with its telephoto lens. I ran back up to the office for the camera, slipped the loupe and the contact sheets I'd been looking at into the camera bag, stopped back in the kitchen to take a roll of film out of the refrigerator, just in case there was something I actually wanted to shoot, and headed for Washington Square Park.

There were eight dogs at the run when we arrived, seven playing, and a black pug lying on his master's coat, which had been spread out on one of the benches for just that purpose. I unhooked Dashiell's leash and watched him join another young male, telegraph his benign intentions with his rounded body language and then begin to wrestle. I chose a bench on the east side of the run, which seemed to have a partial view of the town house I would want to be watching later on, loaded the camera and checked out the view. And there to my surprise was Ms. Peach. She was on the path inside the park that was parallel to where Bechman's office was, and she was limping. She finally found a bench to her liking, the very same one where I'd been sitting just the day before, as if she, too, wanted to watch the entrance to the office where she worked.

Had she come early so that she'd have time to sit outdoors for a while before going in to work? Or was she just sitting for a minute because she was in pain? Perhaps she'd come in early to catch up on her paperwork. Or white out things on some other child's records.

Dr. Edelstein wouldn't be in. She said she was at the hospital in the morning. She wasn't due at this office for another forty-five minutes, assuming her appointments started when her hours did. This would be a good time for Ms. Peach to work, but to work at what, I wondered.

I panned the camera around, as if I wanted a picture of the Washington Square Arch, the people leaning over the fence and trying to get some dog's attention, the black pug still lying on his master's jacket, his front paws crossed, then back toward the bench where Ms. Peach sat in her white uniform, a navy sweater over it, enjoying the sunny day.

There was a homeless man coming up the path, heading toward Ms. Peach. His shoulders rounded forward, his head low, the upper part of his face covered by a baseball cap pulled down over his brow, the lower part by an untrimmed beard, the sign of a man who hadn't seen the inside of a barbershop in way too long. When he got to where she was sitting, he reached out one hand. He was wearing those woolen gloves where the tips of the fingers stick out, the kind the people who sold newspapers in those little outdoor kiosks wore because they keep your hands warm but you can still count money and make change.

When she reached into her bag, I thought she was about to give him money. Don't do it, I thought. He sees your money, he might grab it all and take off, though this one didn't look like he could run any faster than Ms. Peach. But he must have asked for a cigarette, because a moment later I saw him bending toward her, then standing up again, blowing a plume of smoke off to the side. I saw the smoke coming up from where Ms. Peach sat, too.

He bent close again, perhaps to thank her, then turned and walked back the way he'd come, an old sack in one hand, perhaps holding whatever little he owned. He headed toward the southwest corner of the park where the chess players were at it, playing against the clock, feet tapping nervously under the tables as they did. When I looked back to where Ms. Peach had been sitting, the bench was empty. I saw her across the street, an umbrella in one hand, a lady who liked to be prepared. She opened the gate, pulled it closed behind her and stepped down into the entranceway. I couldn't see much after that. There were bushes in the way obscuring my view. I thought I'd let Dashiell play a little longer—there was nothing I could do right now anyway—and then move closer, to where I could see Dr. Edelstein get to the office, to where I'd be able to see Ms. Peach leave.

CHAPTER 32

I was sitting where Ms. Peach had been when my phone rang.

"What medications does Madison take?" It was Dr. Edelstein, talking fast.

"None," I told her.

"You're sure?"

"As sure as I can be. I asked her father. That's what he told me. I also checked their medicine cabinet. And Madison stayed at my house one night. Leon didn't send any meds with her. The whole point of the Botox was that there was nothing else that could do the job, nothing else that was going to help her. The Botox was supposed to be a miracle. It was supposed to—"

"What about early on? What about right after her diagnosis? Did Mr. Spector mention her trying any antidepressants, any antianxiety medication, anything like that? Did he mention risperidone or pimozide? What about Prozac?"

"Why are you asking me, Doctor? You have her records, don't you?"

"Those, at least, I could understand."

"What did you find?"

"Where are you?" she asked.

"In the park. Right across the street from the office. Do you want me to come in?"

"No, no, don't do that. Do you have a pen with you?"

"Yes." Reaching into the camera bag, finding a grease pencil, pulling out the contact sheets so that I could write on the back of them.

"Good," breathless, "then write this down. In Madison's file, Oxycontin, Percocet, Percodan, and six times, injections of morphine sulfate."

"No way."

"I believe you're correct about that, Ms. Alexander. I checked ten other files, briefly. I don't want to be doing this when Ms. Peach returns."

"And?"

"The same."

"No matter what the child's diagnosis was?"

"That's correct."

"I guess we know how Dr. Bechman was supporting Celia and JoAnn. And we know that Ms. Peach was involved somehow, because if not, she wouldn't have altered the files."

"Had I not seen this with my own eyes, there's no way I would believe he . . ." Now silence on the line.

"Would have sold prescriptions for narcotics to take care of his second family?"

"Yes. He was . . ." She stopped again, perhaps thinking about the fact that he *had* a second family.

"The handwriting? It's definitely his?" Knowing it was. Had someone else written the notes, he would have seen them at the following visit. Besides, there were all those forms to file when narcotics were prescribed. He would have had to have done those as well.

"Yes. His. There's no doubt about it."

"And of course Celia knew." Going over the time line in

my head now. "In fact, she was killed after I spoke to Ms. Peach about how Dr. Bechman was supporting Celia and JoAnn. Once she knew Celia was talking to me, that I'd found her, there was no way she could take the chance that Celia might decide to come clean."

"You're saying that Louise, Ms. Peach, killed Celia?" Panic in her voice now.

"I don't know. I don't know if she was doing this by herself or with—"

"I don't want her back here. I can't just leave, I have children coming. But I have a daughter, too, and she . . ." I heard papers rustling, a chair scraping. "I can't take the chance."

"She doesn't know you know anything. And there'll be people in the office."

The line was still open, but there was no response, long enough for me to wonder if I had suggested the right thing. Surely Ms. Peach couldn't think she could get away with killing a second doctor in the office and not have the finger point to her. It couldn't be another suicide. And she wouldn't be able to make it look as if Madison had done it. Who would she blame it on this time, another child? A door left unlocked? All too hinky. No, Laura Edelstein wasn't in danger at work, but if she thought she was, if she acted nervous or jittery, Peach would know something was up. Unless I came up with something fast, this wasn't going to work.

"Doctor?"

"She'll be back soon. I have to put everything away. I have to make sure I leave things exactly as I found them."

"I have an idea, a way to make sure you're perfectly safe."

"Yes?"

For the next minute or so, I talked and Dr. Edelstein listened.

"As for the papers," I said finally, "don't rush. Take your

time and get it right. As I told you, I'm right here, right across the street. I can give you a few more minutes. When I see her coming, I'll make an excuse to talk to her."

I heard her sigh. "Five minutes more," she said. "That's all I need."

"When is the next patient due?"

"Not for another twenty minutes."

"Good. Because I was wondering if you could talk to Dr. Willet and tell him what you found. I was hoping you could get him to change his stand on protecting the patients' privacy. The detectives on the case need to see these files, perhaps, I don't know if you can arrange it that way, with the names blocked. But that's the next step and it should be taken right away."

"I'll take care of it," she said. "But I'd rather do that when I'm out of the office."

"Can you reach him this evening?"

"Yes, I can. I will." Sounding strong now, determined.

"Are you sure you're okay with this?" I asked. "Because if you need me to—"

"Yes, thanks to you, Ms. Alexander. I'm just fine now. Better than fine. I know exactly what to do. There won't be a problem."

"Then I'll talk to you very soon," I said, but she'd already hung up. Just in time, too, because Dashiell stood, looking toward the southwest corner of the park, and there was Ms. Peach, coming not from around the corner as I expected, but cutting through the park, a small bag in one hand, the other on the strap of her shoulder bag. She was walking slowly, still limping I was happy to see, bending now to rub one of her knees. Perhaps it was arthritis, acting up because there was rain in the forecast. Wasn't that why she'd taken her umbrella to work? But she needed more than an umbrella to protect her knees, some glucosamine with MSM on a daily basis, perhaps Celebrex, or when the pain was really bad, something stronger. No problem, at least until a few weeks ago. For a while there, apparently, Ms. Peach had been able to get whatever it was she needed, for a price.

But the great majority, if not all, of the drugs carefully recorded in the patient files, as required by law, weren't for Ms. Peach's personal use. There was no way she could have paid Dr. Bechman for all those prescriptions unless she was reselling them and doing so for much more money. And money, it was clear, was the name of the game, cash for Dr. Bechman, a nice stash for Ms. Peach, perhaps for her old age.

In fact, lucky lady, she worked right across the street from a ready clientele. There wasn't a soul alive who didn't know that Washington Square Park was the Kmart of the downtown illegal drug trade. And for those who didn't know where to sit to signal their desire and willingness to self-medicate life's pain for cash rolled up and stuffed into a film canister or a cigarette pack, say, five minutes of observation would give them the location, on the wall just behind the chess players, one addiction abutting the next, one that would keep you out even when the weather was sending more sensible people rushing to get home, the other a little more serious, the other one people killed for, or in some cases, got killed for.

Ms. Peach was going slowly, stopping every few steps to rest her knee. Putting the camera bag and the contact sheets down on the bench, careful to put the sheets picture side up, I stood so that she'd see me, waving her over, waiting for her to approach before sitting again. It was a little out of her way, but perhaps she was no more anxious to get back to the office than Dr. Edelstein was to have her back there.

"Ms. Peach," I said. "Just the lady I was hoping to see."

She was frowning, less than delighted to see me, but she looked hopefully toward the bench.

"Are you having a problem?" I asked, mustering all the faux concern I could on a moment's notice. "Here, sit down. You look as if you could use a moment to rest."

"It's my knees," she said.

I looked up at the sky. "They predicted rain," as if her knees hadn't made the same forecast. "Is there anything I can do to help?"

She frowned again. "No, I just need to sit a minute." She checked her watch. "The next patient's not due until two and they're always late anyway. You'd think for a *doctor's* appointment, they could manage to get somewhere on time." Shaking her head at the lack of consideration some people had. "What is it you wanted to see me about?" Frowning again, figuring it was me, it couldn't be anything good.

I slid the camera bag over to make room for her. "It's about Madison," I said, winging it as I went along, the way Celia had when she told me how Dr. Bechman earned the money to support his second family. "Mr. Spector was wondering if another pediatric neurologist would be taking over the practice," I said, congratulating myself on the neutral save, "or if you are recommending someone at another practice." I waited a moment, but she was rubbing her knee again, not paying all that much attention to what I was saying. "I told him I was taking the dog to the run," I told her, pointing to the other side of the park, "and that I'd drop by and ask."

"They're still in the talking stage," she said. "Why? Does Madison need an appointment right away? Has something changed?"

I shook my head. "Not a damn thing. She's still got the tics. And she's still not talking." Thinking I needed some damage control now. "The shrink thinks she probably never will." Leaning toward her, just our little secret.

"That's too bad," she said, but I thought I saw a little glimmer of a smile. "And the mother? Any luck there?"

I shook my head. "Turned out to be a dead end. Or rather, a bunch of dead ends."

"I'm not surprised," she said. "After all, the police must have done everything they could at the time she disappeared and *they* couldn't find her. Perhaps she just didn't want to be found."

"We don't even know if she's still alive, Ms. Peach, and now it appears we never will." I checked my watch. It was time to let her go, but I thought I'd go for an extra few minutes, just in case.

"The child must have taken it very hard, your failure to bring her mother back." She shook her head. "I imagine this will drive her even further into herself, don't you?"

I nodded.

"Well, I guess it's time to go. Please tell Mr. Spector that if he needs a referral, he can call me during office hours. And if he can wait, we should know more within a couple of weeks."

"Thanks. I'll tell him." Then pointing to the little bag. "Something for your knees?"

"This? Why, no. It's something for Dr. Edelstein."

"Oh, too bad. Pain like that," shaking my head, "you should be taking something. You shouldn't have to suffer like that. No one should."

She pushed off the bench. I watched her make her way down the path that led out of the park, then wait for a small van to pass before crossing the street. She moved slowly, stopping two more times to take weight off her left knee before finally unlatching the low gate, stepping carefully down the steps and then disappearing behind the iron gate that led under the main staircase.

I picked up the contact sheets again, looking at the list of drugs. I was sure all the requisite paperwork was in the files, too, everything in triplicate whenever a controlled substance was prescribed. Clever, I thought, everything appearing to be on the up-and-up when it was anything but.

Before putting the sheets away, I flipped them over, looking at the pictures of Dashiell and then seeing something else. The earliest pictures on the contact sheets were not of Dash. They were of this end of the park. It appeared that Leon had taken pictures when he got out of Bechman's office after picking up the copies of Madison's records, or perhaps on the way in to get them. Because that's what I was looking at, the very bench where I was sitting, a view of the arch, the corner of the park where Ms. Peach had just been, even a view straight west, as if he stood in the middle of the street to take it.

There was a homeless man on the corner in that last one. Is that why he took the picture, the man the point of it against the background of opulent buildings? There was something familiar about him, not the face, which I couldn't really see without a loupe, something about his hands I thought. No, maybe it was something else, not the hands. Maybe it was the way he held his legs, toes pointing out Charlie Chaplin style. Or his shoulders, not exactly hunched, but slightly forward. Whatever it was, I couldn't put my finger on it. Perhaps he was just one of the men I often saw in the park, no other place to call home. They hung around the chess players, slept on the benches, tried to get the dogs to come over to the fence of the dog run and lick their filthy hands.

I put the sheets away and slipped the strap of the bag over my shoulder. I could see Ms. Peach through the window, on the phone. And then I saw the next patient coming down the block. The mother was tugging her along, as if it might be the child's fault that they were fifteen minutes late. The little girl was crying, even before getting her booster shots or whatever other scary thing she was there for. As I got up to leave, I saw the mother pull the child closer and take her by the shoulders in a not so benign way. "Do you have to always make a scene, Sylvia?" she asked. Then, without waiting for an answer, she opened the gate and pulled the little girl along behind her.

CHAPTER 33

I'd just gotten home when it occurred to me that even on a day without rain in the forecast, Ms. Peach would have had a difficult time getting up the steps to Celia's apartment. Too difficult, I thought. Even if she made it, I'd be hard pressed to imagine her a serious threat to anyone but herself.

The more I thought about it, the more ridiculous the image became. It's not that older women were not credible as murderers. Even after I figured out that Ms. Peach could have self-medicated her pain, rested on the stairs, brandished a gun when she got to Celia's apartment, there was something still off.

I could see her as the go-between. I could even imagine how it might have started, Bechman giving her something really strong on a day her pain seemed unbearable, Ms. Peach commenting, in an offhand way, that the stuff was so good, that it helped so much, she bet people would buy it by the truckload, if only they could. Or perhaps she'd said the stuff was so good she could sell it by the truckload. Perhaps he'd said, "If only." Perhaps they'd had a heart-to-heart about his particular financial need, not that he didn't make enough money, if one could imagine such a thing in this day and age as enough money, but that he needed money from an untraceable source, money he could funnel to Celia without his wife having a way to catch on. He loved his wife, he might have said. But then there was Celia, and JoAnn, his precious JoAnn, Ms. Peach listening, paying good attention, her mind at work.

And maybe that sat in the air between them, his need, her willingness and interest, both of them smart enough to put two and two together.

Maybe he brought it up next. Maybe not. Maybe someone else, someone who could sit on a bench in the park, his persona all the advertising his drug business needed. After all, who in his right mind would think to approach Ms. Peach to buy illegal drugs?

No, there had to be someone else, even to keep Ms. Peach squeaky clean enough to keep her job. She was only the facilitator, because even a doctor with two families, for God's sake, wouldn't keep a drug pusher as his office nurse, would he?

Someone else. Someone who would fit in at the park. But who?

That's when I took the contact sheets back up to the office, turned on the light, moved it low over the sheets and took out the loupe. There was that homeless man standing on the corner, perhaps not the focus of Leon's picture, just a part of it, a part of the scene. A homeless man would fit in at the park. He'd blend in. He'd be invisible. Unless he sat behind the chess players, signaling he had something for sale.

The park was full of homeless men, men most people went out of their way not to notice. But what could any of them have to do with Ms. Peach?

I picked up the contact sheets again, holding the loupe over each picture, the ones taken outside Bechman's office, the ones at the dog run, hoping something would jump out at me, an insight, an answer, something that would tell me who Peach passed the prescriptions to.

But then I put the sheets down. What was I thinking? No way would Bechman have agreed to have the prescriptions sold in the park, to have his name right there in black and white in case of an arrest. In order to sell the drugs in the park, or anywhere else for that matter, someone would have to actually fill the prescriptions first. Someone would have had to take them to a drugstore, probably a different one each time, to pay for them, to sign for them.

Someone dressed well could have done that, filled a prescription for a child. Easy, since under no circumstances would the kid be doing it herself. And anyone could sign for the drugs, scribble a name down, any name. Even if the druggist asked for ID, not a problem in today's world. All you needed was a computer and a few minutes.

Not a homeless man.

Perhaps someone dressed like a homeless man. Someone pretending to be a homeless man. Someone pretending to be some kid's father, poor kid's croaking with pain, a kid who needs Oxycontin, Percocet, Tylenol with codeine, God knows what else. Someone dressed well enough to meet the doctor, unless he only met Ms. Peach, my mind spinning now, seeing how this could work, trying one way, then another.

I went back to the contact sheets again, sitting now, the lamp low over the thumbnail pictures, not looking at Dashiell, looking behind him, remembering the homeless men hanging over the fence, reaching out to the dogs. One brought a bag of biscuits once and came into the run, met by four of us when he opened the bag, told him that no food was allowed in the run because some dogs found the presence of food and competing predators inflammatory. But that wasn't all. No one who loved a dog enough to sit in the dog run every day so that the dog could get a little R & R beyond his walk was going to bet his dog's life on food from a stranger, especially a stranger who looked like a bum or worse, especially not in New York City, where paranoia was the norm.

I started from the top again, the man standing on the corner, the view beyond him toward Sixth Avenue. There was something familiar about him. Was it just that I'd looked at his picture so many times, or was it something else, something more important, something that was visible beyond the outfit?

And then I saw it. It was something about his posture, his stance. I took the grease pencil and marked the other shots where there were people in the background, this time looking only at the way they stood, the position of the head, the articulation of the limbs, something nagging at me, about the way they looked. And that's when I remembered another picture I'd seen, another man who seemed to have more flexibility than the rest of us, more grace, too. Or should I say not another man, the same man?

I turned on the computer and Googled his name. I was sure it would be there, even if it was only part of a cast list, hoping for more, scrolling down past the Web sites for the movies he'd been in, the cast list of a play, then finding one that had actors' bios and clicking on that, and there it was.

There was a list of the films he'd been in. It turns out I'd seen more than a few of them without ever registering his name or his face. And the list of Broadway shows, his agent's name and contact number, a couple of pictures, pictures where his posture was more familiar than the face because his face had been altered, disguised, to put him in character. And then I hit the jackpot, the personal information, the dance school where he'd trained, the fact that his mother had had a short career as a dancer and then taught dance when he was growing up. And finally, more than I had hoped for.

"Theo Fowler, born Franklin Theodore Peach in Zanesville, Ohio, in 1952, moved to New York City in 1971 where he began his career with small dance parts in Broadway and Off Broadway productions as well as character parts on stage, screen and television."

I looked back at the contact sheets. The makeup was so good he could have been all of the men, the one on the corner, the one outside the run, the one who appeared to be bumming a cigarette from Ms. Peach earlier that day. Or none of them. But whatever role he needed to play, he would have played it with everything he had, including his ability to disguise himself from head to toe, everything except the tell, a dancer's carriage, the precise way he moved and stood still as if he were posing. And those feet, as if he'd gotten so used to first position, it had become his default mode.

Ted, of all people. He'd been Sally's savior for a time, the person who offered her respite from her brooding husband and her demanding child. Now, it seemed, he was willing to let Sally's kid go down for a crime he committed. The co-operative neighbor, chatting me up to see what I knew, to find out if he was in danger, not once but twice.

I sat back and rethought the whole thing. Ms. Peach's younger brother. Or an older brother's son? His idea or hers?

His. Sally had told him Celia was leaving what seemed like the perfect job. Isn't that what Ted told me the first time we'd met? What was it Sally had said? Something about access to the doctor's drug samples, something about never having to feel your pain.

Where had Peach been working, I wondered, or had she been between jobs when Ted called her with his great idea, a good job for her, Oxycontin samples for him? And then what?

Had they hatched the rest together one night over drinks, Ted complaining about the diminishing roles available to an over-fifty second-rate dancer, Peach saying, you think you've got problems, wait until you hear what the doctor has gotten himself into, the woman who had the job before me, pregnant with his kid and having it, too. He not only needs money, she might have told him, going on about how it was worse than that, saying the money had to be cash, go solve that one. And so they did.

A perfect role for Ted. He could sell drugs on the set when he had a small part or a role in a commercial. He could sell in the park when he wasn't working. And when he showed up at this drugstore or that to fill a prescription for his daughter or his sister's kid or his niece or nephew, dressed for the part and playing the part, no problem. He might have told a story as he slid a prescription across the counter. "Poor kid, migraines," he could have said. "I didn't even know kids got them." Shaking his head at the unfairness of it all. The man loved to talk. You had to give him that. And expressing sympathy so believably would make him seem more like family. Who would question him, tears in his eyes, his voice breaking?

I could just picture the pharmacist leaning over the counter and saying, "Do you want to come back for this?" And Ted dipping his head, "No, I'll wait. Kid needs it ASAP." He might have worn a mustache and glasses one time, a wig with male-pattern balding the next. He might have dressed as a woman sometimes, carried a cane and limped at others. A different person each time, his singular talent.

But then a hard question came to mind. Why kill the goose that was laying the golden egg?

There was only one way to find out. I pulled out my cell phone. The doctor answered on the second ring.

"Yes?"

"It's Rachel. Mission accomplished?"

"Thanks to you."

"Now I need a favor," I told her. "I need you to make a phone call for me."

I told her what I needed, then went upstairs to get ready for my own next role, grabbed Dashiell's leash and headed out.

CHAPTER 34

There was no answer when I rang the bell. Even better. I waited for someone to come out, pretending to be searching for my key and having the door held open for me, security be damned. When I was inside, I walked down the hall to the right, to Ted's apartment, rang the bell on his door just to make sure, then proceeded to pick his lock, discovering that he was much less paranoid than most. Only one out of two had actually been locked. What arrogance. Did he think he was the only felon in town?

When I got inside, I let Dashiell off leash and went straight for the bedroom closets to see if I could find any of the outfits I thought he might have been wearing in Washington Square Park, finding nothing, then checking his makeup kit, a huge double-layered box. There were several beards and wigs in the bottom part of the box, but not the ones I'd seen him in, not the ones on the contact sheets. I found lots of hats on the shelf in the hall closet, gloves, too, but no fingerless ones, no beat-up boots, no hunter's orange jacket either. He probably never wore the same thing twice, dumped most of it on the way home. He surely wouldn't want to be seen here, where he lived, dressed like that.

I went to check the medicine cabinet next, thinking only

a fool would keep a stash of illegally procured drugs at home, and while I could call Ted a lot of things by now, a long list of things, fool wouldn't have made the list. Most of the drug dealers in Washington Square Park kept their stash nearby, but not on them. Some of them had runners to fetch the drugs when they made a sale. I wasn't sure how Ted operated, but since he'd been doing it without getting arrested for several years as far as I could tell, I was sure he'd figured out a secure place for his merchandise as well as the safest possible way to make the sale. What I hadn't counted on was his own need for drugs, a guy in his fifties, dancing professionally his whole adult life, he would have had a long history of injuries and pain, arthritis by now as well. He might have started out with Advil, some Celebrex now and then, or whatever the drug of choice for pain had been when it had started. There would have been something stronger when he was working, when he had to work despite his pain. He would have done what he had to, taken whatever was available, legal or not. And the need would have grown, more and more help needed to get the job done. Judging by the looks of his medicine cabinet, Theo Fowler was one of his own best customers.

I picked up the first orange container. Oxycontin. Patient's name, Lucy Grubman. And then another and another, Percodan for Matthew Tannen, Valium for Stacy Sussman, Oxycontin for Mark Redmond, each prescription from a different pharmacy, one all the way uptown. There were those little samples, too, the inspiration that started it all—pills to lift you up, pills to calm you down, better living through chemistry.

I remembered the first time I'd met Ted, how sleepy he'd looked when he answered the door, how absolutely perky a few moments later.

I opened the cabinet under the sink, Dashiell's big head poking in there before I got the chance to look. Rubber gloves, the thin kind that doctors use when they take blood or give a shot. My guess is that Ted wore those when he went to do business with Bechman, smart enough not to want to leave anything of himself behind, even long before the "accident."

I could have stayed in the apartment. I could have taken Ted up on his kind invitation to come back, make myself at home, relax, read a book. But relaxing was the last thing I had on my mind. So I hooked Dashiell's leash back onto his collar, took a quick look around to make sure everything was as I'd found it, and went out the way I'd come in, locking the door behind me. Instead of leaving the building, I walked back to where the stairs were, sitting on the bottom step, signaling Dash to lie down. Then I checked my watch, hoping it wouldn't be a long wait. After all, it was starting to get dark outside, and Ted had no reason to wait for Ms. Peach this afternoon. He'd already seen her in the park, bumming a cigarette in his old man costume, a nice touch, just in case anyone was looking.

He was at the glass door now, beardless and wearing an expensive white turtleneck sweater, black woolen trousers, a short black leather jacket, Armani or perhaps Valentino, probably the things he was carrying in the old sack he had with him when he'd stopped to talk to Ms. Peach. He had on loafers now, polished, new-looking, and a scarf tossed around his neck, his signature.

He saw me as soon as he entered the lobby, surprised, then smiling, a little too big for my money, but maybe he was in the habit of projecting to the cheap seats.

"No one home?" he asked, glancing up toward the second floor.

"Actually, I was waiting for you."

"Ah. I was hoping you'd take me up on my offer not to be a stranger."

He turned and headed for his door, unlocking it and holding the door open for me, following me in, slipping off the scarf and draping it over the carousel horse's neck.

"Come. Sit down. Make yourself at home. How about a glass of wine? I have a lovely Riesling chilling."

He disappeared into the kitchen. I sat on the white couch, Dashiell sitting next to my leg.

"Any news?" he asked.

"As a matter of fact, there is." Waiting to see if that would reel him back into the room, if he'd finished whatever it was he was doing in the kitchen.

I heard the refrigerator door close and then he poked his head back into the room.

"About Sally?" he asked. "Don't tell me you found her."

For the moment, I didn't think he was acting. I thought his curiosity was completely sincere.

"Actually, I did."

He came toward me and sat on the closest chair.

"After all these years. I can hardly believe it." Had he gotten paler, or was it all that white around us making it seem so?

"The wine, love." Nodding toward the kitchen. "We need to celebrate."

"Yes, of course," getting up, walking backwards for the first two steps, watching me the way Dashiell was watching him. I heard the pop of the cork. I heard him pouring the wine. I heard the floor in the hall creak once, the medicine cabinet open, then nothing for a moment. And then he was back, the bottle in the crook of an arm, a glass of wine in each hand, that million-dollar grin on his face. He must have been a waiter at some point, the way he juggled the open bottle, the full glasses, not spilling a drop. He put one glass in front of me, one in front of him, the bottle off to the side, everything done as precisely as if he were onstage, everything choreographed and just so.

I picked up my glass and held it toward him, waiting for him to lift his and make a toast. "To Sally," I said, my smile as big as his and twice as phony.

"To Sally," he repeated, taking a small sip. Then, "Tell me everything. Don't leave out a word."

I leaned forward to put down my glass, not paying attention to what I was doing, spilling some of my wine onto the coffee table.

I got up. "Oh, I'm so sorry. Let me get a paper towel . . ."

"No, no, I'll get it. Don't worry about it."

So I didn't. Instead, once he was out of sight, I took the little white packet out of my pocket and dropped its contents into my glass, watching the crushed pills dissolve in what was left of the liquid. I stirred the wine with one finger, then picked up the bottle and topped off the glass, picking it up, wiping off the bottom with my hand and putting Ted's glass in the middle of the spill. Never mix, never worry. The Riesling had a slightly darker color than most whites, a stronger, fruitier taste, too. It was one of my favorites, perfect for a variety of occasions.

Ted wiped the table with a damp cloth, then again with a dry one, wiping the bottom of the glass as I had a moment earlier.

"You found her?" Shaking his head. "You are amazing."

"To me," I said, lifting my glass.

He lifted his as well, touching it to mine. "To you," he said.

And we each took a sip. In truth, I took a sip. Ted was nervous. He took a swig.

"What's that smell?" I said, wrinkling up my nose.

He looked at the glass in his hand, then at mine, then back at me. "I don't . . ."

"Glue?" I watched his face to assess exactly how good an actor he was. Everything perfect, except the eyes.

"Oh," he said, "of course. You're right. The odor always lingers, no matter how carefully you wash. I got that commercial. They're always gluing things on me, a bigger nose, sideburns, a bald pate, something. I'm so used to it, I don't even smell it. Now, don't keep me in suspense any longer. Tell me how you found her."

I sighed, took another sip of wine. It wasn't the kind I bought, that was for sure. It probably cost three or four times as much. "This is wonderful," I told him.

He looked down at his glass, then took another few swallows. "Yes, one of my favorites," he said.

"Then we have that in common. At least, it would be if I could afford it."

"The commercial work," he said, leaning toward me, using a stage whisper, as if we were in a crowded restaurant and he wanted to be overheard by people at the next table. "It's not terribly dignified, but it does pay the rent." He sat back and took another sip. "So she's back?" he asked. "She's here?"

I wrinkled my nose again. "They use that glue for beards, too, right? Bushy eyebrows, mustaches, stuff like that?"

Frowning. "Yes." Nervous. Taking another drink.

"Here, let me top that off for you," I said. And like a good little boy, he drained the glass to make room for his refill. "A little extra hair here and there, a jacket that's too big, maybe a cap, some old beat-up boots, your own mother wouldn't know you, would she? So what's the deal, you just get the old clothes at Housing Works, then toss them before you come home, is that how it works? Maybe the Salvation Army. Their stuff is crappier. Cheaper, too. Am I right? You know, I've done a bit of this myself. I'd have to, wouldn't I, going undercover as a hooker, a homeless person, whatever's necessary to get the job done. It's kind of fun actually, fooling people like that. I find it quite a turn-on."

He stared for a moment, then he put down his glass.

"You didn't find her. You're just fucking around with me, aren't you?"

"I did find her. And I'm not just fucking around with you. I'm dead serious."

"The kid's talking, is that it?"

"Not exactly. But she is communicating nonetheless."

"What did she say?" Wondering perhaps if she'd seen him waiting across the street that last day, if she'd recognized him despite the getup.

I shook my head. "It's not what she said. It's what she drew. But you already saw that, Madison's completed drawing. It was on my lap when I was sitting out front and you were on your way to, what was it you said? A shoot? A commercial? Well, whatever. So now we both know that Madison was only expressing her feelings. She hadn't threatened Dr. Bechman at all. But you already knew that, didn't you?"

"What *are* you talking about?"

Leaning forward, I answered his question slowly so that he'd get the full meaning of what I was about to tell him. "Actually," I said, "by now, someone else is talking, someone who knows a lot more than Madison. Madison only knows what she didn't do. But Louise Peach knows *everything,* doesn't she, and by now, she's making it patently clear to the detectives who did what. By the way, what exactly is the connection, older sister, aunt, second cousin?"

Ted stood and took a step toward me. Dashiell stood, too, but Ted didn't notice, and by then, it no longer mattered. His legs, legs that usually worked so much harder and so much better than anyone else's, were no longer doing what he wanted them to.

"Sit down, Ted. It's all over," watching his left shin bang into the coffee table, then seeing him stumble backwards, ending up in exactly the same place he'd been before. "Answer my questions or don't, it's all the same at this point. Your cousin is already in custody and I'm sure she's giving everything a nice little spin." I paused to let that sink in.

"My aunt," he said, blinking as if something had gotten into both eyes at once, beginning to lose the battle with the double dose of Ambien I'd put in his drink, the same drug Dr. Edelstein had given Ms. Peach, saying it would help her with her bad knee.

"Ah, your father's sister. It's always good to see that family values are alive and well, even here in tough old New York."

He was trying to make a fist but his fingers weren't working any better than his legs had a moment earlier.

"I always thought that if you're going to get caught anyway, it's always a good idea to go down first, before your partner. That way, you can put the blame where it truly belongs. That way you get to be the one offered the deal for cooperating." I shrugged. "Better luck next time," I told him, even though it was too soon for Louise Peach to be cutting a deal. She was as dead to the world as Ted would soon be.

But when I looked at the smug expression on his face, Ted sure he was going to get the last laugh, I realized my mistake.

"She doesn't know," I said. "You never told her it was you who killed Bechman. She really does think it was Madison. And you never told her about shutting up Celia for good either. Damn. You had me fooled, your aunt fooled, too." I shook my head. "By the way, I hope whatever you put into my wine mixes well with what I dropped in." I watched my words register on his face, no acting this time, sure I got the last laugh after all.

I put my glass down and leaned toward him. "I bet you never thought it would go this far, when the whole thing started, did you? First Bechman and then Celia. That's how it is. You take that first step off the path and then in no time everything is out of control, out of *your* control, that is. And then one day you have to look at yourself in the mirror and you have to ask yourself, was it worth it?" I shook my head. "Was it, Ted?"

But he didn't answer me. He was barely moving now, his hands as heavy as lead, his legs like two sawn logs, his eyes getting glassy, his lids drooping the way one of Madison's did. I glanced back at the posters of Ted in costume, then pulled out my cell phone and dialed the precinct.

CHAPTER 35

It was eight-thirty by the time I went up-
stairs and knocked on Leon's door. If he was surprised to see
me, it didn't show.

"Where's Madison?" I asked, still standing in the doorway, waiting for Leon to move out of the way so that I could
go in.

"Reading in her room," he said.

I nodded.

"Do you want to see her?" he asked.

"Not just yet, Leon. I'd like to talk to you first."

He stood looking at me before standing aside so that I
could walk in. There was music coming from Madison's
room, the first time I'd heard that, the first time I'd heard her
do anything that made noise. I guess that's why she hadn't
heard me knock, and for now, though I'd avoided this conversation as long as I could, I was glad she hadn't heard me.
I was glad I could talk to Leon alone.

We walked into the living room. Leon sat on the daybed.
I sat on the love seat.

"I have a lot to tell you, Leon, maybe too much. I don't
know how much of it, how much of the detail, you're going
to want to hear, so I'm going to tell you the bottom line first.

I had a lead about Sally, something old. I had, I thought, the slimmest chance on earth of finding her, but I promised you I'd try my best and I always try to keep my promises. When you and Madison took care of Dashiell, I was in Florida looking for Sally."

He never moved while I spoke, not his hands, not his posture, not anything on his face. Somehow, I thought, it would have been easier if he looked heartbroken, if he showed hope, if I could see what he was feeling in any way. But that didn't happen. Not yet anyway.

"I found her," I said. "So at least we know she's alive."

"At least? What does that mean?"

"She's not going to come back, Leon. If I went back now, or you did, she wouldn't be there."

For a moment, we just sat there, Leon staring into his lap, me wishing I were somewhere else, anywhere but where I was.

Then I asked him how much he wanted to know, and he said he wanted to know everything. So I told him how Sally had left the house to walk the dog because she needed to get out and didn't want to be questioned. I told him how she kept walking, how she kept delaying going home. I told him about Paul, the truck driver, and about Sally going down to the Keys, to the place where she got pregnant with Madison. I told him, as best I could, about the life she was leading, a life with as few demands on her as was possible, a dead-end off-the-books job for subsistence, a library card in another name I was sure, the ocean across the road, her only companion the dog.

"She still has Roy?" he asked. And for a moment, Leon Spector came to life. She hadn't thrown everything of him away. At least she had his dog.

"She does," I said.

I took the digital camera out of my pocket and showed

him the pictures, Roy waiting at the shore, as focused as if he were holding a flock, and then Sally, her mask still on, Roy swimming out toward her.

"That's all?"

"I couldn't take more. It would have made her run sooner. I wanted, at least," there it was again, "to get the story for you. I thought you'd want to know what had happened." Thinking there was no way I could tell this that wouldn't be like driving a knife into his heart, no way at all.

But Leon was no longer looking at me. He was looking past me, toward the far end of the living room. I turned, and there was Madison.

She was wearing pajamas, but she had a baseball cap on and work boots that were several sizes too big for her feet. She wasn't wearing dark glasses and I could see that the droopy eyelid was a tiny bit less droopy, which was good, but the other eye was twitching like crazy and her cheeks were jumping as well. But the worst of it was her right arm, slightly bent and jerking, completely out of control.

I looked back at Leon. He seemed paralyzed. He'd just heard that his missing wife was alive and well and not returning. And his daughter had heard it as well.

When I saw that Leon wasn't moving, I got up and walked over to Madison, putting my arms around her and holding her close. I thought she might kick me, struggle to get away, punch me, bite me, but she didn't. She went limp, so much so that I thought if I let go, she'd land in a heap on the floor. So I didn't let go. I held tight, the arm jerking against my side, her eyelid twitching so hard that I could feel it through my shirt. And then Leon was there, too. I stepped back and he picked her up, as if she were a baby, carrying her back to the couch, sitting down with Madison on his lap, her head against his chest, her face hidden by her father's arms.

Leon was bending, whispering in her ear. Then her arm stopped moving, but she stayed with her face buried in his chest. When Leon looked at me again, I began to speak, quietly, calmly.

"You hired me to find Sally and bring her back in the hope that her return would inspire Madison to start speaking again so that she could tell us what happened that terrible day with Dr. Bechman. I know you both wanted more, and God knows, you deserve more, but the point was exonerating Madison," I said, "and that's done."

Now Madison turned, and they were both looking at me.

"It seems Dr. Bechman needed more money than he was making, and he needed it not to show up with his regular income. Through Ms. Peach, he was selling narcotics, painkillers, to Ms. Peach's nephew, who was then selling the drugs at work and in the park. My best guess is that Dr. Bechman had a change of heart, and when the nephew came for the next batch of prescriptions, that would have been shortly after Madison's last appointment, he told the nephew that it was all over, that he could no longer supply him with the prescriptions that would get him the drugs to sell. The nephew fell into a murderous rage and there on the desk was the hypodermic needle full of Botox that the doctor had had ready for Madison."

I stopped and waited, Madison blinking, Leon staring.

"I'm sorry to tell you that you know the person who did this," I said, telling them it was Ted and how he'd used his knowledge of makeup and costume to help him pull it off.

I didn't say much more. I didn't want to talk about Celia in front of Madison. I didn't want to talk about Jim at all, unless Leon pressed me sometime to find out how I knew about the place in Florida and what had happened there. I thought I'd said enough for now, perhaps too much for both of them to absorb. I thought that would take weeks, maybe months, until they made peace with everything they'd just learned.

When I stood up to go, it was so quiet for that moment, we could have been in Madame Tussauds wax museum. But then Leon thanked me and asked about the money. I told him the last few days were on the house, not what he'd hired me to do, and that I'd send a bill for the rest.

They both walked me to the door, but when I opened it to leave, Madison stepped into the hall, waiting for me and Dash, pulling the door closed behind her.

I waited, thinking she might say something now that there was no longer any point to keeping silent. But she didn't. She made no comment. She didn't go back inside either. She just stood in front of me looking up into my face. I put my arms around her and pulled her close.

"It wasn't because of anything you did," I whispered. "Or didn't do. It wasn't your fault."

After a long while, she stepped back, reaching behind her for the door, glancing down at Dashiell once before backing inside and closing it. I walked down the stairs to the first floor. There was yellow crime scene tape across Ted's door, forming an X.

I'd wanted to ask him what had happened that last day with Bechman. It obviously wasn't planned. You can't plan to kill someone by finding a hypodermic full of Botox to inject into his heart. The cops were right about one thing. The crime had happened in the heat of passion. Had the needle not been there, there would have been some other weapon of opportunity, a bookend, a letter opener, even bare hands, and the strength that comes from uncontainable rage. Whatever it was, whatever he'd picked up to use as a weapon, once he started, he would have had to finish the job. He was a careful man, not one to leave someone around who knew he'd committed a crime, someone who might one day need to soothe his own guilty mind by confessing all to the appropriate authorities.

Had Celia convinced Bechman that they had to manage their finances another way, a way that one day they wouldn't be ashamed to tell their daughter about? Or had it been the doctor's idea to stop cold? Had he simply asked himself what on earth he'd been thinking, getting involved in the illegal trafficking of controlled substances? Had he come to his senses, not knowing it was all too late, and had he wondered what I'd been wondering while waiting for the detectives to arrive, how he'd become the man he now was and what had happened to the man he once was? How he'd forgotten the oath he'd taken years before? In those last days, perhaps seeing clearly for the first time in years, had he asked himself the question that was now on my mind: what the hell had happened to *first do no harm*?

It was dark out, as dark as it ever gets in New York City. I felt a wave of sadness, the kind I felt when my own mother disappeared and I didn't know for what seemed like ages if I'd ever see her again. I didn't think it was true that time healed all wounds. But somehow most people found a way to live despite them.

I was halfway home when my phone rang.

"Alexander," I said.

There was no response, only eloquent silence. I was passing the Bleecker Street playground. I found an empty bench and sat, Dash hopping up next to me, my arm around him, the line open, the phone to my ear, waiting.

ACKNOWLEDGMENTS

Kudos and gratitude to Stephen Joubert for designing and maintaining my Web site and making it an informative and fun place to visit, *www.CarolLeaBenjamin.com,* just in case you find yourself in front of a computer one day with a little time on your hands.

Boundless gratitude is due my agent, Gail Hochman, who goes to the ends of the earth for her authors. And for careful attention to detail and taking good care of her authors—and this author's dog, Flash—my thanks to my editor, Sarah Durand, and to Diana Tynan in publicity.

And since even on bad days I always get great reviews from my dogs, I thank Eugene Sheninger for two of my three, Flash and Peep. I'm not sure whom to thank for Dexter. Someone left him on the side of the road when he was a wee lad and a few weeks later we found each other at the ASPCA and since then have been making sure no one would leave either of us on the side of the road again.

Turn the page for a glimpse of
THE HARD WAY,
the next suspenseful
Rachel Alexander Mystery
from Carol Lea Benjamin

I leaned against the wall opposite the mailboxes and closed my eyes. It was quiet in the tunnel, still cold but out of the snow. Dashiell had run ahead into the garden. I stayed right where I was, pulling off the dirty cap, the frayed scarf, the torn gloves, safe at home now, never, ever even *thinking* out of character until I was.

I'd concocted Eunice that first day, buying the old coat at the Salvation Army thrift shop, using the sneakers I'd worn when I'd painted my office, unraveling the ends of the fingers on an old pair of woolen gloves and digging under the snow for some loose dirt in the garden, rubbing it into my watch cap and old scarf. But the wardrobe, the stick, that was only the beginning. I needed a name, a cover story, a background. I needed to smell right, walk right, speak right. Most important, I needed to think right. Otherwise I might answer to the wrong name. Or not have a smooth answer for a telling question. I might give it all away with a gesture, a grimace, the wrong gait. One small slip was all it would take and I might end up as dead as my client's father.

It had started like any other case. There was always a death, always grieving, always the hope that, in the end, I'd be able to answer the questions I'd been asked. Who did this? Why did they do it?

It had been snowing that day, too, the day she'd called me. It was the first snow of winter, tiny flakes that came down almost too evenly to be real, not sticking when they hit the pavement. Dashiell, my pit bull, and I had just come back from his last walk of the day and I was pulling off my boots when the phone rang.

"I can't sleep," she'd said, not the first time a call for help started that way.

I understood the problem. There'd been a lot to stay up and worry about for the past few years. But Eleanor wasn't staying awake worrying about terrorism, about the war in Iraq. What was bothering her was something private, pain the rest of humanity didn't share with her.

"I can't stand the idea that the man who killed my father is still out there, that he could kill again."

"Can you tell me more?" I'd asked, taking the stairs two at a time to the second bedroom I used as an office, pulling over a pad and a pen.

"You probably saw it in the paper," she said. "He was on his way home from work and he was pushed onto the subway tracks as the train came barreling into the station."

"Gardner Redstone," I said, recalling the article. "I'm so sorry for your loss."

"So are the police. But . . ."

"They haven't been able to find the man?"

"No, they haven't."

"A homeless man, as I recall."

"Yes," she said.

"Described by witnesses."

She snorted into the phone. "Yes. He was. I'll tell you all about that when we meet," not waiting to see if I'd agree to help her, a lady who was used to getting what she wanted, at least when what she wanted was something money could buy.

I met her at her shop the following morning, GR Leather, on West Fourteenth Street, the new mecca of conspicuous consumption. I listened to the click of Eleanor's heels on the white marble floor as she led me to the stairway in back and up to her office on the second floor, facing north, looking over the art galleries, trendy restaurants and other chichi clothing stores that had replaced most of the wholesale meatpacking industry that had occupied the area between Gansevoort Street and West Fourteenth Street for as long as anyone could remember.

She sat behind a brushed-steel table that served as her desk, a well-put-together lady in her forties, designer suit, classic, tailored, stunning, probably Armani, the right jewelry, everything just so, even her ash blond hair, not blond and rumpled like the soldier's, blond from a bottle and not a strand out of place.

"He was on his way home from work," she said, "an ordinary day."

I was sitting across from her in a butter-colored leather chair, although I was sure there was a more expensive description of the color than lowly butter. Dashiell was lying next to my chair on the white wall-to-wall, carpeting so thick I almost felt I might lose my balance crossing the room.

"He took the subway. It was a point of honor with him."

"Meaning?"

"That this," her manicured hand indicating the office, including, I was sure, the lucrative shop beneath it, whatever was above it as well, "didn't change who he was."

Good one, I thought, wondering if poor people ever said that, that their tacky surroundings, their trailer, their empty beer cans, the car up on blocks or the tiny, dark apartment in a bad neighborhood, the one with the view of an air shaft and the pile of unpaid bills on the kitchen counter didn't change who they were.

"He started out forty-two years ago," she said, "making handbags, well-designed, good-quality leather bags that he sold to upscale department stores. His first shop was on Madison Avenue, then another on Fifth, then Soho where he expanded his line, adding jackets and coats. And five years ago, he . . ."

Eleanor stopped, but she didn't take her eyes off me. I didn't take mine off her. All that perfection on the outside? Didn't it often signify something less lovely lurking beneath? Just what that was would be one of the things I might be finding out in the weeks to come, whether I was looking for it or not.

"For years and years," she continued, whatever she'd been feeling the moment before safely stowed away again, "the work and the hours were long. He did well, but it was nothing like it is today, young people spending a thousand dollars for what is virtually a silk T-shirt, nearly that for a pair of shoes, five thousand for a leather coat they want to replace the following year because it's last season's."

"The world's gone mad."

She didn't comment. What would she have said? The particular madness she'd just described had made her a very rich woman.

"There were witnesses," I said.

"Yes." She swiveled her chair around and picked up some papers from the low shelf behind her.

"Only seven people of the estimated forty to fifty who had been nearby on the platform during rush hour claimed to have seen the crime," she said, "but luckily, all seven were able to describe the man who'd done the pushing in great detail."

"Oh." Wondering, in that case, why the police had been unsuccessful in finding the man, an answer I would have soon enough.

"Marilyn Chernow said he was a tall man with light hair, hair that might have been bleached by the unrelenting summer sun, and that he was husky, not fat exactly, certainly not obese, but not thin either, perhaps a little heavier than average, she'd said, and fit enough to run away immediately after he'd committed the crime. Which is what he did, disappearing into the swarm of hot, sweaty commuters trying to get home after work with as little engagement with their fellow humans as possible."

I heard paper rustle as she turned to the next page of her notes. Despite the fact that she glanced at them from time to time, I had the feeling she could have recited the facts in her sleep. I was making some notes of my own, and looked down at what I had written as I waited for her to continue.

"Yes, here it is," she said. "Eleven of the people interviewed, in fact, said they'd been reading the paper and hadn't seen anything, not until they heard screaming, not until a tall, short, fat, thin, black, white man shoved by them running up the stairs, toward the front of the train, across the platform where he jumped onto the local that was just about to pull out of the station, and by then all they remember seeing was the express train and a lot of people with hands over their mouths and one woman crying and a kid holding a hat, his face the color of skim milk.

"The kid, that would be Dustin Ens, who had turned twelve just two weeks earlier." She looked up to see if I was listening, finding me as attentive as a dog begging for a share of his master's dinner. "He said he thought the man was six three, maybe taller, as tall as a basketball player. Except he was, 'like white.' He'd had a cap pulled down over his head so that you couldn't see the color of his hair and

Dustin told the police he remembered wondering why, thinking maybe he was bald from chemo the way his mother had been for the last year and a half of her life, only her cap had fake hair attached to it, long bangs in the front that covered the place her eyebrows used to be and a fringe in the back, just an inch or so, more the color of an overripe banana than the color his mother's hair had been before it all fell out. 'Maybe he was angry that he was sick and that's why he pushed the man,' Dustin had suggested.

"Lucille DiNardo said the man who did the pushing was 'black, African American, whatever the hell you're supposed to say now,' noting that she, for one, had no idea. 'He had a wild beard,' she said, 'and he was wearing gloves, gloves, in that awful triple-H weather we'd been having, you'd have to be crazy.' She remembered looking at them, leather or fake leather, but she couldn't tell without touching them and, 'Lord knows, no one wanted to touch a homeless man's gloves what with where those hands might have been,' and she remembered thinking, 'What kind of a nut wears gloves in all this heat?' And also that she was glad he wasn't standing that close to her because even from two people away, she thought she could smell him.

"Elizabeth Mindell said he was big, that he stood head and shoulders above the crowd, a man of about forty to fifty, really thin, as if he hadn't eaten much for a long, long time and that he had a tattoo on his left hand, in that soft place between the thumb and the forefinger, but she wasn't close enough to see what it was, a bird maybe, or a weapon of some sort, or maybe a heart with initials in it. She thought he was of 'mixed heritage, maybe a black father and a white mother. Or the other way around.' "

Once again, Eleanor stopped to look at me, perhaps to see if I understood what I was up against. Then she checked the notes again before continuing.

"She said when he ran he knocked into her, knocked her shoulder bag right off her shoulder, which is what you get when you don't put the strap across your chest, and that she thought for a minute that he'd taken it, that pushing the man with the attaché case in front of the oncoming train had been a diversion to steal her bag, but then she saw it on the ground, just to the right of her right foot.

"Claire Ackerman always read the paper on the platform, 'to avoid unnecessary eye contact.' But she'd looked up when she heard the train in the tunnel. 'That's when I saw him,' she told the police, 'Mr. Redstone, poor man, flying through the air, almost pausing in midair,' she'd said, 'or maybe it was like when you're scared and everything seems to slow down?' She thought he jumped at first, but then she saw the homeless man running, coming toward her, and she thought she'd die on the spot, his face right in front of hers for a moment, 'small, light eyes, barely blue, steely looking, a bulbous nose, thin lips, a big chin, not as big as Jay Leno's, but bigger than average. Tall,' she said, 'and muscular, too, as if he worked out at a gym, but that wouldn't be possible, would it? Unless he did that before he'd become homeless. He could have lifted the man and thrown him, for God's sake. But they said it was a push, right?'

"Missy Barnes had her cat with her in a carrier and, she said, he'd hissed at the cat. She'd stepped back, to get away from him. 'It could have been me,' she said, 'if I hadn't moved away.' She didn't remember how tall he was because when he was hissing at Bette, her Abyssinian, he was bending, so that the cat could see his face. He had on a batik shirt, she thought, something African, and his skin was so dark, it was almost black. And shiny, but maybe that was sweat, it being so hot out and so hot in the station, too. Or he might have been sweating because of what he was planning to do.' Then she seemed to have a change of heart. 'Maybe he was just trying to get a little space in front of him,' she told the detective who was interviewing her, 'a little air. Maybe he didn't mean to push that man off the platform. And maybe they didn't have pet cats where he came from,' she'd told the police. 'Maybe that's why he'd hissed at Bette, because he was afraid. People do all kinds of things when they're afraid,' she'd said.

"Willy Williams had given the homeless man a swipe, paying for his subway ride. 'I heard this saying once,' he told one of the detectives, 'no good deed goes unpunished. Maybe I hadn't done that, maybe that white guy, he'd still be alive.' Willy, one would think, because he saw the homeless man and even interacted with him before all the hysteria began, should have been the best witness as to the question of the race of the person the police were looking for and would fail to find during the ensuing three months before they informed me they were accepting failure, but that didn't turn out to be the case," Eleanor said, her voice brittle, ready to crack. "When the police asked him about that directly, Mr. Williams said, 'Man, I just don't know. Maybe I just saw him standing by the turnstile with the corner of my eye, you know what I mean? He was a big guy, you dig, and maybe when I looked, I was eye to eye with his shirt buttons. Or maybe I never really looked and just offered him the swipe because he was standing there, not going down to the trains. I figured, maybe he didn't have the bread to pay for his own ride. Maybe he had someplace he had to be. I mean, it's their card, the company I deliver for, so it was no big thing and I guess I just didn't pay all that much attention.' When asked what kind of drugs he used, Willy had shrugged and moved his head slowly in a circle, as if he had a stiff neck and said, 'Let's not even go there. What is it with you people, you see a black man, you figure I'm using while I'm working? Man, I'm here to help you out, and what's on your mind? You're wondering, what crime did the brother commit? You got your eye on me despite the fac' I'm here to help, that I volunteered to help y'all do your job. I got nothing more to say.' "

Eleanor paused for a moment.

"The detective told me that Mr. Williams had refused to talk to them at first and only did so when offered monetary compensation, to make up for the time he was losing from work."

"I know that happens. Some people will use any situation to their own advantage. And witnesses often disagree about what they've seen," I said, understanding why the police had put the case on the back burner.

"In this case, they agreed on four things, that it was hot out, that the man who sent my father off the platform and into the path of the oncoming train had been taller than average, that he appeared to be homeless, and that but for the grace of God, it could have been them."

"How did you get this information?" I asked her, knowing the police normally would not have shared the names of witnesses with a member of the deceased's family.

There was no answer right away. And then, "Through a personal contact," she said.

"In the police department?"

She nodded.

"A detective?"

She ignored my question, glancing beyond me, as if someone had just come in the door. "I need you to find him," she said, "the homeless man who murdered my father."

"You know there's no guarantee I will," I told her. "All I can promise you is that I'll try my best."

"I know you will, Ms. Alexander."

I didn't ask who had recommended me or how she'd checked me out. That was her business. She didn't ask me how I'd go about trying my best. That was my business.

"Is he always with you?" Pointing toward Dashiell with her chin.

"He helps with the work."

Eleanor nodded. She asked my fee and how much of an advance I required, wrote a check and handed it across the nearly empty desk. I thanked her and told her I'd be in touch.

Walking down the marble steps and through the marble shop, I noticed that our wet footprints had already been wiped up. We left without stopping to admire any of the things there that, even if I cashed my retainer and used it all, I could not afford. No matter. What I cared about was something very different. What I cared about was finding the answers to those questions. Who did this? Why did they do it? Though in this case, there might not be a *why*. If the man who had pushed Gardner Redstone from here to eternity was homeless, there was a good chance he was mentally ill. He might have pushed the person standing in front of him because he heard bees buzzing around his head or because someone touched him or because he just did. The real point was finding him and making sure, as Eleanor had said, that he'd never get the opportunity to do it again.

There's no formula for finding the answers I was after any more than there's a formula for getting through life. You make choices and you live with the consequences. I knew right away I'd have to work undercover, that there'd be no way to get credible information from the homeless community, if you could call the homeless a community, unless I was credibly one of them.

It seemed like a good idea at the time. But so far, even crawling around in Dumpsters had netted me nothing. Five days into the job, three and a half months after Gardner Redstone had been killed, the man I was looking for seemed as elusive as smoke on a windy day.

SHIRLEY ROUSSEAU MURPHY

CAT FEAR NO EVIL

0-06-101560-1/$6.99 US/$9.99 Can

A rash of brazen burglaries, from antique jewelry to vintage cars, coincides with the arrival of yellow-eyed Azrael, feline nemesis of crime-solving cats Joe Grey and Dulcie.

CAT SEEING DOUBLE

0-06-101561-X/$6.99 US/$9.99 Can

Wedding festivities between the chief of police and the lovely Charlie Getz are interrupted when two uninvited guests try to blow up the church.

CAT LAUGHING LAST

0-06-101562-8/$6.99 US/$9.99 Can

Joe Grey and Dulcie discover that certain collectibles at local yard sales hold a secret treasure someone will kill to possess.

CAT SPITTING MAD

0-06-105989-7/$6.99 US/$9.99 Can

When Police Chief Max Harper is accused of a gruesome double murder, the fleet-footed sleuthing duo is intent upon restoring an old friend's good name.

CAT CROSS THEIR GRAVES

0-06-057811-4/$6.99 US/$9.99 Can

With retired film star Patty Rose found dead and their tortoiseshell friend Kit missing, Joe Grey and Dulcie set off on the cat's trail.

SRM1 0406

Sign up for the FREE HarperCollins monthly mystery newsletter,

The Scene of the Crime,

and get to know your favorite authors, win free books, and be the first to learn about the best new mysteries going on sale.

To register, simply go to www.HarperCollins.com, visit our mystery channel page, and at the bottom of the page, enter your email address where it states "Sign up for our mystery newsletter." Then you can tap into monthly Hot Reads, check out our award nominees, sneak a peek at upcoming titles, and discover the best whodunits each and every month.

Get to know the magnificent mystery authors of HarperCollins and sign up today!